HEIRS OF VANITY

PART I: ROLAND'S PATH

By: R.J. Hanson

To Brittney,
Thank you so much!
Good luck out there!

Cover designed by Henreitte Boldt

This book is a work of fiction. Names, characters, places, and incidents either are products of the author's imagination or are used fictitiously. Any resemblance to actual persons, living or dead, events, or locales is entirely coincidental.

R.J. Hanson
Visit my website at www.facebook.com/RolandsQuest/?modal=admin_todo_tour

Printed in the United States of America

First Printing: March 2019
Hanson Publishing

ISBN-13 978-1-7970517-8-9

I would have none of what I have if it weren't for the Lord. I owe a debt to my parents, Jesse and Janine, for their patience, my wife, Michelle, for her tolerance, and my daughter, Kaity, for her dedication to this work. I would like to thank my son, Alex, for taking his turn at the head of the table.

I also owe a debt to my friends, Riker, Will, Simon, Doug, Larry, Geary, James, Toren, Michael, Zach, Bradyn, John, Hance, Jon B., Chance, Traff, Straight, Armondo, and Jake. Their input and participation have been invaluable. Also, a huge thanks to Henrie, for her art work for this project.

The RPG character Roland owes the roots of his personality to the Steven King character in the Dark Tower novels; which in turn owes recognition to the Robert Browning poem Childe Roland to the Dark Tower Came. I also owe a debt of gratitude to Louis L'Amor whose books introduces a young boy to a much larger world.

CHAPTER I

Enemies Meet

IN ONE OF THE RICH FORESTS OUTSIDE OF FORDIR in the lord's region of Gallhallad in the eastern parts of the Kingdom of Lethanor, rapid axe blows echoed through the crisp autumn air. It was Tetobier, literally meaning *the tenth sword*. It was the tenth month of the year 1648 of the Age of Restored Great Men Kings, the fifth age of known history.

A large man wearing a battle worn breastplate, and battle worn face for that matter, rode to the edge of the wood. His hair, which had once been black as coal oil, now flurried in the breeze with tints of silver and gray. His eyes were the color of the bracing waters that washed ashore on the glaciers of Janis. Around them deep cracks ran through sun worn skin. Those eyes spoke of brutal days with little food and no sleep. They spoke of miles of marching, and days of battle. They spoke of sorrows known only by the soldier and the warrior and the brutal life they led. This was a man that had traveled.

"Roland," boomed from the man's throat. "Roland, come here!"

A young, but stoutly built and athletically muscled, man walked from the trees with a double-edged axe in each hand and a sheet of sweat cloaking him. He was bare to the waist despite the coolness of the morning. His coal oil black hair, wet with sweat, clung to his neck and forehead. Although decades younger, his father's mark of family could be well read upon his face and in his bearing. Although lacking the evidence of years of toil, his eyes were also his father's eyes.

"Yes, father," Roland replied. In spite of his heavy breathing he sought to reply with control and respect.

It had never been 'Dad,' or 'Pappa.' Always it had been 'Father.'

"I will be riding out of town for a few days. There are a few men that have fled south that I must go after," Velryk said as he shifted in his saddle.

"What of your deputies?" Roland asked letting his curiosity jump ahead of his judgement.

"Did I raise a son that questions his father?" Velryk said.

"No, father," Roland said stepping back a bit and lowering his eyes.

"These men are beyond my 'deputies,'" Velryk continued. "All of our good warriors have gone to the front to seek their fortune. I came by to make sure you continue your exercises and your reading and to tell you to watch the jail."

"I have never shirked my exercises!" Roland replied as the muscles in his strong-boned jaw tightened. His eyes shot back up to meet his father's. The thought that he would grow slovenly in the work of a warrior stung him to his core, and that his own father might think so! He had struggled since the time of his first steps and words to honor his father. He had striven all of his seventeen years to be worthy of Velryk's tutelage. It seemed even in the midst of his attempts to impress he would be forever a disappointment.

Anger washed through the deep and dangerous waters in the older man's eyes. He felt the blood in his veins, blood said to be too strong for mortals, burn with a flash of rage. He rode his war-horse over calmly to face the boy. The gentle way he maneuvered his mount belied the storm in his heart.

It seemed his son not only possessed his father's high cheekbones and strong jaw, he also possessed his inborn pride and quick temper. A vanity, Velryk reflected, that had been deep in their blood and the downfall of a kingdom. A kingdom likely never to rise again. That vanity had been the end of an age.

"Seven feet four inches tall and weighing over four hundred sixty stones. Strong as a bull you are."

Roland, misunderstanding Velryk's air, smiled with a sense of accomplishment.

"Damn your pride, boy!" Velryk barked down at him. "Anyone who spots you on the horizon can tell you are of the race from Lethor. They can calculate your size and your strength, although both be considerable. Listen to me! Open your ears!"

"Yes sir," Roland said, steeling his expression and fixing his faded gray-blue eyes forward. He locked his anger, and sometimes his shame, behind an oft used mask of emotionless flesh.

"This is the weapon you should sharpen," Velryk said as he leaned down from his saddle and struck Roland's forehead with a stiff index, often called the king's, finger. "Your mind will win you more victories than any axe or sword!"

When he could hold in his pride no more Roland said, "but you have taught me so well, father. No one can match your skill with the bastard sword, the axe, or the bow and soon I will be as good with those as you yourself. Perhaps one day even better."

"No one around here can match me, but this is just a small corner of the world, son." Velryk felt his own anger flood to a dull red storm raging behind his eyes. He would have to be better. He must be for his sake and for Roland's. Velryk's anger had cost him, cost him dearly. He did not intend to see his remaining son fall into that trap. A trap that nearly devoured their race.

After a pause, and a look off to the beauty of the world that surrounded them, Velryk said, "an axe is only as good or bad as the man that wields it. I will expect you to have your reading done by the time I return."

"Yes sir," Roland said. Sounding perhaps more resigned that he intended.

"What is a warrior's most valuable weapon?" Velryk asked.

"His mind, sir," resuming his formal tone.

"And what is a warrior's most trusted ally?"

"His courage," Roland answered.

"See that you understand those concepts," Velryk said. "Any fool can regurgitate what is fed to him."

"Yes sir."

Roland watched as his father turned his horse. Velryk's steed cut through the frost on the early morning grass as he began his pursuit to the south.

"'Damn your pride, boy!'" The impression attempted of Velryk's tone was off, but an impression Roland had heard many times. "Your father sounds like a priest of the old religions."

Roland turned and glared at his friend, Eldryn, standing in the trees a few yards away.

"You probably couldn't hear my approach over the grinding of your teeth," Eldryn continued.

"Damn my pride indeed! I am as strong as you, El, and I have a short sword's reach on any man. I am a warrior, and he calls me 'boy!'"

"You are almost as strong as me," Eldryn corrected, raising his finger to mark the point.

Eldryn was another of the Great Man race. Although his stature was akin to the more common, reaching to only six feet three inches in height his strength was undeniable, even by Roland. He was Roland's age with short cropped blonde hair and eyes of deep green. Eldryn's core was that of an oak with a strong build, deep chest, and broad set of shoulders.

"Well, warrior, are you ready for our sparing?"

"Are you ready for me to beat you?" Roland replied.

"You can talk like that once you've beaten me. How about a joust instead? Take up a lance and meet me on horseback and then make your brags," Eldryn replied light heartedly.

The boys trained for death. Trained to prevent their own and cause their enemies'. Eldryn, however, had always had a way of taking things in stride. He always seemed to let words and events wash over him and then away as the ocean's waves would a huge stone on the shore. Roland would not likely admit it, but he always admired that about his friend.

"You know I don't fight mounted," Roland said. "The horses around here…"

"Yes," Eldryn laughed, "your feet would drag the ground."

Both boys had trod the earth for seventeen years and looked their age. However, being of the race of Great Men, they would appear to be seventeen to twenty until well after their fortieth year. Velryk had never discussed his age with Roland, but by Roland's estimation he was around one hundred and fifty years old. It was a topic often pondered by the son about his father.

The two young men walked to their horses that had been staked in tall grass. Roland put on his padded shirt and his old iron breastplate. Eldryn was already wearing his armor. They each drew a six-foot long iron pole from their saddles. The poles were made to resemble the Great swords of old in weight and reach. Shrou-Hayn they were called in the old languages meaning Fate's Hand or the Fate's Decision.

The Great sword was designed so that its sheer weight and momentum could wound as well as its edge. It took uncommon strength just to lift one of the majestic blades, much more to wield one in combat.

Roland held his sparing weapon high above his left shoulder in a more unorthodox position. It sacrificed defense for a stronger attack. Eldryn held his squarely in front of him. The position was much more tactically sound which left him able to block or thrust easily.

Now Eldryn put his humor aside, and Roland his anger. Although only practice, both young men understood that the skills they were sharpening would someday decide whether or not they would walk from a battlefield or, be carried. Both boys were too young to truly remember and properly miss Ellidik, but both had experienced the hole that his death left in the lives of Shaylee, his wife, and Velryk, his brother in arms.

Roland tried his first cut. Eldryn was ready for the move because Roland never held anything back for defense. His first move was always whole heartedly offensive. Eldryn knew Roland held to the philosophy that if a man only defends then he accomplishes delay and exhaustion and little more. Eldryn held to other ideas.

Roland ripped the heavy practice blade through the air, cutting down toward Eldryn's right shoulder. Eldryn swung hard to block, knowing that the weight of the impact could be enough to drive him to the ground even if Roland's pole never got past his blocking sword.

Roland shifted his feet and his grip on the practice sword slightly. As the two weapons collided during Roland's attack and Eldryn's parry, Roland jerked his practice blade in a reverse arc using the power in Eldryn's parry to help drive the sword back above his head. Roland brought the pole high in the air and then brought it back down in a rapid arc away from Eldryn as he spun completely around. This move built momentum in the practice blade and Roland hauled the pole up under his right side toward Eldryn's unprotected lower left.

Eldryn, instead of attempting to stop Roland's new attack, allowed the weight of his weapon to drop it quickly to his lower left as he shifted his feet to the right. His practice blade struck Roland's just enough to knock it slightly off course. Eldryn easily danced clear of Roland's attack.

The two warriors battled on for another three hours with Eldryn landing four minor blows to Roland's one. Both were sweating and the extreme weight of their weapons was taxing their strength.

"One more touch and I will win," Eldryn said with his breath coming in rasps.

Roland tried another lower cut bringing his pole up from a point just below Eldryn's line of sight. Eldryn stepped back and parried the blow to the side.

Roland hauled his pole high above his head, miraculously holding his practice blade in one hand and stretching his left arm out. Eldryn knew that Roland would have to put both hands back on the weapon before attempting an attack. Therefore, he prepared himself for an attack that would come from Roland's middle or left. Roland would have to expose his left side to an open attack if he attempted to put both hands on his hilt and attack from his right.

Eldryn positioned his practice weapon to his right knowing that would be Roland's weak side, and knowing he would have to attack in that hemisphere.

To Eldryn's astonishment, Roland roared and dropped the point of his practice weapon for a thrust at Eldryn's heart, one handed. Since the move was one handed, Roland did not have to bring his left arm across, which meant that his left side was not exposed. Eldryn fought to bring his practice weapon up in time to parry the thrust, but with this move Roland had gravity on his side.

The direct thrust, backed by speed, weight, and gravity, struck its target. The point of Roland's pole struck the left side of Eldryn's breastplate hard enough to dent the iron and knock even mighty Eldryn back several steps.

"I acknowledge the killing blow," Eldryn said between gasps of breath.

"I acknowledge your honor," Roland replied, struggling to breathe himself. Both boys took a knee in the grassy field to chase the breath that had been so elusive.

"Does your father know about that one-handed move?" Eldryn asked. "It doesn't seem honorable."

"I struck you with the blade, did I not? I did not kick, bite, or punch you. I did not throw sand in your face, nor did I use any form of magic."

"Aye, it is true to the Code, but you didn't answer my

question," Eldryn said. "Does your father know about that move?"

"He doesn't think I'm strong enough to wield one of the Great swords in combat, that's why he trains me so hard with the axes. I am stronger than any other man in the valley with the exception of you and my father. He says the Great swords are good for practice, so that one can wield a bastard sword with more ease and finesse. But he says only the old ones could use the Shrou-Hayn as they were intended in battle. Why be a Great Man, if you are not going to wield a Great sword? That's what I say."

"Yes," Eldryn said. "That's what you say, only you do not say it to his face," Eldryn said as a slight barb to his lifelong friend.

"I happen to like the bastard sword. It is versatile, easier to carry, and with the proper level of skill, just as deadly as the Great swords of old. And a bastard sword once swung, does not leave its wielder so badly exposed as would something the size of the old huge blades."

"But the bastard sword is not a Shrou-Hayn of old," Roland said, ignoring Eldryn's attempt to get under his skin. "When I claim my glory from the battlefield it will be as a true warrior like those who strode with the champions and gods."

"So why not join the armies going north? It would give you your chance at those glories and riches you keep talking about."

"I will not take orders from common men with fancy brushes on their shoulders. I have trained to be a warrior and tactician. I will not subjugate myself to a lesser man's whim. Besides," more quietly now, "father doesn't think I'm ready."

"Enough about lesser men and their whims. It's time to eat," Eldryn said as he walked toward his horse. "Will you come into town with me and have a meal at the inn?"

"I have my reading to do," Roland began, but thoughts of the girls and ale at the inn floated into his mind carried on a wind of temptation. "Why not, I will have plenty of time. The

11

old scholars will just have to wait for me a bit longer."

The two young men walked their horses to a stream that cut through the woods nearby. Both stripped to the waist and bathed in the chilling waters. Refreshed and clean, both young men rode into Fordir.

The town of Fordir was busy that day. The boys stabled their horses, dusted their pants clean of the road sediment, and walked toward the Rusty Nail.

The tavern was a two-story building of stone and possessed all of the sights, smells, and tastes one would expect of a tavern right down to the typically fat but cheerful proprietor.

Roland and Eldryn had their goals in order. Both were hungry. After that need was filled, both would want a bit of ale. After that taste was satisfied, there were the tavern girls.

The Rusty Nail was catering to the groups of coffee drinkers during this hour of the day. That group, however, rarely tipped very well. Therefore, Roland and Eldryn were well received when they ordered ale with their noon meals.

These two young men would have drawn young women to them anywhere they traveled. Roland and Eldryn were each handsome in their own ways. Both were very obviously strong, although young. It is often enough that a young girl will be attracted to the future of a man instead of the cut of his brow and cheek. As Roland and Eldryn finished their meals they were greeted with another tankard of ale, served by falsely charming girls accustomed to the tavern life.

The inevitable conversation began, and the usual things that are said between a boy and a girl were said. Roland was not charming, although he thought himself to be. He spoke as most young men do. He spoke of the things that interest him. He had not learned yet that others, those of the fairer sex in particular, preferred topics other than tactics and philosophy.

The tavern girls knew their roles well, however. After all, there were some tactics not found in Roland's books. Seemingly in awe of the boys and their talk of hunting, and warfare, the young ladies listened intently...and kept the ale flowing.

Roland was preparing to dismiss his afternoon and evening plans of further practice and reading to spend that time with a voluptuous young brunette. One that he had spent a few evenings with before. Was Jaqualyn perhaps her name?

He was starting down that path when the sounds of a disturbance in the street made their way through the veil of perfume forming over Roland's eyes and thoughts. He made his way to the front porch of the tavern for a view of the street. The brunette, whose name Roland even now might not be able to recall, bustled along behind.

A large man in polished mercshyeld armor that shone in the sun with its unique smoky tint rode a war-horse down the street dragging three prisoners behind him. Mercshyeld, a composite steel named so for Merc the god that kept the flames of the sun stoked and the old title of Shyeld a knight quested by means of the old Code, was notable to be sure. However, a man that possessed both such fine steel and one of the magnificent horses bred for war...that would be the topic of conversation in this corner of the world for months to come. The three prisoners were tied at the neck and running to keep up with the trotting gate of the mighty horse.

"Who is that big one?" the brunette asked Roland catching up to him on the porch. She hoped to regain the attention of the young man that had been so suddenly taken from her. They watched as the knight rode toward the shire reeve's stout built stone jail and Velryk's office.

"He is Sanderland," Roland replied over his shoulder. "He is a paladin."

"Why does he not wear the colors of the lord of our land, nor those of the king?" She asked.

"He is a Paladin of Silvor, a god of the hunt," Roland said, pointing out the symbol of the Horn of the Hunt on the shield that the man carried. "Paladins only serve their god and their church, not lords nor even kings."

"So, he's the holy sort?"

"Holier than thou, perhaps," Roland said as he stepped

into the street, not realizing the double meaning his words might have had to the young woman. His mind was now on other business. The double entendre was not lost on Eldryn though. He marveled at his friend who in one moment could master a situation and in the next manage to fit both of his feet in his mouth.

Roland, perhaps due to his youth, could be thoughtless. Eldryn knew there was no malice in his friend. He bore this girl no ill will, in fact, Eldryn knew Roland liked her quite a bit. Roland was just sometimes...thoughtless.

Sanderland was six feet eight inches of lean muscle. His hair was short cut and of a light brown. His eyes were of light hazel caged behind lids that wore an almost constant look of disdain.

He had spent his life in the service of Silvor, or of those who claimed to speak for the god, and had received the promotions within the church to reflect it. Paladins, like other officers of the church, were forbidden to own any property. However, he lived in three houses that belonged to the church, he had eight war steeds when most warriors could not afford one, and he had the best armor and weapons money could buy. A breast plate and greaves of mercshyeld adorned Sanderland, while a finely crafted bastard sword of high steel hung at his side rich with the etchings of Silvor's Holy symbols, the signal horn and stag. Of course, all of those items belonged to the church.

Sanderland dismounted in front of the shire reeve's office and stood at the hitching rail expectantly. Roland approached him from behind, still smelling of ale and sweat.

"What can I do for you, sir paladin?" Roland asked.

"You can show me to the reeve," Sanderland replied in an even, if dismissive, tone.

"He is out of town, hunting men. His deputies are far flung. I am the reeve's son; may I assist you?"

Roland hated taking a servant's position for Sanderland. Roland had no reason to dislike Sanderland, but there was something in Sanderland's manner, he was too sure of himself.

Roland would discover later it went beyond that. Although he couldn't articulate it now, he would later realize it was Sanderland's treatment of the common folk that he detested.

"I have three criminals here," Sanderland said as he looked over the boy before him with impatience plainly scrawled on his face.

Roland looked over the three 'criminals.' He saw an older man bent slightly in the back whose long hair and beard were well graying with a definite note of evil in his eyes. He was wrapped in a simple, yet dirty, brown cloak. Although, Roland surmised, the evil look could just be that the old fellow felt the same about Sanderland as Roland himself did.

He saw a young woman who possessed a cold, dead gaze. She moved easily, with agile steps that barely disturbed her short cut black hair from where it had been combed. She carried her six-foot frame ready for combat. She too was dressed simply in a spun dress and well-worn boots. This one would gladly kill you in your sleep, Roland thought. Although it didn't seem to him that she would shy from a battlefield either.

The third was a young, slight man in a green spun shirt similar to the one that the woman wore, and leather pants that barely made it past his knees. He looked like he was trying to be tougher than perhaps he was capable. Less than half way between five feet and six in height, this young man seemed tired and... frightened. Brown eyes drooped beneath his shock of collar length brown hair. In spite of the circumstances, Roland liked this third prisoner. Roland's intuition was rarely strong, or to be trusted, but he liked this third one all the same.

"Spies," Sanderland said. "I picked them up in the mountains to the north, near the coast."

Roland saw that they there were intended to appear as a family, but he noted the details that gave them away. After all, it was at Velryk's knee that he had been taught. Roland approached each of them and examined their hands and faces closely.

Roland mentally listed the calluses on the slight man's thumb and forefinger, most likely from practice at dagger throwing. The small man also had scars on his knuckles and seemed to have unusually well-muscled forearms.

Roland noticed that the old man's hands were soft, except for the part that usually turned a page or held a quill. Here was either a mage, or a scholar. Probably a mage given his apparent mission and the fact that Sanderland had taken the precaution of fixing a collar of green glass around the older man's neck. Lexxmar, a material that was rare and expensive, was said to be able to mute a wizard's abilities in the arts.

No group of spies would be complete without a dedicated bruiser. Roland noted the tightly muscled frame of the young woman. She had hair that was as black as a soulless night and skin as pale as its heavenly companion, the moon. She was wearing a dress now and was beauty defined in it, but Roland could see enough of her shoulder to see the marks from hours spent in armor. Here was a woman with radiant beauty, and a heart of ice to compliment it.

Of the three, Roland could only convict the old man and younger woman in his heart. The young common man looked trapped, if anything.

"From Tarborat?" Roland directed toward Sir Sanderland as much to the three captives.

"I would assume," Sanderland replied. "I'll just want them held here until the local Cleric of Silvor can interrogate them. Just held, do you understand me, boy?"

"I understand, sir," Roland said through gritted teeth.

Sanderland noted the muscles that corded along Roland's jaw and he smiled slightly at that.

"I should be returning in a week to ten days for these three. I will then take them to a prepared priest. See that they are well kept," Sir Sanderland said as he remounted his greater war-horse.

"And boy," Sanderland began with no friendship in his tone, "say hello to your father for me."

"You will be taking their equipment with you then?" Roland asked, thinking that he might already know the answer to that question.

It was Sir Sanderland's turn for anger spawned of embarrassment.

"They had only what you see on them."

"All the way from Tarborat with not so much as a skinning knife between them?" Roland asked.

"I'll not be questioned by a boy," the Paladin said with an edge.

Sir Sanderland wheeled his war-horse and started down the street at a trot.

Roland stepped inside the stout little building behind the three. He moved in front of them and unlocked the cell door to a large iron cage. There were seven inhabitants in that cage already. Two horse thieves from several lands away, one murderer that had three partners that Velryk hunted even now, two purse snares, and two men still too drunk to stand from the night before. He double checked his head count and made correction on the chalk board near the cage to account for the new prisoners.

Roland saw the look exchanged between the mage and the female fighter. He mistook it for some type of plot to escape.

"You will do well not to test me," Roland said as he bowed the iron bars of the cage in his bare hands. "As of now you are simply to be kept, however, should you attempt to escape I would be duty bound to use whatever means necessary to ensure that you remain in custody."

Roland fixed each of them with his gaze. He found, however, that the mage seemed uninterested, the fighter unimpressed, and the slight man, that he presumed was a thief, preoccupied.

Roland, ego bruised, returned to the tavern to find Eldryn standing in the door with an extra mug in his hand.

"I thought you might need a hand there for a moment,"

17

Eldryn said as he looked down the street toward Sanderland's dust.

"A hand with what?" Roland asked, genuinely bewildered.

"It looked as though you were trying to prod him into a fight," Eldryn said.

"Me prod him? He was the one looking to embarrass me. That is always the way with those 'Holier than thou' soldiers."

"Didn't your father teach you anything about respecting a knight's authority?"

"He taught me to judge a man by the man, not by the brush or emblem he wears."

"That chip on your shoulder is going to bear your mighty frame to the ground some day."

"What do you know of it?" Roland asked sharply.

"I know that your pride is as dangerous to you as it is to any other man. Do you forget that we are still boys?"

Roland swelled at that and Eldryn thought for a moment he would strike him. Then Roland let the wind out of his lungs and lowered his head.

"You are right, El. We are still boys and unproven warriors, but not even a pig enjoys being called swine."

"Our time will come," Eldryn assured with a patience that was his custom.

The two young men went inside, finished their meals, and drank three more mugs of ale before rising. Then they walked to the front steps of the tavern where Eldryn took a wrap of smoking leaf from his vest. He offered it to Roland who simply bit the end off of it and worked it into his jaw. Eldryn fired the remaining smoking leaf on the ever-burning lamp next to the door of the tavern. Both boys enjoyed their man's habit in the cool afternoon on the front porch of the tavern watching the time pass with the traffic of the market street.

Across the street in the jail a familiar scene played itself out. This time, however, it ended differently. One of the horse thieves, probably a man of the Great Men line but long since pure by the look of his size, sauntered over to the slight man brought in by Sanderland. The smaller of the spies, who was sitting in the corner of the large cell, seemed not to notice him.

"I am Greely," the horse thief said, looking down at the boy who was maybe fifteen years of age. "While you are here you will give me your food dish when it comes. If you hesitate, or report it, I will beat you without mercy. Is that clear little man?"

"I am The Shanks," the slight man said politely. "I assure you that I will not hesitate."

The Shanks's words were spoken with a calm and agreeable tone. The sort of tone one lady may use to address another in a house of worship. The tone camouflaged the nature of this little fellow.

The Shanks was sitting with his legs outstretched as Greely stood over him. The Shanks hooked the toe of one foot behind Greely's right leg and kicked Greely's right knee swiftly with his other foot. Greely's knee crackled as the kneecap, and the surrounding cartilage, was shattered and separated. The resulting shards of bone pushed into the muscles and tendons that bound the joint.

Greely gasped and toppled to the ground. He held his leg, barely able to stifle a scream as he bit into the cuff of his shirt. They all knew that if a fight broke out and the alarm was raised then they would likely all get beaten, and the ones marked to be hung would find themselves marching toward the gallows ahead of schedule.

The Shanks continued to sit in the same position, and appeared as though he hadn't stirred a muscle. This was not his first time as a captive, and when one is bound by iron the world inside is much the same regardless of the continent.

"Understand this," The Shanks continued in his polite tone. "You will now dance on the gallows with a significant limp. I have not the time, nor the patience, to put up with your foolishness. Therefore, if you so much as cause a foul smell that drifts in my direction, then you will not only dance with a limp, but you will do it gelded."

Everyone in the cell, including The Shanks's traveling companions, reassessed the small man. The Shanks pulled a small root from the waistband of his trousers that had been concealed in the hem. He looked at the root and then looked over the other inmates.

Roland and Eldryn had been friends since their earliest days, even before school and training at the local academy on the east side of Gallhallad. Gallhallad was the city that was home to the lord of those lands, Lord Bessett.

Not many could afford to enter their children in the schools. Eldryn's tuition was a reward to his family for his father's death in service. A death they all suffered from during the battles with Tarborat. Roland knew that his father wasn't rich, but somehow, he managed to pay for Roland's training. This was another topic Roland had often pondered, but Velryk wasn't the sort of man that invited questions. He was sure that it had some tie to Velryk's service in the King's army, but that was another subject Velryk was quiet about.

When Roland and Eldryn were not training at the academy they spent their time learning at Velryk's knee. Velryk and Eldryn's father, Ellidik, were friends during their days together in the armies. Velryk never talked of it, and Eldryn's mother only mentioned it rarely, regardless of how hungry the boys were for stories of their fathers in combat.

Roland's training further included reading of the great scholars, reading that was required by Velryk. Eldryn's reading was limited to the Holy Book of Bolvii and The Code of The Cavalier. Ellidik was a cavalier of the old Code. That book was the only thing of Ellidik's that Velryk managed to rescue from the battlefield the day that his friend fell.

Roland had wondered often why Velryk had returned from the wars to watch over him. It was true enough that his mother had died before he was walking, but there were mothers enough that had taken in the sons and daughters of warriors abroad.

Now, as Roland's thoughts drifted over the past and unanswered questions, the boys enjoyed their habits in the quiet of the afternoon. They knew a peaceful silence that passed between them that only true friends can experience.

After an hour of watching the people in the market and along the street, Eldryn spoke. It seemed Eldryn was always the one to speak first.

"Since you father will be away, you should eat with mother and I tonight. It has been some time since she has seen you."

"I must watch the jail. Father's deputies are not the sort to leave responsible for spies. Especially spies that manage to conceal their equipment, weapons, and symbols from their captor."

The young men shared a laugh at Eldryn's imagined and animated account of Sanderland explaining to one of the high clerics that he doesn't even know for certain who the 'spies' work for.

"Very well," Eldryn began, hoping that Roland would accompany him but knowing that he would not. "I will be off. I have my afternoon exercises and my riding."

"Yes," Roland replied, quietly. "I have my exercises and my reading."

Eldryn started up the street toward his stabled horse looking forward to the talk he and his mount would share. There were many times that a silent animal was just as good in conversation as Roland. Roland spit into the dust, hoping to look older than he was, and walked across the way to the jail.

CHAPTER II

Escape and Pursuit

ROLAND LOOKED OVER THE PRISONERS to find them speaking in low tones among themselves when he entered the jail. He conducted another head count and all were there. He noticed that one seemed very pale and had attempted some sort of field dressing on his right leg. He thought to inquire but remembered one of his lessons. A lesson about a serpent that feigned injury. A lesson about a trap. The fellow would hang before many more breakfasts would pass. A man facing death might try anything. He noted that one of the deputies had brought them food, and, satisfying himself that all was well, went about his own business.

Eldryn, of course, would have been happy to talk at length with any of those jailed. Roland thought about the duality of his friend. Eldryn's studies were focused with no time for ideas or philosophies beyond the old Code and the way of the Cavalier. But, when not at study, his conversation and interest were markedly diverse.

Roland, on the other hand, had no time for the prattling of thieves or cut-throats. In his mind, if they had wisdom to share, then they likely wouldn't be in jail. Roland's views on wisdom, and where to find it, would soon be on a different course. They would soon change as a boy must if he is to become a man.

Roland changed from his one good shirt and trousers back into his deer skin pants and padded coat. He went through the now automatic steps of strapping on his plate armor. Once fully armored, well armored in what he had anyway, Roland took up his helmet and six-foot long practice pole. Roland walked to the small clearing behind the jail and began his afternoon exercises.

After three hours of executing several attack and parry routines with the large sparing weapon, Roland slung it over his shoulder and started his five-league run. His lungs were burning for air by the time he returned to the jail.

Roland regained his breathing pace, and then stepped back inside the jail. He stored his sparing weapon and most of his plate armor in the armory. He kept his breastplate out, and took out two hand axes. He placed that armor and those weapons next to the cot he would sleep on.

Roland looked in on the prisoners again, some of whom had drifted off to sleep. He walked across the street to the tavern again and retrieved a meal fit for any three men and a gallon of goat's milk. He returned to the jail and devoured his meal at his father's desk.

Roland slept an uneventful sleep and awoke the next morning to find the drunk to be released standing at the cell door waiting on him.

"That drink is no friend to you, old man," Roland said to the sobering sot as he rose from his cot and stretched. "I'm sure that we will see you later."

The old man smiled and bowed to Roland as he left the jail. Roland re-secured the cell door, and conducted another head count. All seemed as it should be. He then went across the street to the tavern for his breakfast. He ate well. Once finished, he escorted one of the cooks from the tavern over to the jail to feed the prisoners.

Roland checked them all and did another head count.

They were all present although a few were still sleeping in the back. He left them in the care of a deputy, Tobert. Roland then stretched, and went outside to begin his morning exercises.

He could hear Velryk's voice in his head, as he often did during training. *'You don't train to save your life, boy. You train to save the life of the man next to you. You train to save the lives of your family far away. You train to save your lands. Those, and in that order. Your life is farther down that list.'* This rang as a litany in his head during the repetitions that burned his muscles and forced fire into his lungs.

The day passed without event. Roland checked in on the prisoners at noontime, and returned again at dusk. Tobert reported that the only incident of the day had been the re-arrest of the drunk that had been released just that morning. Roland nodded and relieved Tobert of his duties.

Roland took a thick book from the shelf, 'Arto's Thoughts on War.' Roland began his reading by the light of twin candles. The candles were only half melted when Roland's weary head slumped to the hard wood surface of the desk. Sleep took the boy deep into her arms.

'Awake' screamed in Roland's head and he awoke to find the candles burned to the dish and the jail only lit by the faint light of the ever-glowing lamp from the tavern across the street. He lay very still, as his father had taught him. *'Never jerk awake, boy,'* Velryk had said. *'When you are startled from sleep it is for a reason. Don't let your enemy know you're awake until you are ready to strike him.'*

Roland tried to control his breathing as he slowly scanned the room through one cracked open eye. He had slept facing the doorway to the iron cell. His first thought was the cell door, he visually checked it and it appeared to still be secure. Then he began scanning the shadows within that cell.

Roland found the source of the noise that he assumed had called out to his honed instincts. He watched as the female warrior worked with some sort of tool at freeing the collar around the wizard's neck.

Roland rose swiftly and stepped out of the path of the doorway. He pulled the breastplate over his head and strapped it on to cover his chest and his back. He took up his hand axes and prepared himself. He considered calling out for help, *but what warrior needs to call out for help,* he thought to himself in his own prideful voice. Velryk's voice was now far from his thoughts.

Roland stepped into the doorway to find the wizard preparing what Roland assumed was a type of elemental attack. Roland saw the wizard conjure a ball of black, glowing energy that frosted in the air. Much to Roland's surprise the wizard's target appeared to be the slight man the wizard had been captured with, who was still asleep.

The female saw Roland, and he barely had time to register the fact that she was throwing something before he felt it lodge in his hip just below his armor. Roland felt the stab of the weapon deep into the muscle of his lower abdomen just above his hip, and then a searing pain as the dagger revealed its magical properties. Roland knew it to be a fire blade when he saw the rune glowing on the hilt. If this had been one of the long daggers that the elves favored it would have easily pierced his gut as well.

'*Always search them for yourself, boy,*' he heard Velryk's voice again calling to him from memory. '*Never trust to someone else what is yours to be sure of.*' In his anger at Sanderland, and his own foolish neglect, he had not thought to search the three 'spies.' Now he paid for his stupidity.

The other occupants of the cell did their own personal bests to become holes in the air. Each man melted out of the path between Roland and the wizard by crawling to the corners of the cage.

Roland dropped one of his axes and pulled the blade free from his hip as he had been mentally conditioned to do. He did so without thought. A blade left in the body was never good. As long as it was there it would continue to wound. He was also conditioned for the pain that would accompany the move. However, agony tore through his gut just the same. The burning blade stopped any bleeding, but the jolt of pain caused him to side step and lean briefly against the door. He took the keys from the wall and unlocked the cell door, intent on attacking the wizard before he could unleash his deadly spell.

As Roland swung the door in the wizard wisely changed his target from the sleeping victim to the armed man approaching him. Roland continued forward as the wizard focused three fingers from his right hand and uttered the word *'dactlartha.'*

The dark bolt of cold energy struck Roland hard on the chest and knocked the wind from his lungs. He felt his left shoulder tighten from frost and half of his face went stiff. He powered his way through the blows and continued toward the young woman and the old man, single minded in his objective. He had learned over a few, but very tough, years to put pain in its place.

The woman, surprised at the hard determination discovered in this boy-jailor, stepped in front of the old man and cried out, "Get us out of here!"

Strong though she might have been, and skilled, she had no desire to face Roland having hurled her only weapon into his gut.

Roland made a sweeping cut at the female, but she managed to slap the blade wide with her bare hand as she dodged to the side. Roland had never seen such speed!

Roland called on his left arm to attack, but it would not respond. She struck him hard on the side of the throat, which would have disrupted his breathing if he hadn't still been trying to regain his breath from the magical bolt hurled by the wizard.

Roland prepared for another attack, accepting the idea that the female warrior would get another free swing at him with his left arm out of action.

As he began his attack, he heard the wizard speak again, *'sectlartha.'*

Roland swung his axe blade through thin air as the wizard and the fighter disappeared from his sight and beyond his reach.

Roland turned for the cell door and saw the slight man making his way toward the main office of the jail. His weapon was slick in his hand from his own blood and his shoulder and arm hung at his side like that of a puppet with some of the strings cut. He forced air into his chest.

"Halt or I will hollow your skull!"

The small man's movement went ridged and he slowly moved his hands out to his side and then above his head. Although the two spies he arrived with seemed to have vacated the area without him, the Shanks appeared to also have a desire to depart. The frosted muscles began to thaw, and then to scream in Roland's shoulder.

Roland stepped out of the cell and approached the slight man. His left arm was a beacon fire of pain that he put on a ship and sent to a distance shore.

"Get back in there!" Roland roared.

The young man complied and walked swiftly back to the cell.

Roland secured the door again and then rang the alarm. He did not know the capabilities of the wizard, but Roland knew from what Velryk had taught him that some could teleport only a short distance while others could cover leagues with a single spell. Roland was hoping they would still be in the area.

"I can help you track them," the small man said. "That's what I do. They were preparing to kill me, I owe them nothing. I'd be glad to help you track them down."

"Quiet," Roland said as he worked the stiffness out of his frosted shoulder.

"My name is Ashcliff, I am known as the Shanks," the small man said. "You are Sir Roland, right?"

"I said quiet!"

"Very well, sir," Ashcliff said politely.

"I am just Roland, no Sir to it, not yet."

"Very well, Roland," Ashcliff said in his most compliant tone.

Roland stood in the road in front of the jail. He had worked the soreness out of his arm and Eldryn's mother, Shaylee, had prepared a poultice for his hip wound. Between that and a tea she made for him he was on the mend quickly. Five days had passed since his brief battle in the jail. The scouts had found nothing of the two escaped prisoners. A traveling merchant had brought word that Velryk was on his way into town with the three prisoners that he had set out for.

Velryk rode to the packed earth in front of the jail and dismounted his war-horse. A deputy came from the office and took charge of the three criminals.

"Well, tell me of your reading, boy."

"Father, there were three prisoners that Sanderland brought here about six days ago," Roland began quickly. He hoped to explain and make his case before Velryk's anger went beyond the bounds of reason.

"I said of your reading," Velryk said through clenched teeth. "I did not raise you to disobey my every word. Tell me of your reading."

"'Arto's Thoughts on War,'" Roland began. "'Only the dead have seen the end of war. No man in the wrong can remain against a man that defends the weak who will not acknowledge defeat.'"

"Any speaking bird from Janis can mimic sounds," Velryk said. "What does it mean?"

"War is inevitable as long as men are tied to earthly things. Only the spirits of men will be without strife. No one that fights for the wicked can be victorious over a man that fights for the weak who will not quit. A man that fights for the weak and humble must not quit, because surrender is the only thing that can defeat him."

"Good," Velryk said. "Now what of these prisoners brought by Sir Sanderland."

Roland told Velryk the story from the beginning to the point of the last scout who had returned with no signs or tracks to report.

"Sanderland's prisoners would still be secure if he had done a decent job of searching the woman," Roland said, hoping to gloss over his own failure.

"Do not lay blame, son," Velryk said. He thought of the lessons he had taught the boys about captives, and considered reminding his son. However, the look on Roland's face told him he need not. "A warrior accepts his responsibilities, and takes the scorn with the glory."

"Yes sir," Roland replied with his head lowered.

"They wore no emblem, and possessed no weapons with their symbol or mark?"

"The woman concealed this," Roland showed Velryk the dagger.

"A flaming blade you said?"

"Yes sir," Roland replied, indicating the rune on the handle. "It ignited when it struck my hip, a lucky throw that hit just below my armor."

"I taught you better than that," Velryk said. "Luck did not guide this blade. A man can dodge with his head, or limbs. But to move his hip requires the movement of the whole body. You are a large boy and were in a confined space. She went for the sure strike and did not risk the killing throw at your throat."

"Yes sir," Roland replied, his head bowed.

"Still," Velryk continued, "a magic dagger is no trinket. Sander..., Sir Sanderland also should have taken greater care. Spies from Tarborat are not known to travel with magic weapons, nor do they keep the company of wizards."

"Your wound has been properly treated?" Velryk asked, his thoughts returning to his son.

"Yes sir, Shaylee saw to it."

"Then go home. I will handle the ordeal with Sir Sanderland and the Church."

"Father, it was my mistake. I should be the one to have

to tell them."

"The mistake began with me. I left *you* here to do *my* job." Velryk realized the harsh nature of what he had said, but too late. As he had been taught in his own youth so many years before, and as he had tried to teach Roland, *a word spoken is as an arrow loosed...it cannot be called back.*

Roland's anger was only outweighed by his shame. His father would have to accept the blame from the church and Sir Sanderland, and the debt. No doubt they would expect a payment in gold as retribution for allowing the escape.

Roland led his horse from the stable but walked the twelve leagues to his home. To possess a horse, much more a horse for only riding, was an honor. He did not feel honorable this day. He walked those leagues with shame heavy on his shoulders as his mount trailed behind him.

Eldryn was sleeping soundly when his warrior's mind alerted his snoring body. He had been taught, as Roland had, by Velryk. Eldryn smelled the air and knew that his window had been opened. He also noted the scent of oil on armor and leather. He maintained his breathing, and slowly allowed dim light into one eye.

"I wondered how long it would take you. How could you not have heard me open the window?" Roland noted that Eldryn had done a fine job remaining still. He also observed that Eldryn quit snoring quite abruptly.

"Roland? What are you doing outside my window?" Eldryn asked incredulously.

"Waiting for you to wake up," Roland said. "I assume you're awake now. You quit snoring moments ago. Get dressed, you're going with me."

"With you?" Eldryn asked, avoiding the snoring topic altogether.

"Yes, we are going after the two prisoners that escaped me."

"Exactly how do you plan to track them?"

"I have that worked out," Roland said. "Just get up, get your equipment, and let's go."

"I should leave mother a note," Eldryn said as he rolled out of bed and put his feet on the cold stone floor.

Eldryn had been following Roland his whole life. He was a strong young man of a genuine and good heart. He had always relied on Roland for the mischief and trouble in his life. He had never gone without for it seemed Roland always traveled with plenty of both. What Roland called 'adventure' most referred to as trouble.

"Very well, but make it quick."

Eldryn pulled on his spun trousers and boots, collected his equipment, and wrote a short note addressed to his mother, Shaylee.

Roland sat on his horse chewing his smoking leaf and waiting patiently. Eldryn dropped his bastard sword of iron and shield, both gifts from Velryk, out the window to the soft earth beneath. He climbed out the window behind them hauling his breastplate and change of clothes over his shoulder.

"Do you have time for me to get my horse, or should I saddle myself up and go as your pack animal?"

"Would you quit with the joking?" Roland asked, pleaded.

"Very well," Eldryn said as he started toward the barn with his gear.

Both young men rode away from the stone home toward Fordir with the midnight moon hanging over head.

"So, what exactly did you have in mind?" Eldryn asked after the two had traveled for a few leagues.

"I have a tracker," Roland began. "We will use him to track them down. Once we have them in custody we will return. Then as a warrior I will have corrected my failure and redeemed myself."

"Did I ever tell you that you take yourself too seriously?" Eldryn quipped.

Roland smiled a little.

"I know, but I have to make up for this," Roland said dropping his officious tone. "My father is going before Sanderland to tell him it was his mistake to leave me to handle things for the few days he was gone. How can I let my father do that, bringing shame on us both, without doing something about it? My father trusted me and I have disgraced both our names before Sanderland and the lord of the land."

"I see your point, but do you really think your father's opinion of you is so low?"

"What else could he think of me? It was my first test in real combat other than hunting down a few purse snares and slaying the wolves that come after our livestock. I failed. I won't face that sneering Sanderland again until I have proven myself."

"How long do you think it will take?"

Eldryn had often questioned Roland on his motives and his plans. However, those questions had always been asked after he had happily joined him. From stealing cookies from the kitchen jar at the age of five, to sneaking off to trap wild boars at the age of eleven, to 'procuring' ounces of smoking leaf from Velryk's bag at the age of thirteen Eldryn had always followed without any hesitation.

Roland had always counted on Eldryn without even realizing it. Eldryn had always been there for him and always willing. Eldryn had a steadfast friend in Roland. Roland had always come to his defense without question or hesitation. Each young man had a great friend in the other. It would be years before they realized just how deep and strong their friendship was, and by then it would be too late.

"The number of moons is for Father Time to count," Roland quoted from the holy book of Bolvii.

"So, you don't know," Eldryn said more as a statement of fact than a question.

"No, I don't. I plan on taking as long as it takes."

Two young men rode up to the hitching rail in front of the jail. Their soft leather boots were silent on the hard-packed earth.

"Hello in the jail," Roland called.

"Yes."

"Tobert, it is Roland. Father sent me to watch the jail. He said he wants you to meet him at the south pass as soon as possible."

"Velryk said he wanted me?" Tobert asked, a little doubtfully.

"You are a deputy of Fordir, are you not?"

"Yes," Tobert's tone was uncertain. "Yes, I am," a bit more confident now. "Very well. You will watch the jail?"

"Yes, that's why I'm here."

Tobert tightened his breastplate, hoisted his shield and checked his sword to make sure it was in its place in his scabbard. Tobert nodded to both boys as he started the short run toward the south pass.

Roland stepped into the jail and went straight to the keys for the iron cell. As Roland moved for the cell Eldryn made himself busy gathering waterskins and extra provisions kept aside for the deputies in case of long rides with no warning.

"Ashcliff," Roland whispered into the dark.

"Yes?"

"It is Roland. Gather yourself, you are going to lead me to your friends."

"As you say, Roland."

Ashcliff moved to the door as a silent breeze. Roland unlocked and opened the iron door.

"You won't regret this," Ashcliff said as he walked into the free air of the early morning.

"If I do regret this, you will never again walk nor find pleasure with a woman. Do I make myself clear?"

"As Lexxmar."

Roland looked Ashcliff over again. A spy, and he

couldn't be older than Roland himself.

Roland went to the coin box where the fines paid and drunkard fees were kept. He had seen Velryk pay deputies from this box and he saw this as no different. Well, perhaps a little different but they were riding in the service of the Reeve. He gathered a few coins and dropped them in his purse. Roland stepped outside into the night and mounted his horse next to where Eldryn sat his.

"No horse for me?" Ashcliff asked.

"Point to your horse and you may take it," Roland replied, gesturing to the empty street. Roland had placed a great deal of trust in Ashcliff, but to give a possible spy a horse? Not just yet.

"Very well."

Ashcliff began to jog down the street heading west out of Fordir and the lands of Gallhallad. He ran easily as the two boys rode along behind him.

They traveled for twenty leagues before Roland called a halt. Both Roland and Eldryn were surprised at Ashcliff' abilities to cover distances on foot.

"We should rest here for what is left of the night. We'll only get a few hours of sleep before sunrise, but it should be enough to keep us going most of the day tomorrow."

Ashcliff began unpacking the saddlebags and Eldryn unloaded his gear. Roland watered the horses at a stream nearby and picketed them in tall grass. When he returned to the campsite Roland found a very weary Ashcliff sound asleep, and Eldryn watching him.

"I don't know if I trust him," Eldryn said quietly, not taking his eyes from the sleeping figure.

"Well, they were set to kill him the night the woman warrior and the mage escaped me. The bolt of dark energy that hit me in the chest was meant for him. I think at the least we can trust him to hate them. As in 'Thoughts on War', 'the enemy of my enemy is my ally.'"

"That's pretty thin logic," Eldryn replied, "even for you."

"It's the only move I have, El'," Roland said, dropping his typical tone of knight-errand and speaking as the boy's friend instead. "I must try."

Eldryn nodded and rolled into his blanket.

They all slept. Eldryn and Roland were both relieved to wake and find Ashcliff preparing a breakfast of fried pork and eggs seasoned with something unknown to the boys. A breakfast that surprised both of them due to its delicious taste.

"How exactly do you plan to track them?" Roland asked Ashcliff.

"I don't exactly know how to track," Ashcliff began, speaking quickly so as to explain himself. "Well not exactly. I'm decent at it, but tracking a teleporting wizard? I do, however, have an idea of where they will head first. We buried most of our equipment before being ambushed by the elves. I would imagine Yorketh, and Dawn will go there first. If we cannot catch them there, then I know of their destination."

"Now that we have the time and inclination for it," Eldryn said, "what was your destination, and purpose?"

"I was an apprentice and my master sent me to the great land of Lawrec, the land of Prince Ralston. I was to observe the movements of a wizard there called Daeriv. I was captured by his men and made a slave. I told them I was a lost sailor and for two years I worked in slavery for them. I let them see some of my skills over the course of time and I was eventually promoted out of slavery to be a watcher for Daeriv. He is the one that Dawn and Yorketh work for. He has nothing to do with Tarborat, although Daeriv is no less evil than those in that land. He had obtained a map that I took the opportunity to memorize. The map showed the location and pathways of a ruined city of ancient times. It was a city that was uprooted and cast into the depths of the earth during the Battles of Rending. There was rumored to be great wealth there from the days that champions and gods walked among men, and an item that Daeriv wants. I don't know exactly what that item is. Only Yorketh and Dawn know what he seeks there," Ashcliff said.

These boys were strong and he had seen Roland demonstrate his sturdy constitution in the fight in the jail, but, fortunately for Ashcliff, neither was a skilled interrogator. Although even a skilled interviewer would have trouble spotting the truths left out. Most who came to question the likes of him were looking for lies present, not truth absent.

"Wait," Roland said. "Elves captured you?"

"Yes," Ashcliff replied. "We decided to remove all of our identifying items and we concealed them along the route to the ancient city. The elves came upon us during my watch. I saw them come and hoped that they might capture my companions and then I would be free. However, after catching them the elves realized that it was a camp for three and they began searching for me. I eluded them for a few days, but one does not escape an elf in his own forest. As it turns out they are not fond of trespassers in their precious wooded realm. They kept what equipment we still carried with us, and turned us over to Sanderland. He was eager for us to admit that we were spies from Tarborat. We all knew that telling the truth to man who already knows what he wants to hear will only get you tortured further, so we did not respond to his questioning. He wasn't very skilled in that regard anyway. He decided to take us before a cleric and have our minds dissected by his 'Holy' ways."

"What is the name of this city?" Eldryn asked.

"Nolcavanor," Ashcliff replied, expecting disbelief and perhaps derision.

"Nolcavanor? That was one of the old capitals. The Book of History said that it was consumed by molten rock hurled by the gods," Eldryn said. Both boys had heard the stories of magnificent cathedrals and impenetrable castles. They had heard the tales of Lord Ivant and his friends. They had played as children pretending to be those heroes of old. Could it still stand? Could remnants of that great city remain?

"Not totally destroyed," Ashcliff said. "Some areas of

the city were encased in lava, preserved. Daeriv does not act on whim. His information came from a fallen champion servant. He brought an artifact from the city for Daeriv to examine."

"This wizard, Yorketh, is he powerful?" Roland asked, trying to hide his excitement at the possibility of Nolcavanor.

"He can be. Without the trinkets he usually carries he is not so dangerous, but he has certain items that augment his actions and spells."

"And the woman, Dawn?"

"She is a marvelously attractive woman to look at, but a deadly one to touch. She is very capable. It is said that she has a sister even more beautiful, but I find it hard to believe she even had a mother, much less a sibling."

"How far ahead can they be?" Roland asked.

"Yorketh, as I said, has his limits. His ability to travel by magic has a number of parameters. He must know his destination well. To attempt to travel to a place he has never been before would most likely be disastrous. He is also limited by distance and the expended energy traveling like that requires. They shouldn't be too far ahead, I think. Given the distance to Nolcavanor, we have time to cut their lead significantly."

"We have your word to be loyal to our cause until they are secured or dead?" Eldryn asked.

"If you do me the honor of accepting my word as a binding oath, then I give it with gratitude," Ashcliff said smiling.

"I don't know if I like your answer," Roland said.

"Then let us speak plainly. My word is worth nothing for I deal in lies. However, I want them dead or captured as much as you. I owe you my freedom. You spared me from torture and worse. I owe you that much and I always pay my debts. I also want to find that city."

"Nolcavanor?" Both boys asked again, as if trying to confirm their wildest dreams might be at the end of their chase. Dare they believe?

"Yes, I have it all here," Ashcliff said as he pointed to his head clad in sandy brown hair.

"What of your master? What exactly are you an apprentice of anyway?" Eldryn asked unintentionally leaning forward a bit, chasing childhood dreams from his mind.

"I have been honest with you thus far," Ashcliff said, in a different, more quiet tone. "I do not want to be forced to lie to you this early in our partnership."

"Fair enough," Roland said. "Your business is your own. But do not forget, friend, that you do owe us for the freedom you enjoy now."

"I will not forget. The Shanks does not leave debts unpaid," Ashcliff said with a confidence he did not feel.

"What is this business of 'The Shanks?'" Roland asked.

"In my line of work, it is best to be known, but not *known*. It is a name that will one day be whispered in alleys and dark corners of taverns with fear. It is a name that someday will command a good deal of coin for services rendered," Ashcliff said, "and great respect."

"What is a 'Shanks?'" Eldryn asked.

"I know what a shank is," Roland said. "It's a type of weapon sometimes made by those jailed. They take a nail, a piece of crockery or dish and sharpen it. Father showed me some that he's collected over the years when I started taking on duties in the jail."

"Just so," Ashcliff said. "In my case it is a nickname that resulted from my first notable act on the street. The first man I killed. In most cities those of my ilk aren't allowed weapons and, to be fair, I was also a child at the time. By stature at least. It would have garnered all of the wrong type of attention if I should have walked those alleys and pathways with a dagger on my side. So, I taught myself to make shanks. I had several made out of nails and a couple I made out of the broken handles of clay cups. The main reason for them was to keep the larger boys and girls from taking whatever food I had been able to find. There was a man in those times that had the idea that most of what us kids took belonged to him. He called it taxes for his protection. Lord of the Pups is what they called him. He had a habit of beating us on occasion as well. One afternoon he was shaking me down for what I had stolen that day. I had attempted to hide a silver chain from him. He said it was the last time I would hide anything from him and began to beat me fiercely. I had taken beatings before but it was clear to me that he meant it to be my last. Therefore, I had a choice to make. The beating would either be my last or his. I took a sharpened piece of cup, made for just such work, and sliced the insides of his legs where the blood flows the heaviest. You may not know this, but that part of the leg, the thigh, is also called a shank. As I was saying, I sliced his legs and drew the blood I was hoping for. The Lord of the Pups bled to death at my feet. After that the bigger kids left me alone and the others started calling me 'Shanks.'"

Roland and Eldryn were quiet then for a time. Both chewed over Ashcliff' tail as it in turn wore away their innocence. Ashcliff, who might be their age but likely a few years younger, had killed a man. Had killed more than one actually. They had known of killers and thieves, but not of such abuses of children.

Eldryn began to wonder how dark the world around him might really be. He had known of wars and strife, of course. He had known that sometimes fathers don't come home to their sons. But to hear of such things being told in a matter of fact tone wounded him. It hurt him to think of children stealing food to eat, or being extorted by the likes of The Lord of Pups. It hurt him that it was accepted.

"How could the guard of any city allow such things to go on?" Roland asked finally breaking the silence.

"There are many orphans," Ashcliff said. "The wars have created their share but there are many from happenstance and just plain bad luck. Those orphans are left to make their own way if they don't have family. Most fall to stealing food from merchants or scrounging what they can from the trash behind taverns. Some make it to adulthood, like me. Most don't."

"The guard," Ashcliff continued, "do what they can. Most mean well I suppose. But the care of the taxpayer must be seen to first. Those on the bottom must look out for them-selves."

"Could they have reached their buried equipment by now?" Eldryn asked attempting to change the subject. This new view of the world did not set well with him, and he would just as soon not be reminded of it.

"I seriously doubt it," Ashcliff responded. Perhaps glad of the change of subject as well. "However, I would say that it is likely that they will arrive there before we do. Yorketh, how-ever, requires a great deal of rest after exerting himself. If they beat us to the burial site, then we should be able to track them on land from there. I know the general direction they will be traveling in, and that will make tracking them much easier."

"Well then, we waste time by talking," Roland said. "Ashcliff, you will take my horse for the first two hours while I run. Then you will switch to Eldryn's horse for two hours while he runs. Then you will run for as long as you wish."

"He rides?" Eldryn asked, incredulous at the idea of a sneak riding his horse.

"We need our exercise anyway. It will keep us all sharp, without tiring anyone more than necessary. We will be travel-ing in the wild and it would be good for us all to be in the best shape possible. Furthermore, the horses will fare better as well not having to carry riders of our size all day. Ashcliff' light frame should give them the break they need."

"As you say," Eldryn replied, resigned. This was Roland's quest, and therefore his decision to make. If they succeeded it would be Roland's triumph. If they failed it would be Roland's fault. Eldryn didn't consciously think this, but it was more just the pattern of thought his mind had traveled in since early childhood. In truth, even if this whole thing was Eldryn's idea, he would gladly let Roland make the calls.

The three packed their few belongings and began on their journey west. While Roland ran they covered ground quickly. Roland was quick for a man of his size, and his stride al-lowed him to run almost as fast as some horses.

"Why do we travel west when Sanderland said he captured you to the north east?" Roland asked.

Ashcliff made a mental note to himself that although running at a moderate pace, this Roland's wind came to him easily as they talked. He would do well to remember this fellow's deep well of endurance.

"First I would remind you that Sir Sanderland did not capture us," Ashcliff replied. "Second, he took us from the elves in the west. I can only assume, but I would guess that anyone attempting to back track him and verify his story would come up empty handed by traveling north east."

"'Believe none of what you hear, and only some of what you see,'" Roland quoted.

"Yes," Ashcliff said with a look of appreciation. "You are more wise than you look, Roland."

"It is borrowed wisdom. It's from the book 'Thoughts on War.' It is a book I was reading."

"A warrior that can read?" Ashcliff said. "Will wonders never cease?"

Roland's anger built immediately, and then fled when he saw the smile on Ashcliff's face. He was embarrassed to have shown the traits he so despised in Sanderland and some of the others of his ilk.

"El, you are right," Roland said. "I take myself too seriously."

Several leagues and lands away to the southeast a lone rider approached a stone house and barn. Velryk rode to the barn, unsaddled his horse, and forked some hay in the stall. Velryk saw smoke rising from the kitchen chimney of the simple dwelling. He approached the house and knocked three times on the aged wood door. A beautiful woman appearing in her late thirties opened the door. Her hair and eyes were the faded version of the shades reflected in her son.

"I was wondering when you would come," Shaylee said.

"I had some things to take care of involving the church,"

Velryk replied.

"I assumed so. I suppose you know that Eldryn went with him. He left this note."

Velryk took the note and read it.

Mother,

I haven't much time. I am leaving with Roland, as you have always known I would. I am sorry not to say this in person but time is against us. I will send word when I can. I will make my father's spirit proud.

I love you,

El

Velryk looked up from the note into Shaylee's tear rimmed eyes. Her lips trembled with fear for her son, but she was the definition of the Great Women. Shaylee was strong, healthy, reserved, and rarely lost control. Ellidik had been a lucky man.

"I told the church that I sent the boys after the escapees. I also told them that the other prisoner was pardoned by me by mistake and released. They didn't believe a word of it, but did not wish to question my word. The questions ceased, of course, after I made a donation of fifteen gold coins to 'The Cause.' Our King is so eager for a victory against Tarborat that he refuses to see the real battle between good and evil being waged in our own churches," Velryk spat, as the rage at the hypocrisy mounted in his heart and throat.

"Still the same Velryk. You cannot judge a religion by a few people who abuse the authority it gives them. The same thing happens with some lords and knights. You know that to be true. No kingdom or church will be perfect until men can leave their pride and vanity dead behind them."

"I know," Velryk acknowledged, softening his voice. "But they are just so self-righteous," he offered as a feeble defense. His son Roland had never heard Velryk get this close to an apology or an excuse. There were many things about Velryk Roland had yet to learn.

"To change the course of this often-practiced conversation," Shaylee skillfully redirected, "I take it the boys are not wanted for their crimes then?"

"It is no serious offense against the laws to be stubborn and proud," Velryk said.

"That is good, otherwise they would have had you in chains decades ago."

Both smiled and Velryk nodded his agreement.

"Still that boy can be so hard headed," Velryk said. "Why would he do this?"

"Are you going after them?" Shaylee asked, knowing the answer to Velryk's question. An answer he wouldn't admit to himself.

"No," Velryk said with a resigned sigh. "If I go after them it will give the church something to base a criminal charge on. And if I did find them, I don't think it would do any good. What would I do? Order them to come home?"

"You have yourself to blame," Shaylee said. "Don't give me that surprised and innocent look. It is your blood that runs in his veins. Do you not remember the days when you and Ellidik would run off after your crazy causes?"

"They are, neither one of them, old enough for this sort of thing. They were taught better than Dik and I were. They should have known better. How will they learn anything by running off into the world without a notion of what real war is about? Roland doesn't have his feet on the ground solid. He needs to learn more about the nature of men before fighting those types of battles. He's not ready to learn what it is like to take the life of another man. He's not ready for what it can do to your soul."

"You don't fear for his safety, do you? You're afraid that what happened to your first son will happen to him," Shaylee said, taking Velryk's hand.

She had loved her husband dearly. They had all been such good friends. Now, holding Velryk's hand... "You're angry you didn't have more time to teach him. You have to let go of what happened to your first born. No one blames you for that but you."

"Roland's not ready!" Velryk barked, harsher than he intended. He pulled his hand away from her gentle touch.

It had been his poor luck to live on when a man as good as Ellidik fell on the battlefield. Ellidik would have made the proper teacher. Dik was the patient one. Dik was the one always centered and calm. Why had Bolvii let Dik fall and leave Velryk here. His own wife had been dead for years, why was it not Dik here to comfort Shaylee? Why did Velryk love her?

Shaylee's voice brought him out of his thoughts.

"If he's not ready then he never will be. There is only so much you can teach a child before he has to learn the hard way for himself. You remember the day when he and El were babies and just barely walking and playing near the cooking pot? You told Roland not to touch the pot because it was hot. What did he do? The first thing he did was put his hand to the glowing red iron. He even burned his other hand on the pot just to spite you. You have done a good job raising the boys, Velryk. You have to trust in them now. Give them their room and let them understand the reasons behind the lessons you have taught them. If you go after them now then they will touch the burning pot again, just to spite you."

"I suppose you are right," Velryk said. "You always have been. If you hear from El will you let me know? I think Roland would be too proud to send a message to his father unless it be to tell me he has defeated all the armies of Tarborat single handedly."

"I will certainly let you know. Would you like some breakfast? I just can't get used to cooking for only myself. I'm afraid I have prepared too much."

"I'd love a good meal."

Eight hundred leagues away, in the city of Gallhallad, a paladin and cleric of the church of Silvor the Huntsman enjoyed a much more lavish meal.

Gallhallad was the home of Lord Bessett and overlooked the eastern shores of the Kingdom of Lethanor. Gallhallad had been the least effected by the wars with Tarborat and it's dark general Ingshburn. Within its walls each of the twelve gods was honored with their own cathedrals and grounds. The properties of the churches here did not rival those found in Ostbier, the capital city of the kingdom, however they possessed their fair share of gold fixtures and tapestries of silk.

Sitting in the chambers of High Cleric Barnam, Sir Sanderland pled his case for charges to be brought against that arrogant boy and his father, Velryk.

"I understand your thoughts on the matter," Barnam said. "You must understand that the church has other concerns, other plans, in the offing. If we can seem indulgent now it will strengthen our standing in the future. A future in which we will demand, or perhaps take, power from a weakening throne."

High Cleric Barnam was born of the Great Man race, as most in the upper echelon of the churches were. He appeared to be in his late fifties perhaps which could put his actual age anywhere from two to four hundred years. His blonde hair bore a good deal of gray now as it curled around his silken cap. He was possessed of a kind face and easy smile which stood in sharp contrast to eyes of blue that could be merciless. His frame was large, as was usual for those of his race, but his soft hands and bulge of a gut belied his even softer lifestyle. A lifestyle paid for by the faithful.

"Your Holiness," Sanderland said, "this Velryk's name doesn't carry the weight that it did in former years. Many have said in hushed voices how his courage must have failed him for him to live such a humble and safe life in Fordir."

"Ah, but they do keep their voices hushed, do they not?" Barnam replied. "Those prisoners were of no threat to the church. Of that I am sure. Furthermore, nothing should come in the way of your engagement with Lady Angelica."

"She still puts me off," Sanderland said. "Has she no thought of how mighty our children could be?"

"I have assurances from her High Cleric that you will

be wed," Barnam said. "In the meantime, make your way to Lawrec. If the tide is turned there against this Daeriv, then the Church of Silvor should be among those that take the glory for it. If Daeriv is successful in driving the prince from there then I will need a good man who can attest to the failings of the prince and therefore the failings of his bloodline. If the prince should fall in battle then the Church will need you there ready to assume command, for the good of the people or course."

CHAPTER III

The Wild Lands

THE THREE YOUNG MEN TRAVELED for a few days and were beyond the borders of Gallhallad. Gallhallad enjoyed a peace that few other regions could match. Now they were moving into the borderlands. The untamed fringes between those places known as civilization. The leaves and grass were browning in preparation for winter's sharp touch. They traveled for weeks avoiding towns and strangers. Roland wanted no word of him returning to his father unless it be of his victories.

They passed shacks and cabins here and there inhabited by the huntsmen that roamed these less tamed lands keeping their distance. All the boys, for boys is truly what they still were, enjoyed the time. They enjoyed discovering places unknown to them, and drinking water from foreign streams. Eldryn, Ashcliff, and Roland talked a great deal during that time. Ashcliff was always very careful when discussing his own past. They spoke in turn of tales they had read, or mischief they had gotten up to in their recent-past youth.

Roland and Eldryn fell into their talks with the ease of a lifelong friendship, with Eldryn talking for both of them most of the time. Ashcliff's veneer, although well-conceived and undetectable by Roland and Eldryn, began to fade. He caught himself time and again telling them stories of his life without his usual careful guard. He told them of his life on the streets of various cities as a beggar and a thief. He told them of his captivity and time as a slave. He found he was becoming their friend rather than posing as one.

Roland and Eldryn discovered that Ashcliff could match even their endurance, if not their stride, when it came to the daily runs. They also discovered that he could produce surprising results when hunting with only a dagger borrowed from Eldryn. Ashcliff, however, insisted on hunting alone. He did have secrets he must protect. The other boys protested this idea in the beginning but, as their trust grew, so did Ashcliff's freedoms.

Eldryn stalked, and harvested, several deer with his bow. Roland was as skilled an archer as Eldryn, but his bulk countered his attempts at approaching wild game quietly. He rarely got within bowshot of anything worth eating. Roland did find that he was skilled at hunting wild boar and bears, however. He developed a method that consisted of angering his prey, and when they charged, he would cut them down with his axes, or bastard sword. That tactic seemed to suit Roland well.

Ashcliff had displayed a remarkable knowledge of herbs and eatable plants. The small group ate well for trail food, however, not nearly in enough quantity to please Roland or Eldryn for that matter. The diet and travel seemed to lean Roland and Eldryn's physique. Both, however, gained in strength and constitution with the increase in exercises and the life in the wild.

In their camps of evening Roland would instruct Ashcliff in the use of the hand axe, or short axe as it was known to some. Eldryn taught him archery. Ashcliff attempted to pass on the tricks of manipulating and throwing a dagger, but the alien nature of handling a weapon in that fashion was difficult for Roland. Eldryn politely paid attention but did not practice. It seemed Eldryn was satisfied with the weapons he knew.

As they strayed farther and farther from the settled

lands the terrain became more broken and wild. The closer they came to the mountains the more evidence they saw of the Battles of Rending that literally tore lands apart. They labored over sharp embankments of ancient lava and carefully negotiated rushing streams of near freezing water from the snows far above. The trees became shorter and more sparse. They heard the cries of unknown beasts in the night.

The boys began taking turns at watch during their slumber after a curious creature none of them could identify attacked, killed, and attempted to eat Roland's horse. The creature, which looked something like an evil cross between a tiger and a raccoon, died with a dagger in its right eye, an arrow in its heart, and one of Roland's axe blades in its skull. They didn't realize it at the time, but this was their first stand together. A quick act of instinct by all toward a common goal. An act which became a corner stone for a friendship.

When the beast fell dead Eldryn, much to Roland's dismay, noticed that Roland's pants were most of the way down leaving only his shirt tail to scarcely cover his genitals.

"Why are your pants off?" Eldryn asked.

"They're not off!" Roland said as he worked to pull them the rest of the way up. "I was...I was taking a dump if you must know!"

Both Eldryn and Ashcliff tried to stifle laughter.

"I haven't read as much of the old tales as you have, Roland," Eldryn said as his laughter began to over flow his lips. "But, tell me I beg, do they talk of the great Shyeld of old 'taking a dump' in those wonderous stories?"

This sally broke the dam and Eldryn and Ashcliff burst into a laugh fueled not only by the state of Roland's pants but the release of the fright the night creature had brought on them so suddenly.

The rough winds and rougher terrain began to take its toll on their spirits. Sleep became harder to come by and less restful. But, as it is with most men, shared misery became a shared bond.

The moon was declining as Roland's shift on watch, he always took third watch of the three, was coming to an end. It would be time for him to prepare breakfast soon. Roland heard something in the brush approaching their shelter in a dry creek bed. Winter was in full force now, and the boys did what they could for shelter from the wind in these wild lands.

Roland, dressed for warmth and battle, took up his two axes and listened. He considered waking his friends, but what warrior wakes his friends at the slightest bump in the night. He considered taking off some of his armor to move more quietly, as Ashcliff had begun to teach him. He dismissed that thought as well.

Roland walked into the dark, relying on his ears and nose, as he had been taught. He did smell something vile on the wind. He heard the twist and bind of leather to his left and he spun to meet the attack he felt was coming.

Roland took the full force of a hammering blow on his left leg that buckled his knee. If he had not turned when he did his knee would have been broken by the blow instead of only buckled.

Roland cut out in a reaction to the painful strike. He saw the outline of a large humanoid being in the shadows and the faint glow of disease yellow eyes. The creature howled as Roland's axe blade bit into its upper thigh. It swung at Roland again.

Roland saw the blow coming this time. It was not in Roland to block the attack. 'If one only defends, he will not be victorious, he will only be tired.' Roland heard the quote from 'Thoughts on War' run through his mind. It seemed he was quite good at remembering the quotes that agreed with his own philosophy.

Roland dug in the toe of his left boot and forced himself inside the arc of the club that swept towards him. He crashed into a fowl smelling beast that was at least two feet taller than his seven feet four inches.

Roland cut for the inner thigh with one axe, and the collarbone with the other. He felt the club strike him on the back and he knew it would leave a bruise. However, a bruise was better than a broken limb. He felt his axes bite flesh and break bone. The creature howled again and Roland pushed away from it drawing his iron free of the wounds they had cleaved.

Roland set himself and the beast came at him again with an overhead chop. Roland had just enough time to side step the swing. He moved to his right and caught the creature's arm between his axe blades, one rising and one falling onto the beast's forearm. Roland had practiced that attack on trees four to six inches in diameter and had splintered them. This time he cut through a few inches of muscle, and brought another howl of pain from the beast's throat.

The large beast kicked out at Roland and struck his breastplate just above his abdomen knocking him back eight feet. Now his breastplate was dented in and was pushing on his diaphragm, cutting off his air.

Roland dropped an axe and drew his flame blade dagger. He sliced through the leather straps on his armor as fast as he could as he kneeled on the ground.

The beast approached, one arm hanging in a grotesque and unnatural bend, the other arm holding the small tree it was wielding as a club.

Roland had to drop his remaining axe to get the killing armor off. Using both hands, one wielding the dagger, he managed to get free of the death grip the bent armor had put him in. Once freed he looked up from his kneeling position to see the creature standing over him.

The beast swung another overhead chop directed at Roland's skull. Roland caught the swinging club in one hand and strained with all the might that he could summon. Roland forced the club back up into the air and pushed the large beast back.

The creature sneered and leaned its maw toward Roland to bite at his face and throat. As it drove its head forward Roland launched the dagger in reply. Risking his hand, Roland thrust the dagger between the creature's teeth and into its maw. Driven by Roland's strength, the blade traveled through the roof of the beast's mouth and into its brain. Unclean teeth scraped the iron surface of Roland's bracer.

The beast slumped to the ground, dead. Roland collapsed beside it with exhaustion, his chest heaving for breath.

Eldryn was running into the trees with a torch lit and held high.

"Roland!"

"I'm here," Roland said between gasps, "with our visitor."

"What is that thing?" Eldryn asked as the light from the torch shined on the intruder's damaged corpse.

"An ogre I believe. It matches the descriptions I've heard," Roland said, between gasps.

"Yes, that is indeed an ogre," Ashcliff said from the shadows with a belied calm.

"Why did you not wake us?" Eldryn asked angrily.

"Should I wake you at every noise of the wind?" Roland offered. He had thought this response a reasonable retort, but it felt weak when he heard it out loud.

"Your pride will not only be the death of you, Roland," Eldryn, calming now, said. "What if the creature had killed you? That would have left Ashcliff and I at its mercy while we slept."

"I bow to your wisdom, and ask your pardon," Roland said in his infuriating knight-errand tone. Roland had meant every word not really understanding how that tone so enraged Eldryn at times.

"Get up and let's eat breakfast," Eldryn replied exasperated.

"Give me a minute, to catch my wind," Roland said.

"Are you injured?" Eldryn asked concerned for his friend. His anger passed as if it had never been as the idea that Roland might have been hurt replaced it.

"Not seriously, no. A bruise or two, that is all."

"Let's see what this big fella has on him," Ashcliff said,

smiling. "Ogres are known for their fondness of anything shiny."

Ashcliff searched the ogre's corpse while Eldryn stood over him with the torch. Roland sat next to them on the ground examining the severed leather straps and disabling dent on his armor.

"Take a look at this," Ashcliff said as he removed loot from the ogre.

Ashcliff showed Roland and Eldryn what he had discovered in the ogre's purse. Four daggers, twelve silver coins, three silver tipped arrows, and an assortment of teeth from various creatures.

"These arrows are something," Ashcliff said examining them. "One is designed to magically slay men, one to slay giants, and the last is blessed. That means that it would be most effective against a fallen champion or evil sorcerer."

"What would an ogre want with those types of things?" Roland asked.

"Ogres like shiny things," Ashcliff repeated. "They will treasure a piece of rock candy as much as a gold coin. It may only be pretty rocks, but let's remember, young lords, that diamonds are just shiny rocks.

I would like to keep the pack, the daggers, and the coins. I have only these clothes and a borrowed dagger. I could use the others."

"I care not, take them. El, do you want the arrows?"

"You are an archer as well," Eldryn replied.

"I am, but I cannot get within bow shot of anything quietly, and by the time a creature sees me I would rather be within arm's reach."

"Very well, I thank you. What are you going to do about your armor?" Eldryn asked.

"We don't have a kiln, or blacksmith for that matter. I suppose I can place it on the ground and have your horse step on it to bend it back into shape."

"You know it could split easily."

"Yes, but split armor is better than none. I'll use the hide

I kept from my last bear kill to repair the straps."

The three ate their breakfast of broiled bear meat and potatoes along with peanuts that Ashcliff had found.

The boys traveled with Roland riding a large portion of the time resting his injured knee. They had minor encounters with beasts along the way, some of which defied description. They would hear strange cries on the wind, even in the day time now, and would catch glimpses of fur or scale passing from one shadow to another. Ashcliff found the feces of a large predator and, after some argument, scented the three and their horse and gear with it.

"How do you know it was a predator?" Eldryn asked, hoping to make a good argument against the idea of smearing himself and his horse with crap.

"Teeth," Ashcliff responded confidently.

"Teeth?" Eldryn, as Ashcliff predicted, responded.

"Yes, teeth. The teeth I found in the dung were that of a large cat. Now it is possible that the pile I found belonged to a scavenger of some sort but scavengers usually have the time to be selective. Predators, on the other hand, tend to bite off and swallow whatever they can. So, teeth. Also, based on the, um, size of the pile, I would say a fairly big predator."

Nine days had pasted since the fight with the ogre when the group was traveling along a creek bed, using the walls of the creek as a partial shelter from winter's onslaught. Eldryn was riding their one horse when the group rounded a turn in the creek bed.

A rock the size of cow's head flew toward Eldryn. All of the boys knew their mistake for what it was.

They had been traveling in the wild lands, talking and singing like drunks on Sobriety Day. Their attempt at lifting their spirits might end with their spirits separating from their earthly bodies. Whatever had attacked them had probably heard them over the winds of winter for several hundred yards now.

Roland and Ashcliff both thought Eldryn had been struck a deadly blow, seeing him disappear from the back of the horse as swiftly as he did. Eldryn, however, had seen the rock coming just in time. Instinctively he kicked his feet free from the stirrups of the saddle. He swung himself under the neck of the horse to dodge the attack, and continued around the horse's neck and chest until he was upright in the saddle again. The move astonished both Ashcliff and Roland. The maneuver was a true mark of a skilled cavalier.

Eldryn drew one of the practice poles, this one of wood, he and Roland had used so many times as mock Great swords. This pole he had sharpened and capped with an iron point. He could not afford a formal lance, but this would do the trick. Eldryn dug his spurs into his mount and the horse leapt forward, hitting the ground at a full charge.

Ashcliff saw Eldryn's target and slipped out of the creek crawling up a wash, unseen by the monster.   Roland saw the giant that had thrown the rock. It was a great creature standing almost seventeen feet tall. Even Roland at his great height didn't quite reach the giant's waist. Roland was confident in Eldryn's abilities, in fact Eldryn was his superior with most weapons, but one giant was enough to be concerned about in a battle. Three giants could be considered by some to be suicide. Roland counted four giants gathered along the edge of the creek.

The first giant that threw the rock had taken up his club and set himself for Eldryn's charge. The next two hoisted rocks and hurled them at Roland. The fourth took up his club and headed into the woods in the direction that Ashcliff had disappeared in.

Roland, for his size, had always been quick. His length of stride also lent him a surprising speed. Roland used that stride now and stretched his legs out in a full sprint for the group of three giants on the small ridge at almost the same speed as Eldryn's charging steed. One of the rocks thrown at him missed cleanly while the other clipped his shoulder spinning him slightly off course. He drew both of his axes. The roar that came from Roland's throat would have been recognized by any fighting man of any language or culture. In fact, it was also recognized by the beasts they faced. It was a sound that came from the depth of his gut, a primal noise that many before him had made and many more after him would. It was the roar of a man intent on shedding blood. Roland roared, and continued his charge.

Eldryn reached his giant with his makeshift lance on target. The giant swung the heavy club to clear Eldryn from the saddle, but Eldryn's determined, and well trained, steed was too quick and charged inside the arc of the giant's swing.

Eldryn stabbed his 'lance' deep between the giant's ribs. The wooden pole shattered under the force, but not before burying a foot-long section of iron and wood in the giant's torso. The piece broke off under the skin and sunk into the beast's organs. The giant gurgled in pain as he dropped his club to scratch with futility at the bloody hole the 'lance' had left.

Roland reached the two giants just as they retrieved their clubs. Roland ran between the creatures, faking a cut at one, and digging both axes into the calf muscle of the other. As Roland passed them, he dropped into a crouch, set his feet, and turned to travel away from the giants at a right angle. He had hoped that his cuts would have disabled the one's mobility but the giant didn't seem to mind the minor wounds.

Eldryn plowed the ground with his horse's hooves as he turned him on a sharp arc to make another pass at the giants. He dropped what was left of his 'lance' and drew his bastard sword. As he rode in the giant did something unexpectedly clever. The giant struck low and caught the horse's front legs, sending both horse and rider flying. Eldryn struck the ground with a thud and rolled over the edge of the creek to fall to the soft creek bed below. The horse was lucky. It tumbled over the ledge of the creek and regained his footing on the way down to the sandy creek bed. Miraculously nothing was broken.

Now Roland faced three giants. One unmarked, one

sporting a minor wound delivered by Roland's axe, and one slowly bleeding to death from Eldryn's broken lance. He baited one into a swing at him. Once the giant began his swing Roland swiftly stepped between the legs of the other, causing the first giant to strike his companion on the knee. By the sound that blow made, Roland judged at least the kneecap broken, and perhaps more. What he did not consider, however, was the giant he was under. Once its leg was struck, it collapsed to the ground, with Roland under him. Roland dropped both axes and caught the creature as its weight bared down on him. He was able to guide the creature's fall slightly, which kept him from being crushed to death.

The fall still knocked Roland to the ground. Before he could regain his wits, he was slapped with a heavy wooden club that sent him flying twenty feet from where he sat. As Roland flew through the air, he saw that the giant with blood seeping from his lance wound and bubbling at his lips had managed to find his club. Roland hit the ground, again, the air already gone from his lungs. His battered armor had saved his life...again. Roland rolled over to see two giants approaching him with malicious grins on their faces. Their companion was rolling on the ground holding his injured leg.

Roland's bastard sword had been stripped from him at some time during the exchange. He drew his only remaining weapon, the flaming dagger. Bleak did not begin to describe his odds at survival. The giants demonstrated their scant wit by sneering at the small blade in the large man's hands.

Eldryn regained his breath and struggled over to the nervous horse. Whispering to the animal Eldryn took his bow, which somehow survived the tumble, from the saddle. He carried the bow and his quiver of arrows back up the creek bank swiftly. He rose from the bank to see the two giants approaching Roland, and one on the ground struggling to get up. Eldryn began trying to string his bow feverishly.

Roland took the flame blade in his right hand and stood up to face the two monsters. Both monsters laughed at the ridiculous sight of a man facing them with a knife.

Eldryn finally got the loop over the end of his bow and searched for the special arrow he had taken from the ogre, the one that Ashcliff said would slay a giant.

Roland watched as both giants hefted their clubs high in the air. He was amazed when one of them winced and then roared. Blood spewed out of its mouth and the giant's eyes rolled back into its head. Eldryn's slaying arrow had struck its target well.

The other giant, already breathing up froths of blood, turned to see what new threat had come from behind. When it turned Eldryn sunk an arrow into its chest. The monster laughed again at the puny effort as the arrow barely broke through its tough hide.

Once the creature turned, Roland seized his opportunity. He jumped onto the back of the giant's ankle, holding onto its leg with his left arm. Then he began sawing with his dagger on the tendon that ran behind the ankle and linked the calf muscle to the foot. The flame blade ignited when it tasted the blood of the giant and the tendon was scorched in two. The giant attempted to turn and get Roland in a position that he could strike him, but as the beast turned and tried to use his foot, he found that it did not respond as it should have. The giant fell to the ground with a howl. Roland began searching for one or both of his axes.

Eldryn sunk an arrow into the first fallen giant's right eye, just to be sure. The giant that had suffered a broken leg from his companion's strike had pulled himself up to his knees and was taking a large rock from their pile of ammunition.

Roland found one of his axes and attacked the giant lying near him with the severed tendon. Roland dodged several punches and was finally successful in leaping onto the creature's back. Roland heaved his axe blade down with all of his might striking the giant at the base of its skull. Roland heard a snap and the creature fell still instantly.

Eldryn put two arrows into the giant before it had the

rock prepared for a throw. However, throw the rock he did and with gruesome accuracy. Eldryn was knocked flying again, the wind forced from his lungs. Eldryn came to rest on the ground ten feet from where he had stood, his bow had been knocked far from his reach. He felt wetness on the side of his shirt. He could only pray that there was no internal bleeding as well.

Roland saw Eldryn's desperate situation, but also heard Ashcliff yelling. He could hear the giant hunting Ashcliff crashing through the trees.

"Go," Eldryn said through the blood on his lips. "I am a warrior. You go and defend the weak one, I'll handle this."

Roland had his doubts but respected his friend's decision. To help El now would be to dishonor him after he had refused assistance. Roland saw his other axe, took it up in his left hand, and whispered a quick prayer to Bolvii for Eldryn as he ran toward the sounds of battle in the trees.

Eldryn pulled his bastard sword from its scabbard on his side and began hurling every curse he could think of at the giant. The giant hoisted another rock and then anger flushed his face. He apparently understood some of the things the man was saying. The giant pulled himself up, took up his club, and limped toward the fallen man. The giant reasoned that the man could not walk, otherwise he would have risen to attack him or would have gone to help his friends. The giant smiled widely as he limped his way toward the man. This one would pay for the pain he felt in his leg.

Eldryn positioned his left leg underneath him. He took his bastard sword in his left hand and took an arrow out of his quiver and held it low in his right. Eldryn waited for the monster's approach.

The giant limped toward Eldryn. Eldryn held his sword up over head as if in a weak block against the crushing blow the giant would deliver. The creature smiled again and lifted his club high. The club came down with incredible force. Eldryn lowered his sword and then struck upward with all the strength he could muster to parry the club. As he did this, Eldryn pushed himself up with his left leg and spun himself to stand under the giant's wide spread legs.

Eldryn's sword was knocked to the ground but he was no longer in line for the giant's attack. Eldryn took the arrow in his right hand and stabbed it upward into the giant's crotch. The beast screamed in pain. Eldryn let go the arrow, leaving it stuck in the giant's organ, and grabbed the giant's good leg. He braced himself there and delivered a powerful kick to the inside of the knee on the creature's broken leg.

Eldryn quick-stepped back as the beast toppled to the ground again. The giant grabbed at itself trying to remove the biting pain coming from its groin. Eldryn retrieved his bastard sword and swung a two-handed chop that severed the beast's head. *My attack was not honorable*, Eldryn reflected. *Forgive me father.*

Roland ran into the tree line to find the giant crashing through the brush swiping at an unseen enemy. Roland noticed three daggers buried in the giant's face, one of which was in its left eye. Roland charged toward the giant head on. Ashcliff suddenly appeared on a tree limb behind the giant and sunk another dagger into the back of the creature's head. The creature spun about and seemed very satisfied to finally have his opponent in sight.

"Strike it in the back!" Ashcliff yelled to Roland. "Take him quick!"

Roland lifted both axes high and continued his charge. Roland struck the giant in the lower back with both axes carrying the full force of his charge. The axes sunk in deep and severed the giant's spine.

The large beast fell to the ground, paralyzed. Ashcliff dropped from his perch in the tree. He retrieved one of his thrown daggers and sliced the giant's throat.

A battered Roland and sweating Ashcliff walked from the forest to the edge of the creek where Eldryn was sitting.

"Oh, for something stronger to drink than water," Eldryn said with blood shining brightly on his lips.

"How bad is it?" Roland asked.

"Most of the bleeding is on the outside, which is good. But I've got a few broken ribs, I can feel them moving when I breathe. Also, some good bruising, and I've lost blood."

"Let me see what I can do," Ashcliff said.

Ashcliff helped Eldryn remove his armor and shirt. They all saw the large bruise forming and the piece of rib sticking out of Eldryn's bloody side. Wounds much worse that Eldryn realized.

"I have been taught about field dressings. We could try to set the bones right, and then wrap it tightly," Roland said. "It will take some time to heal."

"I know something of medicine," Ashcliff said. "Roland, can you start a fire and boil some water?"

"Certainly," Roland said.

Ashcliff took a wet cloth and wiped blood away from Eldryn's wound.

"I need to gather some things," Ashcliff said. "I'll be back shortly."

After Roland had the water boiling, he retrieved all of the fallen, lodged, and lost weapons of the group. Ashcliff returned with a few plant roots, five mushrooms, a small pile of leaves, and mud from the creek bank.

"Chew on these leaves," Ashcliff said. "They will help with the pain. I'm going to make a poultice out of these roots and this mud. This mud was around a plant we passed a little ways back. The poultice will stop the bleeding and heal the bones faster."

"What of the mushrooms?" Eldryn asked.

"These were a lucky find," Ashcliff said. "They will be useful."

"Indulge me," Eldryn said.

"When you eat one it will quicken your blood, and speed your muscles. It will allow you to attack and react much faster than normal."

"I see," Eldryn said with a doubtful look on his face. "I'll just hang on to these leaves. I don't need them right now."

"Prizes such as these herbs are to be found just lying around?" Roland asked doubtfully.

"We are nearing a magic place," Ashcliff said. "Think on the creatures you've seen. The gods struck this ground with pure power. That sort of power has a residual effect. Some good, some bad. El, are you sure you won't eat of the leaves?"

Roland noted the familiar, concerned way Ashcliff spoke to Eldryn. He smiled.

"No," Eldryn said, wincing. "We may need them further on."

"As you wish. We are getting close," Ashcliff said. "We should be at the burial site in a few days and that is only three or four days from the entrance to the sunken city."

"So, we are within a week of the entrance?" Roland asked, his sense of adventure renewed at the thought of Nolca-vanor.

"Yes," Ashcliff said.

"I will need some rest," Eldryn said.

"Yes, you will, I could use some myself," Roland said. "We will camp here for a few days. I'll take the giant heads and mount them on poles in a perimeter around us. That will hope-fully discourage any more visitors. At least for a short time."

Ashcliff's hands worked deftly yet gently around Eldryn's wound. He cleaned it with a cloth soaked in the hot water and applied the poultice, comprised of the mud-root-moss combination, around the exposed bone.

"Don't we need to reset the bone first?" Roland asked.

"The poultice will do that," Ashcliff said. "El' will need time to heal, but this should mesh the bone back together and close the wound in a day or two. El', let me know if your stom-ach begins to hurt or feels hard to the touch. That could in-dicate bleeding on the inside. I didn't see any, but you should watch for it just the same. The main thing is that you're not coughing blood which means there's most likely no damage to the lungs."

Roland and Eldryn marveled at their friend and the secrets he must know.

The three young men camped for a few days resting and healing. Eldryn's wounds healed at an extremely accelerated rate. Roland and Eldryn were both amazed.

"I've been trained in many things," was Ashcliff's only answer to their questioning looks.

They began their trek again after all had rested well. Their traveling was slower now, but they pushed on steadily.

By sunset of the third day after leaving the encampment near their battle with the giants, the boys came upon the hole in the earth where Ashcliff's equipment had once rested. They found a bare hole and a cold campsite. They were well upon the mountains now and could see the western end of the northern range.

"And what now?" Eldryn asked.

"Now we head toward Nolcavanor," Ashcliff said. "This site is cold, but only a few days old. They will travel afoot from here. Yorketh will have to conserve his power for what lays ahead of them so he won't be teleporting them any farther. Two of us travel afoot, but we have a horse to carry our equipment and a rider. Dawn has a remarkable endurance, but Yorketh runs like an aging bartender with lung rot."

All three laughed at the thought of the old wizard scurrying over these rocky climbs.

"So, we will gain time on them," Roland said. "Ashcliff you ride from here on in. You run like a deer, but you don't have the wind that El and I do. Eldryn and I have healed tremendously, thanks to you. If we do catch them, I don't want to be tied up on horseback anyway."

"What about me?" Eldryn asked.

"I know you treasure the idea of fighting from horseback, but you can't use that longbow of yours from horseback. If we come upon them you will need to get an arrow into that mage. Your first arrow must incapacitate him. I know better than to underestimate my female opponent this time, but I cannot calculate what a wizard might do."

"Very well," Eldryn said. "You can reason well enough, Roland, when it suits your purposes."

Now only two of them laughed.

"Have you a better idea?" Roland asked.

"No, no," Eldryn said. "I was just remarking on your skill at fortifying your heart's desire with reason and philosophy."

"May I ask you two a question," Ashcliff said.

"Of course," both boys answered in unison.

"Does it really burn? Your blood I mean," Ashcliff said. "I assume from what I know of the two of you that you are both of the Great Man race and likely pure in the blood."

"What do you mean, 'burn?'" Eldryn asked.

"Legend is that the Great Man race is from the times when champions and gods took on human lovers," Ashcliff continued. "Some scoff at the idea, but I have seen other things..." Ashcliff trailed off at that realizing what he was about to say.

"I've heard the same stories," Roland said missing the fact that Ashcliff almost divulged something he wished to keep hidden. "About the beginning of our race anyway. I'm not sure what you mean by our blood burning though. You've seen us both bleed and it's as red as your own."

"Not actually burn," Ashcliff said. "I've heard that the blood of champions and gods was too strong for their offspring and that it drove some of them mad and made others into giants and ogres. I've heard that the rage and vanity of the old kings is the result of that power. Some say that it is too much for a human body."

Roland and Eldryn exchanged a look.

"I'm not sure how to answer you," Roland said. "I have a quick and dangerous temper sometimes..."

"Sometimes?" Eldryn said.

"As I was saying," Roland continued while cutting his eyes at Eldryn. "I've seen horse thieves and cut purses with bad temperament as well. Is that different? I don't know. I can tell you that as far back as I can remember father has taught us to control ourselves. When we were younger, I sometimes got so angry that I lost time. When I would come to, I had struck or broken something. I would go into what father called a 'black rage.' He said it was a family trait although I can see where some might call it a curse. I've never known El' here to lose his temper though. He is always, has always been, steady."

Eldryn opened his mouth to say something when the fact that Roland actually complimented him struck. Eldryn's words were lost while his mind went over again what Roland had just said.

"What method did your father use to teach you to control it?" Ashcliff asked.

"He taught us about Bolvii," Roland said. "It began with teaching and reading which led to faith and understanding. Most of the time you can feel it coming, the rage I mean. It's just a matter of understanding that it's your enemy and not your ally. It is an enemy to your friends as well. Father likened it to a blindfolded archer. When the arrow of anger is let fly there is no calling it back. The arrow strikes wherever it will and the wound it creates is upon the soul of the bowman."

"As it comes you focus your will and try to let the anger flow away from you and not through you. As I got older the philosophies of Arto helped as well. He was a master of tactics, to be sure, but few know that his core belief was that a mind and soul must be at peace before the body can act with precision."

Eldryn marveled at Ashcliff. Eldryn had been taught just the same as Roland, but Eldryn had never needed that training. He didn't have the temper that Roland and Velryk seemed possessed by. Eldryn was amazed that Roland was talking about it though. He had asked Roland about his anger before, but Roland would rarely discuss it, and when he did it was never beyond single syllable responses.

For the first time Eldryn began to understand that Roland was ashamed of his temper. For the first time Eldryn began to understand that Roland envied him for what Roland must assume was masterful control when in truth it was not. Eldryn couldn't remember any time that he was angry. He had been sad, of course, and disappointed at times. When training, and more recently in battle, he felt his nerves tingle at the prospect of combat. Never anger, though. He wondered if he would have ever realized those things if it had not been for Ashcliff and his open question. In these weeks on the road Eldryn had learned more about his friend than he had in their years growing up together.

"Roland," Ashcliff said, "you continue to surprise me."

The boys traveled two hours past sunset along their path. Two more days of traveling brought them past five more campsites, the last still had warm embers. That night, on a ridge high above them they all saw the fire of a distant camp.

"Cold camps from here on in," Roland said.

"Chew on these," Ashcliff offered the others a few leaves he had collected during their journey. "The dark green ones will help you sleep, and the tinted blue ones will help keep your blood warm against the winds of the cold nights."

"What are these?" Eldryn asked.

"They are simple leaves, with some unusual powers."

"I'm not sure I like the idea of ingesting all of these leaves that possess 'unusual powers,'" Eldryn said. "They helped heal me well enough, but magical plants. I don't know if I like the idea."

"Salt has the power to dry out hides and kill snails. Pepper has the power to make a grown man sneeze. This is no different."

"Very well," Eldryn said with an acceptance that had, thus far in his life, been reserved for only Roland's wild ideas. "This is different than salt and pepper, though."

Each of the three looked up toward the distant fire with mixed emotions. Revenge, fear, uncertainty, and a desire for redemption blended in their hearts.

CHAPTER IV

Ruined Nolcavanor

T HAT MORNING THE AIR WAS BRISK and the sun was still an hour from the land's brim. Each boy rose, shook the frost off of his blanket, and stretched the stiffness out of his muscles.

Roland laid his axes and his bastard sword out on his blanket. He began to work the blades of each weapon with his whetstone, and then oiled them. Roland strapped on his breastplate, arm bracers, and leg greaves. Then he slung his axes on his weapons belt, placed his sword in its scabbard on his back, and stuck the flame blade behind his weapons belt on his side.

Eldryn oiled his bastard sword, and strung his bow. He made a careful count of the arrows in his quiver. He had taken the time to mark the three arrows that were taken from the ogre with their special purposes. Eldryn then fastened each special arrow to a different spot on the edge of his quiver with a rawhide strip and tied each with a slipknot.

Ashcliff put his cloak and light jacket on the horse. He took cloth and tied his loose-fitting woven trousers tight to his legs. He did the same with the deer skin shirt Roland had fashioned for him.

They had barbed Roland about his potential career as a seamstress should being a warrior not suit him. But the shirt was well made, and Roland was beginning to learn how to take a joke.

Ashcliff counted out his five daggers, one borrowed from El, and four taken from the ogre. Four very special daggers taken from the ogre. Ashcliff dug into the cold ashes of Yorketh and Dawn's fire that marked their previous campsite. He smeared ash on his hands, exposed forearms, and face.

"From here, I will be in the shadows," Ashcliff said. "I can serve you better from there. If they see you two approaching, I may be able to provide them with an unexpected surprise."

"Very well," Roland said. "Be in the shadows, but be close."

"If you cannot track them from the fire that we saw last night, the entrance to the caverns leading to Nolcavanor is concealed in an ancient lava flow. Look for the black sharp rock from the old flow. It will have been partially covered by sediment and over growth, but the black rock is there. Along the trail you will find where it forms a wall next to the path. Follow that wall, tracing it with your hand. There is a crack there, just big enough for a large man, but it is concealed by an overlap of the wall."

"If we need you to track?" Eldryn asked.

"Then just call, I will remain within ear shot."

Roland threw his cloak over the back of the horse so that his arms would be free of it in case he had to move quickly. Eldryn threw his strung bow over his shoulder and hung his shield on the saddle horn. Then Eldryn mounted their remaining horse. The mark of the firelight from their prey's camp led them all to believe it unlikely they would run across Yorketh and Dawn on a mountain trail. They would be in the caverns soon. Ashcliff disappeared into the brush to their north without a sound.

Roland began walking and Eldryn rode behind him. Both young men were edgy, but the years of training for moments like this one had them better prepared than most.

It took Roland and Eldryn longer than they expected to reach the point of the fire they had seen the night before. They found the familiar remnants of a campsite, and nothing more. Eldryn was able to identify a few tracks around the camp, but nothing leading more than ten yards from the area.

Roland could see the change in the shape of the mountain. It would have been easy to miss for the casual eye, but Roland knew what he was looking for and more importantly how to look. Velryk had taught them many things and this knowledge among them. *Most read from left to right. Those that don't read still develop a habit of looking something over from one side across to the other in a consistent pattern. You must learn to see, not to just look. When scanning the horizon, or a trail from a trap, look from left to right. But then go back from right to left. See what is before. Don't just point the lamps in your head this way and that.* He spotted the area where the lava flow had slowed between two peaks and formed a wall between them. Tracing that wall back with his eye he found the entrance to the path leading up the mountain face.

"You may as well leave your mount here," Roland said. "Even if you manage to get him up the trail much further, we will still have to leave him at the lava wall."

"You're right," Eldryn said with a resigned sigh.

Eldryn dismounted and took two waterskins off of the saddle. He handed one to Roland and then shouldered his shield. Eldryn stripped the rest of the gear off of the horse and released him. On this mountain a horse tied up was a meal lashed to a tree. At least this way the horse could defend himself, and might even return to his master's call, *if we get out of this,* Eldryn thought.

Roland watched Eldryn removing the saddle and saddle bags. After a quick evaluation of the gear he already carried, he took seventy-five feet of rope, a heavy tarp, five tent pegs, another waterskin, a piece of flint, and a seal skin filled with lamp oil. He placed most of those items in one of the saddlebags and threw it over one shoulder. Eldryn, seeing this, took up three prepared torches, extra cloth, and another seal skin of lamp oil.

Eldryn grinned at Roland, "some adventurers we are. We almost forgot that it gets dark underground."

Roland smiled back at him. It was a smile that showed a confidence that he did not feel. This battle would be different for Roland. In the jail against Yorketh and Dawn, and on the plains against the ogre and then the giants, Roland had no time for thought. He reacted to a violent situation without thought, allowing years of conditioning to do their work. Now he had plenty of time to think. Now Roland considered the taking of a life. Now Roland was afraid.

He had never killed a man, or woman, before. Velryk had taught them much, but, according to him, no words or books could completely prepare a man for the taking of a life. Defending himself was one thing, instinct. Now he set out to capture or kill. Those he hunted were evil, of that he had no doubt. What he must do was clear before him. However, how it might affect him was not. He had heard of soldiers and knights who developed a taste for killing and had heard of others that it had broken.

He was not a killer, nor was he broken by shame or guilt. Not yet. He desired the life of a knight. All his life he thought of nothing but the honor of standing for the weak against the wicked, of taking his place in the stories and legends of the heroes of old. Roland faced his true fear now. He was afraid to fail.

Both young men started up the path that Roland's eye had selected. After climbing for what they guessed to be three hours they found a sign. Eldryn spotted a bush bearing thorns that had snatched a piece of cloth from a dark cloak.

The altitude was getting thinner, and both boys were feeling the bite of winter. The night before they had used the leaves given to them by Ashcliff. Now they each took a tinted blue leaf and began to chew.

Once those were consumed, Eldryn produced a smoking leaf from his dwindling supply. He tore off a portion and gave it to Roland and then decided that lighting his own would be too much trouble and perhaps not tactically sound.

Eldryn bit off his own piece of the leaf and began to work it into his jaw. Roland took the piece of smoking leaf and began to chew. They spat into the snow, and both boys continued on their way to the wall of frozen lava and black, sharp glass.

They reached the path that led along the side of the wall. Eldryn noticed a tracing in the dirt along the wall made by what he assumed were human fingers. They followed those tracings until the markings disappeared.

Roland took the leather gauntlet off of his left hand and began to trace where the marks had left off. Immediately he noticed a slight draft and could feel the sharp curve of the overlap. The path was all but invisible. The pattern of the rock flowed together and was concealed in shadow, eluding all but the sharpest eye.

Roland looked around for Ashcliff, but to no avail. If Ashcliff was out there, he was well hidden. Roland took his axes from his belt and began down what he considered a very narrow path. From time to time both boys would stop and hold their breath after one or the other's armor would scrape the wall of the narrow passage. After another hour of stalking along the path they came to a clearing.

Roland looked up for the first time after being in the passage and understood the clearing.

"It's a bubble," Roland said.

"What?"

"A bubble. When the lava ran through here it began to cool quickly. It was still very hot, and boiling. This clearing was a bubble that was forming and didn't burst before the lava cooled to a solid. Look," Roland said as he pointed upward.

Eldryn looked up and saw what Roland was talking about. He could see where the top of the bubble had soared toward the sky and then was frozen in place. The crest of the bubble was shattered now, which explained the shards of jagged black glass among the sediment in the clearing. Eldryn could see the sharp and irregular rim of what was once molten rock above them.

"So, what now?" Eldryn asked.

"Now we find the entrance to fame, glory, and riches," Roland replied jovially.

"You shouldn't attempt to joke," Eldryn said. "You're no good at it. Leave the joking to me."

Roland hung up his axes and took out his bastard sword. He began searching the perimeter of the 'bubble.' Eldryn took down his long bow and knocked an arrow. Eldryn then began searching the interior of the 'bubble' for signs of an entrance.

The two searched for several minutes when Roland heard something thump past his ear. He looked up to see a throwing dagger still vibrating after striking a nearby tree. He recognized the dagger as being the one Eldryn had loaned to Ashcliff.

Roland began examining the tree and found that it was not rooted to the ground. It appeared to have been sheared off at the ground somewhere else and placed here. Roland grabbed the tree and flexed the muscles in his arms and chest. The tree tipped over, and Roland noted that it was hinged beneath and somehow rigged to a counter weight. Roland discovered a large hole leading into a tunnel below. Roland shoved the tree over to expose the hole to daylight. He left the dagger where it was, sunk into the wood, and peered down into the tunnel.

Eldryn approached him and looked down into the tunnel as well.

"How did you find that?"

"Just lucky. A borrowed dagger showed me the way."

"I see," Eldryn said. "So, what now? We don't know how deep it is, or if it's burdened with traps. Do we tie onto something up here and then lower ourselves in? Do we drop a lit torch down first so that we can see what we're getting into? Does one of us lower the other down on the rope while…"

Eldryn was answered abruptly when Roland dropped his sword in its scabbard, drew his axes, and jumped into the hole, feet first.

"I guess you just jump in and we go from there," Eldryn said to himself as much as to anyone else.

Roland dropped for fourteen feet before he struck the ground with a thud. He looked around him in the dim daylight that shined down from above.

"I feel a bit of a draft," Roland said. "I think I see a tunnel leading off to the north."

"Well, move out of the way," Eldryn said. "I'm going to light a torch and drop it down. Then I'll jump down there with you."

Eldryn dropped the torch and Roland retrieved it. Eldryn slung his bow over his shoulder and lowered himself into the hole. He and Roland both winced when his armor scrapped the rock surface on the inside of the hole. Once he was hanging down into the tunnel arm's length from the surface, he let himself drop. They both looked at the tunnel. It was roughly ten feet tall, and eight feet wide. Plenty of room to walk through but much too tight a space to fight in.

Roland started into the cavern with the torch in his left hand and one of his axes in his right. Eldryn followed. Eldryn had unstrung his bow and had drawn his bastard sword.

"You're putting up the bow?" Roland asked.

"Yes," Eldryn replied. "A bow is no good underground. It requires too much of an arc during flight to be good at any distance."

Roland nodded, seeing the truth of it, and continued forward. Suddenly he felt a shift in the ground beneath him.

"Back," Roland yelled. "Quick!"

The floor beneath them fell forward at a steep angle and a rush of oil poured down the steel plate they had walked out onto. Eldryn tried to jump back but there was oil on his heals before he could react. He slid, and fell to the surface of the steel plate.

Roland slid forward, struggling to remain standing and his feet rapidly skidded toward the edge of a large pit. As Roland approached the pit, he saw razor sharp shards of lava glass mounted and pointing up from the bottom. Roland looked across the pit and estimated it to be about twenty feet to the ledge on the other side.

"Leap when you hit the edge," Roland yelled as he slid forward.

Roland's barely controlled slide continued to pick up speed. He bent his knees and crotched low as he reached the edge of the steel plate. He threw the torch across the pit and it landed on the other side. He leaned forward and the weight of his body brought him forward and over the edge. He looked down the sheer face of the pit and pushed off with all the strength his legs could muster. Roland jumped vertically across the hole.

Roland saw that he would not make it to the landing. He stretched his long body and struck out with his axe. The axe blade caught just over the edge and Roland, gripping the haft, crashed into the far wall of the pit. He looked back in time to see Eldryn, with his sword in one hand, leaping toward him. He was not sure how El' had managed to get his footing but was glad that he had.

Roland stretched out his left hand and Eldryn caught it. Eldryn swung beneath Roland in a short arc that slapped him against the wall of the pit. Roland could hear the iron of his weapon begin to bend and scratch and he felt it edging toward the lip of the pit. Both boys hung on the blade of an axe.

"Grab on," Roland breathed to Eldryn. "I need my arm."

Eldryn grabbed Roland by his weapons belt and Roland pulled both bodies up to the edge with one arm. Once within reach, Roland grabbed for the edge of the pit with his other hand. He secured his grasp just as his axe slid off of the side.

Hanging by one handhold, Roland tossed his axe over the edge of the pit and hoisted his and Eldryn's weight up the side of the pit to the ledge. Once his elbows were hooked over the edge Roland looked down toward Eldryn.

"Climb over me to the landing," Roland said. "Once you're up there, pull me up."

Eldryn began to climb over Roland slowly, finally reaching the landing and relative safety. Eldryn rolled over and, lying flat, began pulling Roland up and over the side. Both boys finally made it to the level surface of the tunnel.

Both were breathing hard. Roland and Eldryn leaned over the edge to look down into the pit. Roland noticed a small ledge, no more than six to eight inches wide, along the side of the pit.

"I guess that is the way to cross," Roland said, indicating the ledge.

"That was close," Eldryn said between breaths.

"Close indeed," Roland said. "Let's move on."

The pair continued down the passage until they came upon two bodies lying in the tunnel. The corpses were fresh, dark skinned, lithe of build, and possessed short cropped white hair. Roland examined one, Eldryn the other.

"These are dark elves," Eldryn said. "They are said to be among the most evil creatures ever to walk or breathe."

"This one is wearing some kind of symbol," Roland said, eyeing what looked like two off set triangles. One of the triangles was at the base of the symbol, and the other askew to the side. The details were hard to make out in the torch light. "I don't recognize it."

"This one is as well. They must be part of a clan, or army in these tunnels and caverns. Great."

Eldryn looked both ahead and behind them down the tunnel. From what he had heard of the dark elves they were the things of nightmares.

"They have been stripped of most of their equipment," Roland said. "Both were killed by a single dagger stab to the throat. Only one injury each and the blows appear to have been immediately fatal. It is my understanding that dark elves are virtually impossible to sneak up on, and the injuries are on their front. That means they probably saw their attacker or were at least looking in the attacker's direction. That implies great skill."

"Ash?" Eldryn asked.

"I hope so," Roland replied.

The two moved further down the tunnel and found a ladder cut into the stone leading down. Roland began climbing down the ladder while Eldryn continued to scan the tunnel behind them. Both young men reached the lower level and saw that they were in a room roughly thirty feet wide and thirty feet across. There was a hallway leading out of the room on each of three walls, and one door on the north wall.

Neither boy knew much about the formation of natural caverns or the crafting of mine shafts, but the unusual nature of this room would be easy to mark for even the uneducated. They both noted that the floor, doorways, and some of the walls were clearly crafted by hand, a skilled hand. However, much of the tunnel they had come from looked more like a crudely cut mine shaft. They also saw that the stones in the floor and forming the door jams was marble.

"Well, which way?" Eldryn asked.

"We can't depend on Ashcliff. He may not even know for sure. Let's just travel and see what we find."

"Very well," Eldryn said as he approached the door.

Eldryn tried the knob and discovered that the door was unlocked. He threw the door open prepared for a demon or some other such creature. He found five crossbow bolts loosed at him instead. Three of the bolts struck his shield, one his breastplate, and one his bracer, bruising his wrist. Eldryn dropped his sword from the pain in his hand and began to yell a string of obscenities when he remembered where he was.

"Are you alright?" Roland asked.

"Only hit me in the pride," Eldryn said.

Eldryn looked into a small closet that had apparently been designed for the single purpose of this trap. He saw the crossbows mounted on a wooden frame and a thin wire that ran from the door to the trigger mechanisms.

"How about this way," Roland said as he walked toward the hallway on his left.

"One is just as good as another," Eldryn replied as he picked up his sword.

The boys continued in a direction they guessed was west for another thirty feet into the black with only their torch to push back the heavy dark. They came into another room about the size of the last one. This room had a hallway across from them, a door on the south side, a hallway on the north side that appeared to turn west, and another door on the north side that appeared to turn to the east.

"Shall I try the door this time?" Roland asked.

"No," Eldryn said. "Surely they won't booby trap the entire place. Eldryn walked to the door on the south side of the room and pulled it open with his shield held high.

Five crossbow bolts flew out of another trap soaring at Eldryn. Four of them landed squarely into his shield, however, one was mounted low and struck his greaves. The bolt's head was broken off by the iron armor but it skidded up and struck him soundly on the knee. A knot began to rise on his knee, and Eldryn could feel a small trickle of blood begin within his leg greaves.

"Curse these dirt dwellers," Eldryn said as he rubbed his knee.

Roland approached the door, torch in one hand and axe in the other. He looked inside to discover a large room with what looked to be the same symbol they discovered on the dark elves drawn on the floor. There were four torches in the room, mounted on the walls and a brazier in the center of the symbol where the upper point of the triangle reached toward the point of the other triangle that sat askew.

"What is this place?" Roland asked.

"It looks like a summoning room. A place where wizards call and control fallen champions and their spawn. The symbol on the floor matches the one we found on the dark elves in the tunnel."

"Well, it's not what we're here after," Roland said. "Let's get going."

"I'm going through that door," Eldryn said indicating the door on the north wall near the east corner.

"Do you think that's a good idea?" Roland asked.

"No, I do not," Eldryn said, displaying a rare stubbornness. "But I am not going to allow them to make me afraid of simple doors."

Eldryn took hold of the door and jerked it open hard. To Roland's amazement five more crossbow bolts struck Eldryn in the upper body. Three lodged in his already burdened shield, two slid just past the edge of his shield and pierced his breastplate. Eldryn fell back to the ground with the force of the blows.

Roland ran to him and began working to get his armor off. Roland got the straps loose, being careful not to move the armor that the bolts were sticking through.

"I think I would avoid any games of chance that involve betting, at least for the rest of the day," Roland said. "Today you are not lucky."

Eldryn winced as Roland worked.

"I told you once, Roland. Leave the joking to me. You're terrible at it."

Roland took up Eldryn's bastard sword. He braced one of the bolts in the corner formed by Eldryn's blade and the hilt guard on his bastard sword. Roland snapped it quickly, breaking the bolt off cleanly. Eldryn struggled to contain a scream. Roland broke the other bolt off in the same fashion.

Roland removed Eldryn's breastplate and looked at the wounds. Eldryn had been remarkably lucky.

"Perhaps today is your day for cards after all," Roland said.

Roland was looking at the heads of the bolts and noted that the first barbs of the bolts hadn't made it past the armor. Roland had been worried that if the heads of the bolts were deep inside the flesh, he would have to cut them out, possibly causing even more damage than the bolt did initially.

Roland remembered a time as a child when he had fallen while running with a fishing spear. Velryk had come to his cries and cut the barbs of the spear free of Roland's leg. Velryk, always teaching, spoke to Roland then of conducting a similar operation on a fellow soldier who had been struck by an arrow. Roland had been lost in the tale of that battle when the sharp pain of Velryk's dagger in his leg reminded him of his predicament.

Roland grabbed a bolt in each hand.

"El, did I ever tell you about the time that father told me about an ambush by archers?"

As Eldryn began his reply Roland jerked the bolts quickly out. Eldryn gasped for breath.

"Get up," Roland said, hoping to encourage his friend. "You're not really hurt."

"The heads didn't go in?" Eldryn asked as he looked down at his chest.

"No, they did not."

Roland took some extra cloth from the tail of Eldryn's shirt and wrapped his chest, stopping the small amount of blood that was seeping out of Eldryn's wounds.

"There," Roland said. "Now get dressed."

Eldryn pulled his armor back on slowly, not wanting to disturb the dressing on his puncture wounds. Roland looked down the hallway that ran from behind the latest trapped door. It appeared to run roughly forty feet and then open into a T intersection. Roland started down the hallway with Eldryn following him closely.

Roland came to the intersection and looked east and west. Looking east Roland only saw hallway for as far as torch light would reveal. Looking west Roland saw that the hallway turned back to the north about twelve feet in. Roland started west.

Roland turned north and followed the hallway for another thirty feet before coming to a door. At the sight of the door Eldryn raised his shield.

"Hold this," Roland said extending the torch toward Eldryn, "and move back."

Roland lifted his axe and struck the doorknob, knocking it cleanly out of the door while holding the door its self in place. Both young men heard several thumps strike the door on the other side. One of the crossbow bolts struck the door with such force that part of the head protruded through to their side of the doorway. Roland and Eldryn exchanged a tired look. How many traps could there be?

The boys entered and found a descending staircase that ran into the dark as far as the light from their torch would travel.

Roland began down the steps placing his feet lightly as Ashcliff had shown him. He had climbed down twenty feet when he heard some type of movement, and could see a landing approximately forty feet below him. Roland continued, axe in one hand and his retrieved torch in the other.

Eldryn followed with his shield up and sword in hand. Eldryn moved quietly as well, but in his excitement, he scraped his shield against the stone wall. Both boys held their breath for a moment. When there seemed to be no response from around them, they continued.

Step by step, controlling their breathing and fighting the urge to leap, they finally arrived at the landing. They saw that they were in a large round room with a single door on the far side. Between them and the door they discovered two very surprised creatures. Creatures of a squat, but mighty, build and skin the color of old bruises. Fangs protruded irregularly from cracked and stained lips.

"What are those things?" Eldryn asked as the creatures lifted stoutly built crossbows and leveled them at the boys.

Roland charged forward with Eldryn closely behind.

"Gray Ogres," Roland yelled. "Shorter than their above ground kin, but just as strong."

Roland charged forward and both creatures took aim

at him. Both triggered their stout crossbows and the bolts cut through the air toward Roland. One bolt glanced off of his helmet rocking his head back. The other bolt struck Roland's knee, felling him.

Eldryn watched both bolts strike his friend and his rage flared. His rage? Well, perhaps not rage, but Eldryn felt the stirring of anger deep within him. He was, however, a well-trained warrior and he tried to immediately put his feelings away and continue toward the ogres with a layer of frost around his heart.

Roland toppled to the ground, his knee bent in a direction that was not intended. He did, however, maintain his grasp on his axe and the torch. One of the gray ogres began preparing another crossbow bolt, the other hefted a heavy thick blade.

Roland pulled himself up to a sitting position despite the strength sapping pain that stole lightning quick up his injured leg. He held his torch to the side and his axe at the ready.

Eldryn, sword in hand and shield up, charged for the ogre with the large cleaver. He feigned an attack, and then ripped his sword away from the first ogre to strike the one still loading the crossbow. Eldryn's attack was not meant for the ogre, but rather his weapon. Roland could still defend himself against a melee attack, but with a crossbow one could just stand back and slowly execute the fallen warrior, his fallen friend. The crossbow was reduced to nothing but a collection of wood and cable with one great swipe of Eldryn's bastard sword.

The ogre with the large sword grinned at his open chance. The ogre cast aside all thoughts of defense and raised his enormous blade high in the air. Eldryn, with his sword too far off course to use for attack or defense, utilized the only other attack available to him. Eldryn struck up hard with the steel edge of his shield against the ogre's exposed chin. Blood sprayed from the ogre's mouth as his jaw sagged away from the roof of his mouth in two distinct pieces.

Eldryn attempted to quick-step back to put both of his opponents in a smaller angle for combat. The broken jaw injured the ogre, but his sword still fell with wicked accuracy. The edge struck Eldryn's shield and shoulder, knocking him down to one knee and shattering his shield.

Eldryn whipped a cut between the ogre's legs aimed at the inside of its thigh. The cut was true and blood spewed out of the creature. The ogre fell back, now bleeding profusely from two different places. The beast attempted to stem the flow of its life out of its body, but had no success. The ogre was bleeding to death, and rapidly.

The second ogre had retrieved his club now, seeing that his crossbow was beyond repair and of no use.

Eldryn tried his shoulder and was relieved that it worked smoothly. He did, however, grieve the loss of his shield. He took up his bastard sword in both hands to improve his control and speed with the blade. He prepared himself for the fight. The ogre could out match even Eldryn in strength, but not in agility. Eldryn was strong, but also quite skilled.

The creature came in and swung its brutal club toward Eldryn. Eldryn struck the club twice attempting to beat it off of its course. Seeing that the strength in his attempted parry would fail, Eldryn rolled over backward and outside the arc of the club. Eldryn regained his footing and attempted to come in behind the path of the club to attack the ogre. The remaining gray ogre, however, brought the club backward along the same arc catching Eldryn in the same position he had just barely survived a moment before.

Eldryn braced himself, and struck out hard against the blow of the club. He shifted his feet and, when the powerful strike from the ogre came, Eldryn used the force to drive himself in a circle around the creature. Then Eldryn noticed his advantage. He continued his feigns and allowed the attempted parries to drive him around the room as the last one had. The ogre believed that he had Eldryn on his heels and that victory would come as soon as Eldryn was backed into a corner that he could not retreat from. The ogre could already taste his flesh.

Eldryn continued to back away and allow the attacks

to drive him in circles around the room. The creature finally had Eldryn backed against the west wall of the room.

The ogre prepared his attack and his shock was complete when his right leg folded, dropping him to the floor. The creature looked behind him as he fell to see the other man, the one that the ogre had thought was out of the battle, sitting behind him with a bloody axe in his hands.

Eldryn wasted no time. He stepped forward and cut a deep furrow in the ogre's throat. The creature collapsed, dead. Eldryn went to Roland's side.

"Can you walk?" Eldryn asked.

"I don't think so," Roland admitted through gritted teeth. "Judging from the angle, I don't even know if I can set my knee aright."

"I can," Ashcliff said, startling both boys. "I apologize for being late. There were some things I needed to gather."

"Things?" Eldryn asked.

"Yes," Ashcliff replied. "While I was in jail in Fordir I sent a message to someone I trusted to have some supplies hidden near the entrance to this place. I needed to retrieve them."

"How did you get a message out from the jail?" Roland asked.

"I have my ways," Ashcliff replied.

"I am in no mood for your secrets," Roland said sternly. "This is something you will tell me, one trusted friend to another. If you will not, then I care not for your help or your friendship."

Eldryn surprised himself by readying his defense of Ashcliff. There was no need for Roland to take such a tone with a friend, with their friend. Ash was his friend now. It had been true for some time, but not fully recognized by Eldryn. He was not as close to Ash as to Roland, of course. But Roland was in the wrong, and Eldryn meant to tell him so.

"I mean you no dishonor by my quiet nature," Ashcliff began. "Please understand that it is part of who I am and what I do. This particular secret I will tell you. I have some limited magical capabilities. Very specific capabilities. It was through those skills that I escaped your jail for a short time by appearing as another who was to be released. You remember the drunk that you released, and you had to jail him again that very evening? I disguised myself as that drunk. I only had a short time of freedom because I knew he would eventually awake from the ground root I put in his food. If he were to awake and ask why he had not been released, then I would have been in some very hot water. If, due to his clamor, you had conducted a head count then I would have been discovered missing. Then I would have you hunting me too."

"What would you have done if I hadn't released you and solicited your help?" Roland asked, genuinely curious now.

"I would have escaped Sir Sanderland before he presented me to his cleric. I would not want the likes of your father, Lord Velryk, on my trail. Therefore, I decided that Sir Sanderland was the weaker of the two. If I was forced to make an enemy of one of them by escaping their custody, I would prefer that enemy to be Sanderland. One of two things would have happened should I have escaped Sir Sanderland. Either Sir Sanderland would have told of my escape from him and I would be hunted by him and the church, or he would have kept quiet about my escape, and his failure to bring me in, and I would have been truly free."

"You called him 'Lord Velryk.' What do you know of my father?" Roland asked. "He is the local reeve and was once a soldier, but I have never heard him called a lord."

"I make it my business to know about every legend that still walks. You never know when that knowledge might save your life. I assume that your father has not hunted us thus far because he has duties where he is, and he did not declare my 'release' as an escape. To do so would have indicated his son in the escape and made you two wanted criminals. I assume he came up with some story to tell the clergy."

"You didn't answer my question," Roland said. The pain in his knee was severe, however, he burned with curiosity about his father. "What do you know of my father, and why do you call him 'Lord Velryk.'"

"I've heard enough to know that I don't want him for an enemy. It is said that he fought viciously during his time in the wars with Tarborat. He was counted among Tarborat's greatest enemies at one time. The 'Lord' in his name is just a courtesy, of course. He does not hold his own lands, but the King considered him of equal or more importance as those that do hold lands and bring their own armies to the front."

"He has never said anything of it," Roland said.

"Do you want to talk, or fix your leg?"

"The leg first," Roland said. "I do, however, want to finish this conversation later."

Ashcliff took a potion from his newly acquired backpack and handed it to Roland. Then he prepared a yellow paste out of several berries he took from his pack.

"Do you want something for the pain?" Ashcliff asked.

"No, just get it done."

"You will need to hold his upper body, El. I'm going to pull the leg back in line."

Eldryn held Roland, and Ashcliff took Roland's leg just below the twisted knee. Roland and Ash exchanged looks and Roland nodded. Ashcliff jerked and turned Roland's leg brutally. Roland gasped, but did not cry out.

"There," Ashcliff said. "Now drink the potion, it will heal the muscles around your knee rapidly."

Roland's face was still flushed from the effort. He took the potion and drank it without question. A few moments slid past and suddenly Roland felt relief from the crippling injury. Roland relaxed his gritted teeth and stood shakily. He tried his knee and stood more firmly.

"You are truly an amazement," Roland said to Ashcliff.

"I am well trained, as are each of us, in certain areas. That is all."

"If you are just now catching up to us," Eldryn said, "then it wasn't you that took the two dark elves we found in the entrance tunnel?"

"It was not I," Ashcliff said. "I was hoping that the two of you had felled them."

"I suppose Dawn is more to be reckoned with than we had assumed," Roland said. "When we face her, we must close the distance quickly. We cannot give her the opportunity to hurl daggers at us while we advance."

"I think I should take point from here on in," Ashcliff said.

"Good idea," Eldryn confirmed.

"What about that door there?" Roland asked indicating the door that the two ogres seemed to have been guarding.

"We don't want to stray down there. What we are here for is in this upper level, and I don't think we could open it anyway."

"What's down there?" Eldryn asked. He looked over the door more closely now and saw carved runes and magical warding surrounding it.

"An evil that you do not want to know."

CHAPTER V

A Question of Time

ASHCLIFF BEGAN UP THE STEPS LEADING out of the room that Roland and Eldryn had trod down. He led them back to their left and they traveled east for about seventy feet and turned back to the south. They followed the hallway along its winding path until they came to a T intersection. The hallway ran north and south.   They all heard the sounds of battle coming from the northern hallway.

"I'll take a look," Ashcliff said. "I'll be right back."

With that Ashcliff trotted silently down the northern hallway and turned out of sight just before reaching the edge of the torchlight.

"How will he see in the black?" Eldryn asked Roland.

"Your guess is as good as mine."

Roland and Eldryn waited impatiently for Ashcliff's return with their weapons ready. The minutes went by slowly. The damp air of the deep cavern filled their noses with a tangible dread. Finally, Ashcliff returned as softly as a breeze up the hallway.

"We may have encountered some luck," Ashcliff said. "Yorketh and Dawn are outnumbered and locked in a battle with twelve of the dark elves. If they aren't killed, we will at least have the time to get part of what we came here for."

"I came here for them," Roland said.

"We can go back and get their corpses in a while," Ash-cliff said. "If they are not felled in combat then they will at least be weaker so that we can take them with more ease."

"What else are we here for?" Eldryn asked.

"Treasure," Ashcliff said, grinning.

"There is no treasure here or anywhere that I want more than I want those two in irons and on their way back to Fordir," Roland said.

Ashcliff's grin dropped.

"Look, the items I was sent for are of great value," Ash-cliff began. "I am not talking of silver and gold. They could change the outcomes of wars and save many lives. If in the wrong hands, Daeriv's hands, many will die. Which do you want to pursue? Two spies who have thus far failed in their mission, or something that could change the tides of kingdoms?"

With that Ashcliff took up the lead again and began south down the hallway. Roland and Eldryn exchanged a look. Neither possessed a magical telepathy, as some did, but they did have a more natural means of communication. The type of communication that comes from years of friendship. They turned and followed after their friend.

Ashcliff froze thirty feet into the hallway.

"Trip wire," Ashcliff said, pointing out the thin wire running across the floor of the corridor.

Roland and Eldryn carefully stepped over the wire with their breath held, and then continued on following Ashcliff. Ash pointed out three more traps along the way that the other two young men would have certainly fallen prey to without him to guide them.

Ashcliff led the boys down a series of hallways and through several hidden doors. The boys trod on into the dark. Roland and Eldryn had lost track of time and distance in this heavy blanket of dark that rested around their struggling torch. Finally, they reached a large iron bound wooden door.

"Through here is our goal," Ashcliff said. "There is a

great beast within. Beyond it is another room. In that room we will find the treasure we seek."

"And what about Dawn and Yorketh?" Roland asked.

"If we can obtain what is in that room then they will come to us. That is why they are here and they will pursue that item until they have it or they are dead."

"What is it we seek?" Eldryn asked hoping this time to get more than generalities about mystical powers.

"There is an ancient holy book, The Book of Fate. Next to that book should be a large hourglass. The Hourglass of Time. Both items are artifacts and are pursued by some very powerful individuals."

"And this beast?" Roland asked.

"That is for you to figure out as you go. I'm afraid I won't be much help against the creature. As you may have already put together, that is not exactly my specialty."

"Well, there is no time like the present," Roland said. With that he went through the doorway.

Eldryn prepared himself and stepped through behind Roland. Neither boy noticed where Ashcliff went.

Inside they discovered a large, hair covered creature that resembled a lion with the exceptions that it possessed two heads, and its back was almost twelve feet from the stone floor. A smell of stale musk oil filled their noses. The beast was enormous and immediately vicious. Both boys felt an uncommon fear shake them to their cores.

Both young men were courageous. Either from a birthright of strong blood, years of training, or the fact that most young men lack the ability to fathom their own demise, these two were sturdy in the face of danger. This fear was not that. This was somehow magical in nature and stole throughout them until it reached their center. Until it crashed into the minds of two warriors and the will forged within.

In less than a second this struggle of magic versus determined minds was fought. In less time than the flap of a bird's wing was the power of this creature repelled.

The beast came for Roland and then veered away rapidly. When Eldryn entered the room and began to circle it, the creature turned its attention on him.

Both heads struck at Eldryn in turn. Eldryn could smell the decaying meat on the beast's breath as he struggled to parry the bites with his sword. Roland struck the creature's hindquarter with his axe and it whirled on him. It bared both sets of its great fangs, and then turned to face Eldryn once again.

Roland struck the beast again and again, sinking his axe deep into hide and muscle. However, it maintained its attention on Eldryn. Eldryn dodged several swipes from the great monster's claws before it defeated his defenses.

The creature's large claw caught Eldryn squarely, knocked him back and crushing him against the stone wall. Eldryn dropped to the ground, breathless and disoriented. The creature prepared its maws and started toward Eldryn's fallen body, preparing to rip him in two.

Roland, desperate to save Eldryn, threw down his torch, and drew his other axe. He leapt between the creature and his fallen companion. The creature began attacking Roland with its massive forepaws and Roland found himself hard pressed to avoid and parry the blows.

Two large claws came in for Roland and it took all of his strength and speed to dodge certain death. He realized too late that the paws were just a distraction. The large creature's right head came down swiftly, not to bite, but to ram. The creature struck Roland's helmet with its own head knocking him to the floor. Roland grasped for his consciousness with weak hands.

The teeth came in now. Roland's vision cleared just enough to see the monster's mouth coming for him. He rolled quickly to the side and slapped out with one of his axes as he did so. The blade somehow nicked the creature's gum just below its fangs. The two-headed beast jerked its wounded head back and eyed Roland dangerously with the other.

Roland wondered why the creature faced him now. It had avoided him before even after he had dealt it several bloody wounds. The view of the flaming torch on the floor gave him his answer.

Roland rolled again traveling underneath his vicious opponent. One of the creature's paws slapped him across the floor. Roland skidded until he slammed into the stone wall of the room.

Roland retreated around the room and positioned himself behind the torch. The creature stepped back away from him and then returned to Eldryn who was still struggling to stand.

Roland took the seal skin full of lamp oil from his pack. He sprayed oil across the beast's back and hindquarters. The creature turned both heads back toward Roland in time to see Roland hoist and throw his torch.

The great monster ignited in flame and roared. Roland ran as best as he could around the edge of the room attempting to avoid the enraged creature. He made it to Eldryn's side and helped him up from the ground. They both watched as the beast burned as if made of kindling. The temperature in the room climbed rapidly. The smell of the burning, otherworldly, flesh turned their stomachs.

Roland and Eldryn stood for a few more moments catching their breath and wondering how much Bolvii had a hand in their survival. Neither of them knew, or could know, that even Fate herself was dumbfounded at their fortune.

They walked toward the other door to the inner room that Ashcliff had told them about. It was of sectot wood and bound in steel, not iron. Although the years had made their marks on the great portal it still maintained a vestige of what must have once been great majesty.

They were sweating from exertion before, but now sweat soaked their clothing from the heat of the burning beast. Both boys watched the burning monster cautiously as they moved around it.

They arrived at the door and found Ashcliff there, already working on the lock. Ash labored his way around the door frame with a small set of tools.

"What are you doing?" Eldryn asked.

"Disarming traps. We can't merely walk in."

Roland and Eldryn kept their eyes on the dying creature and the door leading into the room on the other side. Both were beginning to realize the danger they had put themselves in.

"How much longer?" Eldryn asked.

"Give me about ten minutes. I think I have them all disarmed, but I must be sure."

"So, it is unlocked?" Roland asked.

"Yes, but..."

Ashcliff had barely begun his answer when Roland struck the door with his shoulder, knocking it wide open. In spite of age the door moved smoothly on hinges masterfully crafted.

The three young men smelled dust that had been collecting for eons. They looked in upon an ancient altar room designed specifically for the worship of the Infinite Father and Fate, his bride. A battle had been fought in this room many thousands of years ago. The boys saw mangled skeletons still clad in their regal armor and clutching majestic weapons.

"What are those scorch marks on the floor?" Ashcliff asked.

"My father told me of a battle in which several of the faithful that he served with were fighting a fallen champion," Roland said as he lit another torch. He went through the chore of flint on steel not wanting to get too close to the still burning creature.

"They defeated the demon only to lose a fellow warrior to the flames that the creature burst into when it died. He said that the ashes fell into piles that traced unholy symbols on the ground."

"There are holy and unholy symbols here," Ashcliff said. "What does that mean?"

"That faithful and fallen champions faced each other in this very room in battle," Eldryn said. "This fight must have taken place during the Battles of Rending. This room must have been buried here, untouched, ever since that battle was fought."

All three looked on the scene in amazement. Roland thought of the books he had read. Books written by men and women who had traveled far and knew much. He wondered how envious those authors would have been of him and his friends at this moment, viewing the scene they now over looked. So much history. So much evidence and story from a time of such destruction, from a time so many knew so little about.

Ashcliff noticed that dust had settled on everything in the room except for two items.

"Look," Ash said indicating a book and an hourglass sitting atop the altar in the center of the great worship hall. "No dust has collected on them. The Book of Fate and the Hourglass of Time. They don't have so much as a cobweb on them."

"Is this a good idea?" Eldryn asked.

"If we do not take them then Dawn and Yorketh might," Roland said. "If they do, then these items will end up in the hands of evil. We have a duty as honorable warriors to protect such items."

"No need for dramatics," Eldryn said, smiling. "A simple 'yes' would have been sufficient."

Roland smiled and then laughed at himself.

"You make a good point El," Roland said. "Yes, it is the best idea."

"This will take some finesse," Ashcliff said. "I'm going to work on the traps surrounding the two artifacts. You two might look around. I would be surprised if you didn't find a great many useful items in here."

"I don't see any wires or trips on the artifacts," Roland said. "I wouldn't think it would be that difficult."

"The traps I'm referring to don't necessarily require wires and pressure plates. You don't think it would be difficult because you don't understand the nature of the traps. Please leave this to me," Ashcliff said remembering the door Roland had crashed through not so long ago. "If this is done wrong none of us will walk out of this room."

"Very well," Roland said.

"Look at this," Eldryn said. "This is a weighted bastard sword. You can wield it in one hand, but it is weighted on the end so that it strikes almost as hard as one of the Shrou-Hayn of old! I think they were called Shrou-Shelds. Many smiths have tried to duplicate the design but none have been successful. And look at this, it is marked with arcane runes!"

Eldryn took up the black bladed Shrou-Sheld and replaced his sword in his scabbard with his new find. Eldryn then removed a dust covered shield and breastplate made of an almost pure white steel alloy from a cobwebbed skeleton. Both items were inscribed with an arcane language that he did not understand. He also retrieved a full quiver of arrows that had shafts of still shiny black wood and possessed tips of pure Rorkor, a smoke colored silver said to have a magic of its own. Each arrow tip was marked with a different rune or holy symbol. He found a bow carved of sectot wood that the string had rotted off of long ago. Eldryn wiped the dust from it and tied it onto his back next to his own unstrung bow.

Roland watched as Ashcliff mumbled to himself and circled the altar where the artifacts sat. Roland decided to look around the room and greed struck him to his core. Roland didn't like the idea of being around so many dead bodies. It didn't scare him, he just felt that they were disgusting and, although, pilfering through these corpses' belongings was work that needed to be done, it was work that was beneath a warrior. However, he saw something that made all of those thoughts, prideful thoughts, fade from his mind.

Roland walked to a skeleton in the corner that was surrounded by five more, and the remains of what must have been three unholy champions. Roland took the Shrou-Hayn from the bony clutch of the fallen warrior and reverently wiped the dust from its blade. Roland had never actually seen a Shrou-Hayn before, although he had heard that there were a few men on the Tarborat front that used ancient ones. Under the dust was a blade that was made of a steel alloy that left it the color of smoke, mercshyeld. It was inscribed with holy symbols and, inlayed with pure silver and Roarke's Ore, were words in the old language of the original Great Men, *Bleda o A Bleda Shuik*. Roland's knowledge of the language was limited but he was able to understand the words 'Swift Blood.' The pommel was wrapped in a fine black leather, a leather that must have been enchanted, with a single emerald mounted in the hilt. Inside the emerald there seemed to be a bubble or chamber that held something that was red and appeared to be swirling. Blood. A true Great sword of old.

Roland hefted the sword and, although heavy, it sliced through the air with a magical speed. Roland put the sword through a few short attack routines and found that he could wield it as easily as a bastard sword, and much more quickly. He could feel the magical energy from the weapon pulse through his veins when he held it.

Roland took the weapon, and the scabbard for it, from the skeleton. He also noticed that the corpse was in possession of a rather nice replacement for his worn and split iron armor. Roland removed a set of mercshyeld halfplate from the same corpse. The breast plate, greaves, and bracers, were a matching set. The helmet was fashioned of the same mercshyeld but sported a green gem of Lexxmar in its forehead.

Roland hoped the armor would fit him. These were, after all, the original Great Men. However, Roland was a bit larger than your average Great Man. Roland stripped his armor off and as he began to strap the fine armor on, he was amazed to see it soften to the pliability of wet leather. Roland pulled the armor on with ease and, once it was in place, it hardened immediately. A perfect fit.

Roland pulled the helmet on and as the visor past his face his vision became startlingly clear. He could see every inch of the room in great detail, even into the black corners and shadows that the torchlight had not penetrated. He also saw the heat that radiated from each item in the room in the same vision. The combination of the two was a bit dizzying.

Roland noticed a skeleton, shorter than the others in the room, that was clad in remarkable full plate armor head to foot. He found a double headed hand axe made of black lava glass much like they had seen on their way into this cavern. It was a sturdy weapon and razor blade sharp with a jagged rim to both edges. Roland also found a brace of ten daggers sheathed in a belt. He took this belt, slung his new scabbard on it, and strapped the Shrou-Hayn across his back. He replaced his bent bladed iron axe with the double headed axe of black lava glass. These were truly the trappings of a great warrior.

"I will attempt to bring the glory to your weapon that it was accustomed to when it rode into combat in your hands," Roland whispered, almost praying, to the fallen corpse. "I will not allow my actions to bring any shame on these fine armaments. You have my word as a warrior."

Roland knew it was a little ridiculous to speak to a corpse in such a manner, but he preferred to view the weapon and armor he had found as providence from the deities rather than grave robbing.

Grave robbing has no honor and is done for wealth alone. Roland sincerely hoped to win glory and demonstrate the best qualities of a warrior with help from these mighty allies he had discovered. He believed Bolvii had placed these in his path. In this belief he was not wrong.

Roland rose and saw Eldryn clad in shining white alloy armor and bearing a magnificent sword and shield. They exchanged looks of admiration.

"I almost have it," Ashcliff said.

The spoken words slightly startled both Roland and Eldryn. In their discoveries of such wondrous things both had forgotten Ash was even in the room.

"There," Ashcliff said. "That should do it. Roland, I need a pack to put these things in."

Roland began checking the corpses in the room, but

most anything made of simple material or leather had been eaten away by the ages. In his search, however, Roland discovered several hundred gold coins, and a few valuable gems. Roland pocketed those and in so doing discovered the tarp he had placed in his pack.

"Here," Roland said unfolding the tarp. "Place them in this. We'll wrap them tightly and secure it with my old weapons belt."

Ashcliff looked the artifacts over again. He knew of the legendary curses, but had originally thought them to be just ghost stories to frighten would be thieves. Now he was not so sure.

"You two did find a few useful things I take it."

"Indeed, we did," Eldryn said, failing to control the sound of giddiness in his voice.

"These weapons were meant to be used in defense of the weak by warriors that are true. We will help these majestic items return to the service of their purpose," Roland said in a solemn tone.

Eldryn and Ash looked at Roland.

"I know," Roland said. "Dramatics. But it is the way I feel. It is the truth."

"Very well," Ashcliff said. "I am going to need some help with these," Ashcliff said indicating the ancient holy items. "It might be just tales, but I don't think it would be a good idea for someone of my back ground to handle them. Could you two help me figure out a way of placing them in the tarp?"

"Is there some kind of curse on them?" Eldryn asked.

"Well, there might be a very good reason why none of the cavern dwelling elves here have disturbed them," Ashcliff replied. "The drow, after all, are said to be a cursed race."

Roland seeing the hesitancy of his friends grew impatient. He stepped to the alter and took up the book. Eldryn, shocked at the action that seemed rash even for Roland, took two quick steps toward his companion before he realized Roland was unharmed.

Roland laid the book on the heavy tarp with reverence.

"You see?" Roland said as he reached for the hourglass.

As Roland's hands gripped the relic a power as old as the galaxy itself seized his nerves. Eldryn, seeing Roland in trouble, ran to his aid. Ashcliff tried to slow Eldryn, however, his weight was nothing more than a breeze to the determined cavalier.

Eldryn gripped Roland's hand and then tried to pull the artifact from his grasp. Both boys were conquered by the un-yielding force that rested in the sands of the hourglass... the actual Sands of Time.

Ashcliff watched with great concern as both boys seemed to age ten years in only a few seconds time. Time is, however, a relative creature. In those few seconds Roland and Eldryn lived lifetimes.

They found themselves bound in struggles strange to the mind yet familiar to the heart. In a moment Roland wore animal skins and wielded a sharpened stick, protecting his cave and family from a large toothed cat. Eldryn recorded a battle with a neighboring tribe by painting its images on a stone wall with a fallen enemies' blood.

Roland, now much older, felt the pride of seeing his great-great grandson born as age began to rob him of his own vigor. Eldryn knew great joy as he and his men finally con-quered the waters with a magnificent vessel that defied the drowning waves by floating atop them.

Roland experienced the birth, life, and death of a land mark mountain in hazy recognition. Eldryn's mind raced through the brief, yet brilliant, life of a snowflake.

Roland found himself looking through the slits of an unfamiliar helm at a mounted paladin of Silvor who faced him with a lance. Roland felt the sting of the paladin's lance as his own black blade struck the rider from his saddle. Then his mind was swept away. He sees a terrible beast of bone and magic. He watches as his blade is broken by the grasp of the dragon's claw. He feels the lightning pain as his flesh is being pierced again and again. He sees Eldryn fall.

Now Roland watches as a young man, one nearly his own size, takes the hand of a lady warrior, a Templar of Silvor, before a priest. He watches with a pride and love that he doesn't understand as they share their first kiss as husband and wife. He sees the two of them years later as they play with their toddler son who would one day become king of a united land.

Roland's mind is opened to the nature of the artifact. He sees how the shape of it is as a family tree, spreading both upward toward ancestors and downward toward children's children. He comes to understand how he is the middle, how he is the narrow focal point of the Glass through which the sands pass. He learns how the sands flow backward and forward in time and in lives. He understands how he is seeing the lives of his father's fathers and the lives of his son's sons.

Roland sees a man outfitted with richly engraved armor and shield, a man he first thinks to be Velryk, as this man banishes a disgraced son. He thinks of the older man as father, but his face is not that of Velryk, although the resemblance is distracting.

Roland sees the rising of a terrible beast, the one that will kill him. He knows that it is brought by evil but that it will cleanse the land in the purpose of good.

The Sands of Time bestowed them with a gift of prophecy. Their lives, and the lives of their children's' children, were laid out before them. They saw their own deaths. Much of what Roland saw could have saved lives, but alas remembering it all was beyond his capacity. His mind was like a bucket being used to catch a waterfall. Glimpses of the past and of the future.

Time had become a living creature, a being. It had shown both boys more of its nature than most men could stand, and aspects of eternity that no man could comprehend. Each boy lay on the floor of the dusty stone chamber living thousands of lives and dying a thousand and more deaths. Some were violent, some peaceful. Lives of men, animals, the earth, and the stars. Both boys began to fade into the sheer magnitude of creation. Roland felt his own soul drifting apart, being spread into nothingness. Eldryn felt himself floating among the constellations as his mind began to free itself from his mortal ties.

Eldryn's consciousness swept across the patterns of the great burning stones of the night sky. Then there was another. There was another with him as he drifted. He felt Fate point his eyes to the Horseman, the constellation of the cavalier. He remembered the tail of the Horseman, first told to him by his father. His father! What was his father's name? What was his name? Fear tore through his heart. The Horseman, Cavalier, his father had been a cavalier. He was a cavalier, a horseman of the old Code. He was Eldryn, son of Ellidik. He was a warrior with a warrior's life to finish yet.

Eldryn ripped his mind and focus from the beauty that surrounded him. *I am Eldryn!* Screamed in his mind. **YOU ARE ELDRYN, SON OF ELLIDIK** Fate spoke to him in a voice that traveled through his flesh, nerves, and mind. *I am Eldryn and not even the vastness of the universe will sway me!*

Eldryn spent ages forcing his mind to focus. Then he found him. His friend. He could not remember his name but he knew he had to save him. Eldryn continued to sharpen his will into a needle point. He pushed himself into Friend's path. His will pried between Friend and the Universe. *Eldryn, son of Ellidik...Roland, son of Velryk...Eldryn, cavalier...Roland, warrior...*

Both boys fell to the ground. The hourglass dropped from their hands, however, Ashcliff's speed saved the relic with a quickly placed cloak.

Roland and Eldryn sat up from the dusty stone floor. One hardly recognized the other. Both had visibly aged nearly a decade which to the Great Man race could mean close to a century. Moments ago, in this world, in this life, they had been boys. Now two men stared across at one another.

"Are you alright?" Ashcliff asked.

"I'm not sure," Roland said, not recognizing the sound of his own voice. "That was..."

His pause sat heavy on the air.

"That was something," he finally managed to finish.

"You are both much older now, at least by the look of you."

Eldryn examined his own face in the reflection of a shield.

"At least fifty years," Eldryn said.

"That is a lifetime to lose," Ashcliff said, ashamed that he had allowed his friends to endure such a horror.

"A lifetime for those of common blood," Roland said as he attempted to come to terms with the cost of his impatience. "It is not so severe for those of the Great Man race."

Roland struggled to remember. He knew it was important! It was just in his damn head and now it has slipped away like camp smoke through the leaves. Fate had her plan and Roland had been offered a glimpse of it.

"We've lost years of our lives to that thing!" Eldryn exclaimed shaking Roland from his reflection.

"The price for disturbing such an artifact," Roland replied, attempting to remain stoic. "Now we know why the drow wouldn't touch it."

"They are immortal," Eldryn said. "Why would they be concerned about the loss of a few years?"

"Because only those of purest purpose and heart can survive the trials concealed in those grains of sand," Ashcliff said. "Friends, I am sorry."

A boy and two grown men stared at the quiet and seemingly benign holy symbols.

Roland struggled to remember. The faces he saw were so familiar and so strange to him. The images drifted away as a dream, but the emotions left behind in his soul remained. He had never thought of a family of his own, but now felt the pride in his heart of his sons and of their sons. Such strong emotion, such strong love, for family that he had never met...perhaps never would. His mind clamored at the memories, prophecies, like a fish in the net struggling to get back to the stream.

"We must move," Eldryn said finally. "I'm sure that bonfire we started in the outer room will be attracting onlookers before long."

"We should pick a spot to regroup if we get separated," Ashcliff said. "We must get the book and hourglass out of here and out of Dawn and Yorketh's grasp. I can do that, but it means leaving the two of you behind."

"The priority is getting those artifacts to safety," Roland said, now with a deeper understanding of what they carried. "We are twice the warriors that we were when we entered this cavern. We will fight our way clear, and if luck, and Bolvii, are with us, we will bring Dawn and Yorketh out and in chains."

"The campsite where that thing ate Roland's horse?" Ashcliff asked.

"It sounds like as good a meeting place as any," Roland said. "I'm sure we can all find it and it should be far enough from these mountains and the creatures that dwell here."

"Very well then. I'll see you there if we don't meet before then."

Ash trotted across the room and disappeared through the door on the other side. Roland and Eldryn walked with more confidence now bearing the weapons of the ancient Great Men. They strode to the door leading out of the outer room. As they approached the door four drow slipped into the room with them, weapons drawn.

CHAPTER VI

The Test of New Allies

ELDRYN DREW HIS NEW BLADE AND HOISTED his fine shield. Roland pulled Swift Blood form the scabbard on his back. The hallways would be too confined for battle with a Great Sword, but in this room where the monster still smoldered, he had plenty of room.

The drow fanned out. One carried a broad sword, two others carried paired short swords, and the last sported twin maces. They began to circle Eldryn and Roland.

The dark elf with the twin maces started in at Roland feigning with one mace and striking with the other. Roland was amazed at the speed with which the sword in his hands responded to his will. He slapped aside the feign and was still able to parry the strike with ease. Roland found that he was moving much more swiftly than his elven opponent. After the two parries Roland struck the dark elf on the right shoulder. The mortal blow cut the elf from shoulder to navel in one smooth stroke shearing through his silent chain armor like paper.

The cavern elf with the broad sword executed an exact thrust toward Eldryn. Eldryn dipped his shield and battered that attack away. He swung his Shrou-Sheld in a side cutting arc that the drow attempted to block. The swiftness of the cut and the weight of the weapon knocked the drow from his feet when the weapons collided. The dark elf scrambled to his feet barely in enough time to parry Eldryn's second attack.

The two dark elves wielding paired short swords stepped in circles around Roland. Roland found that, due to his new helmet, he had no trouble watching both attackers at the same time even though one was before and the other behind him. Roland feigned forward knowing the drow behind him would attempt an attack at his exposed back. Without turning his head Roland clearly saw the double thrust coming at his lower back. Roland spun the mighty weapon under his arm and thrust out backwards with his smoke colored blade. The reach of the Shrou-Hayn was more than a full yard further than that of the short swords coming at his back. The smoke colored tip of the Great sword gouged a gory hole in the dark elf's chain armor above where his heart lay. The elf slid from Roland's blade lifeless.

Eldryn continued to force the drow on his heels, pushing him back. The drow looked above him to the mighty rafters that supported the room and kept the weight of the earth from collapsing in on them. With remarkable agility, and magical assistance, the elf leapt up the twenty feet to the rafter, catching hold and hanging from there. Eldryn considered stringing his bow but realized he would not have time. He watched as the dark elf smiled and drew a small handheld crossbow from his side. The drow whispered something and the crossbow drew and loaded itself magically. Eldryn knew that he and Roland would be dead at this coward's hands. Roland would be able to strike the hanging archer from the ground but Roland had his hands full. Anger, an anger that Eldryn was unaccustomed to, burned through him and his arm stabbed the blade of the Shrou-Sheld high in the air. Lightning built rapidly in the cross piece of the sword, danced down the length of the blade, and ripped from the tip of the Shrou-Sheld. The blinding light continued through the dark near the ceiling and blasted into the frail frame of the dark elf. The remains of its corpse collapsed, smoldering, to the stone floor.

Roland heard the lightning blast from behind him and through the magical qualities of his new helmet he watched as Eldryn seemed to throw a bolt of lightning from his sword into the hanging would-be archer. Roland was, however, very busy with the final drow. This dark elf seemed to match his quickness and every move that he made. They parried and thrust back and forth at the speed of thought. Roland saw the drow chewing on something and a familiar smell came to his nose. The mushrooms! This drow had a mushroom like the ones that Ashcliff had given Roland and Eldryn.

Roland had the advantage of a significant reach on the drow, but the dark elf was very skilled. He continued to work inside the arc of Roland's blade. So close to Roland that Roland did not have the chance to bring the force of his mighty weapon against the drow. Roland found himself parrying and striking with only the first twelve inches of the blade from the hilt of his Shrou-Hayn.

It was not honorable fighting, but as Velryk had said, '*Fight honorable men with honor. Fight evil men with everything you have.*' Roland parried a double chop from the short swords and, instead of making a short strike with the blade as he had been doing, he reversed the majestic weapon at the hilt and struck the drow in the face with the pommel of the heavy weapon. Roland's pommel strike mashed the dark elf's nose flat into his face. The drow staggered back briefly blinded and parrying wildly. Roland stepped back away from the cavern elf and finally got the distance he needed.

Roland swept the Great sword in a rapid arc over his head and cut down with magnificent force. The dark elf, vision blurred, saw something and he raised his swords to block. Roland's momentum forced the drow's short swords down and the end of his blade sunk eight bone-searing inches into the top of the drow's head parting his eyes.

"Did you see that?" Eldryn exclaimed.

"El, I think I see everything," Roland said with an astonished tone in his voice.

"We'd better get moving."

"El, you remember those mushrooms Ash gave us?"

"Yeah."

"They are potent. You might want to consider using one if we get into very much trouble."

"Is that what caused your serpent like speed?"

"No, my speed found its source in this mighty weapon. I think the drow I fought at the end, however, was chewing on one."

"I'll keep it in mind," Eldryn said. "Now, let's get out of this place."

"Agreed."

Eldryn slung his shield over his shoulder and repositioned his pack. He took up the lit torch in his left hand and continued to carry the Shrou-Sheld in his right.

Roland sheathed Swift Blood in its scabbard on his back. He took his new black glass axe in his right hand and his old iron one in his left.

The two young warriors started off again into the dark hallways. Eldryn led the way with his torch held high as his eyes searched their path for the traps Ashcliff had pointed out earlier.

"Shouldn't I lead?" Roland asked. "This helm is amazing, El'. I can see through the dark."

"Does it shine off of the metal wire?"

"No," Roland asked more than replied.

"Well, the torch does," Eldryn said. "Now that I have an idea what to watch for, I can see the shine off of the wires and plate hinges."

Roland nodded his head and followed with an axe in each hand. He felt much more comfortable now that his helmet allowed him to see through the heavy black curtains of dark surrounding them.

As they walked Roland saw a panel on the ceiling above, cleverly disguised as rock, behind them slid open. He kept his stride not wanting to alert the ambushers to his observations.

Roland watched as the first dark elf lowered himself to the ground behind them in absolute silence. Roland had no doubts that this warrior would have murdered them easily in the black silence that surrounded them if not for his helm.

Roland mentally prepared himself and visualized his first and second move. What happened after that would depend on the dark elves. As the second drow began lowering himself Roland wheeled and swung an overhead cut toward the drow's unprotected right leg.

The black glass of the lava axe sliced through the dark elf's leather pants and continued through the muscles in his thigh. Roland, in his inexperience, counted that drow as no longer a danger and focused his next attack on the first one to drop into the hallway.

Roland made a quick cut with his iron axe at the other drow. The drow, a broad sword in his hand, parried the attack and stepped back quickly drawing Roland directly under the passage in the roof of the hallway.

The dark elf with the severe cut on his leg had pulled himself back up into the passage beyond the tall man's reach. His leg was badly wounded but medical attention would have to wait. He prepared his short sword and dropped from the hidden passage onto the big man as soon as he was in view.

Eldryn heard the sound of battle behind him and whirled around. He saw Roland advancing toward a crouching figure. Eldryn moved up beside Roland when Roland suddenly yelled and threw himself into the far wall.

Eldryn didn't know what trouble Roland had but he had to trust in him to handle it while he took care of the drow before him.

Eldryn discovered that although he was much stronger than his opponent, the small dark elf was a very skilled fencer, and very quick. Eldryn attacked and parried furiously trying to keep the talented drow at bay. He thought of the mushrooms in his pack but with blade in one hand and torch in the other... *Torch,* Eldryn thought to himself. *Elves see in the dark by infravi-*

sion! They see heat!

Eldryn began to use the torch in the same fashion he had been taught to use a dagger paired with a sword. The drow handled the addition of the attacks from the torch with ease. Eldryn waited for the right sequence and then it came.

Eldryn, leaving his left flank exposed, swung the torch in his left hand from his right to his left. The blade of the Shrou-Sheld came in following the blinding heat from the torch.

The dark elf facing Eldryn knew the ancient blade of the Shrou-Sheld was cutting toward him. However, he couldn't see the attack through the intense heat glaring from the torch. He attempted to parry the strike, but his broad sword traveled too highly and the edge of Eldryn's weapon cut deeply into the dark elf's side.

Eldryn attempted a follow up attack but the skilled drow parried and countered, forcing Eldryn back. Eldryn went back in toward the drow and he noticed that the dark elf was moving much slower. He could see the wetness of blood on his opponent's lips.

Eldryn pressed his attacks and backed the drow away while he moved around him to put the dark elf between him and the wall of the hallway. Eldryn thrust the torch toward the face of the tiring drow. The dark elf slapped the torch from Eldryn's hand with his broad sword. Eldryn caught the broad sword with the blade of his Shrou-Sheld and forced both blades wide. He quick-stepped in close to the drow and caught him by the throat.

Eldryn gripped the drow's throat in his callused hand. The drow clawed at the hand at his neck and struggled to get his broad sword free. Those efforts dwindled as the might in Eldryn's powerful arm squeezed the life from the battling dark elf.

Roland felt the canary weight of the drow's body as the dark elf dropped onto him from above. Roland cursed himself for counting the foe out when he had not made sure that he was incapacitated first. Nevertheless, when the drow fell on him it startled him to his core. In those slow-moving moments Roland also had time to realize that the helmet did not show him what was directly above him. That was a fact he would have to remember, if he survived this mistake.

Roland dropped his iron axe and began grasping for the dark elf that had dropped onto his back. He was unable to get a hold on the drow and his foe would soon be finding a home for the short sword he wielded, likely in Roland's neck or chest.

Roland resorted to the only attack he could think of. He slammed his four-hundred-pound frame into the stone wall, trapping and crushing the drow's frail body in between. The dark elf was resilient, but after several blows he fell from Roland's back, unconscious.

Roland looked at the drow on the floor of the hallway. He would be sure this time. Roland retrieved his iron hand axe and sliced the throat of the fallen dark elf.

"Are you injured?" Eldryn asked.

"No. You?"

"No," Eldryn replied. "I think I could use a good meal though."

Eldryn took a water skin from his pack and handed it to Roland. Roland took a long drink and handed the skin back. Eldryn rinsed his mouth with the refreshing, if warm, water. He took two drinks from the skin and replaced it in the pack.

"I think we still have a long way to go," Roland said.

"I'm afraid that you are right."

The two embattled friends continued on into the damp dark with Eldryn's torch a lonely glow of light against the black that surrounded them.

They traveled for hours through the maze of hallways and tunnels marking the stone with Roland's iron axe. Several times they had to back track and begin again. Three times they feared they were lost, but luck, or Fate herself, saved them when they would see a mark on the stone that Roland had left.

Roland's helm also allowed them to avoid several pit

falls. In one of these Roland made a surprising discovery.

"El," Roland said. "Someone is in there."

"A drow?"

"I think a prisoner," Roland said. "Hello there in the hole," Roland said with his voice raised slightly.

"I heard you come, but I have heard many things," came from the deep pit. The voice was cracked. Whoever it was spoke in the common language of Lethanor, but with a distinct accent that neither Roland nor Eldryn could place.

"Are you real or more ghosts of my mind?" The voice was harsh and low. Roland heard a man who was afraid to hope.

"We are real enough to pull you from your pit," Roland replied. "We'll throw you down a torch and then lower a rope."

"Do not bother with the torch. Drop the rope and may whatever gods you worship bless you for it."

Roland did as the voice requested. He dropped the rope for what he estimated was forty feet before it struck the floor. He held tight to the rope and then a light weight pulled at the rope's end.

"Are you secure?" Roland asked.

"I am."

Roland and Eldryn began to pull, noticing that the man, whoever he might be, was very light, probably less that one hundred and twenty pounds. Roland and Eldryn saw the old man that came from the deep hole, which turned out to be another cavern altogether. They forgot their own woes when they looked upon what was left of the man. They guessed that he was Slandik by his look and by the bone charm that he wore on a leather strap around his neck. Roland remembered reading of the tribes of the tundra of Janis. Mostly a nomadic people of will and excellent hunters and sailors. This one had long blonde and gray hair and was clad in worn animal skins. His eyes were milky white. He was blind. The old man was built on a large frame for a common man but was emaciated and starved.

"How fare you, old man?" Roland asked.

"I have been worse," the old man replied. "I am Lucas. I

come from the cold spans of Janis. I came here looking for glory and riches. I found only darkness."

Roland noticed that the pouch the old man wore was full of gems, mingled with rocks. He carried a hand axe that showed long and terrible use.

"How long have you wondered in these darks?" Eldryn asked.

"It was the year of the birth of your Prince Ralston when I came here," Lucas said. "How long ago was that?"

"Prince Ralston has reached his twenty second year," Roland replied. He thought Lucas would weep, but there was a steel in this man that was extraordinary. "We will lead you clear of this place, Lucas. We will see you safe back to your people."

"I would be eternally grateful and in your debt."

Eldryn dug in his pack and produced the remains of a bear steak, part of a potato, and a handful of nuts. He placed those in Lucas' hands along with a water skin.

"Meat," Lucas said taking his first bite of the steak. "Real meat and not rat or snake. May all the gods bless you."

"Take my hand," Eldryn offered.

"I have survived these years alone. I hear, and I smell. I eat what I catch, and those dark elves haven't taken me yet. I'll be fine. Just show me the path from this place if you know it. And gods bless you for the meat."

Roland led the three down the dark corridors. Eldryn found that, although blind, Lucas moved with the grace of a cat and passed through these halls as silent as the drow that inhabited it.

Voices drifted to them from one of the corridors ahead of them. They made a left turn and discovered the room that they first entered when coming into the caverns of Nolcavanor. Eldryn remembered well the door on the north wall. A door that led to many crossbow bolts. They discerned that the voices were coming from the east, and one of them was Ashcliff's.

"I will go first because I can see in the black," Roland whispered. "You remain here with the torch and watch over Lucas. I will continue into the next room and see what the matter is. Then I will come back here, and we can decide our actions from there."

Eldryn gave Roland a doubtful look cocking one eye brow.

"You are right," Roland said. "I probably wouldn't come back. Very well, if the situation requires combat, I will yell out to you before I charge in. Fair enough?"

"What of Lucas?" Eldryn asked.

"I have fared down here for over two decades," Lucas said. "I think I should be alright for a few minutes."

"Very well," Eldryn said.

Roland walked off into the dark. Eldryn observed the hallway that Roland had entered. He counted the steps from that opening to the tunnel that led to the outside. Then Eldryn went back to the opening and tried to memorize the exact angle from the doorway that would put him on a direct path for the tunnel leading out. He didn't want to do this blind, but he might have no choice. Eldryn paced the steps off again and arrived at the same number. That confirmation made him feel a little better. He led Lucas to the pathway out and told him about the pit in the entrance tunnel. Even from this far away from the entrance Lucas drank in the smell of fresh air. As he completed his third walk and registered the number in his head Eldryn heard Roland call out.

Roland continued into the hallway thirty feet and discovered one of the rooms he had been in before. He continued another thirty feet into the hallway beyond this room. There Roland could still here the voices coming from ahead of him, but he saw a dead end to the corridor. Roland had watched Ashcliff open similar secret doors on their way in and he tried some of the same tricks now. However, none of those tricks worked for Roland so he stopped to listen.

"We are growing tired of this, little man. Yorketh will resort to attacking you if he must, but none of us want any harm to come to those precious items you carry. If you force me to chase you down, then you will not like what happens to you. You would only go to the torture chamber tired."

Roland knew the voice, it had to be Dawn, and somehow coming from the other side of this rock. Roland tried the tricks he'd seen Ashcliff perform one more time. Nothing worked. Roland stepped back and looked the dead end over. He called out to Eldryn, "Battle!"

Roland looked again at the dead end and kicked out at it powerfully. The rock gave slightly but did not open. Roland remembered a lesson his father had taught him. *'Do not punch the bag, son. Punch behind it. It is the same with any strike. Aim a few inches beyond your target.'* Roland took in a deep breath and kicked out again, aiming his boot three inches beyond the surface of the rock. The hidden door crumbled underneath the might of Roland's boot.

Roland looked beyond the settling dust to see that the dead end had only been a sheet of rock less than half an inch thick. He saw that the hallway continued another fifteen feet and turned both right and left. Roland walked down the hallway with an axe in each hand. He stopped before he reached the edge of the intersection. Roland put away his iron axe and took one of Ashcliff's mushrooms from his pack. Roland stuck the mushroom inside his mouth in his jaw where he usually kept the smoke leaf he chewed. He took his iron axe back up and continued. Roland reached the turns in the hallway and saw a movement that could have been no more than the gust of a vapor off to his right. Roland set himself and then began down the hallway leading right.

Roland walked for twenty more feet and entered a round room set with tables, bunks, and furniture. A barracks. Roland scanned the room for movement or a sign of the voices he had heard before but saw nothing. The voices had stopped. That meant something. However, it probably meant something bad.

Roland could hear Eldryn coming up the hallway behind him. He had to get them out in the open before Eldryn got here. If one of them was ambushed, they would still have a chance. If both of them were ambushed, then they might very well be lost.

Roland strode to the center of the room. He looked around him again and then he felt the hair on the back of his neck stand on end. Roland dropped to his knees and spun in time to see two daggers fly over his head. Dawn, who was now suddenly easy to see, rushed out of the darkness toward Roland with a falchion in one hand and a mace in the other. Roland stood, but just barely in time to begin to parry Dawn's attacks. She was quick, and vicious. Roland struggled to keep his footing and knew he was being pressed back in a particular direction.

He bit into the mushroom and began to chew. Roland could feel his muscles tingle with the sensation of speed. This was a different feeling than the one he got from the Shrou-Hayn, but the quickness in his movements was the same. Roland held his ground, but he was still parrying more than attacking.

Yorketh appeared from a corner of the gloom where he had somehow been concealed. Roland saw the movements of Yorketh's hands, but he could do nothing about it. Yorketh chanted, and his voice rose with each word toward the climax of the spell.

Eldryn bolted into the room with torch in one hand and Shrou-Sheld in the other. He saw Yorketh in mid cast and charged him. Yorketh changed targets with ease and uttered the final word, 'dactlartha.' The frosty bolt of dead fire shot toward Eldryn who could only accept the blow.

The cold fire struck Eldryn in the chest and flowed along the edges of his new armor. The impact and effects from the attack were lost among the inlay of arcane letters in his breastplate. Eldryn was still holding his breath when he came out of the cloud and it was a few moments before he realized that no damage had been done. He had suffered no injury.

Yorketh looked at Eldryn in disbelief. He immediately began another chant. Eldryn smiled and stalked toward the now nervous wizard.

Roland and Dawn struck blade upon blade, and hilt upon hilt. Roland fought harder and more desperately than he ever had in his life, but he could get no attacks through Dawn's defenses. She seemed invulnerable.

Yorketh, in desperation, cried out a rapid spell, which shook rocks and earth all through the caverns. The floors churned, and the ceilings buckled. Stone and dust fell from above, and all could hear different hallways collapsing outside the room. Eldryn was knocked to his knees when the floor bucked underneath him. He steadied himself, and then continued toward the mage.

Roland and Dawn were locked together in a blur of steel flashes. Both were knocked from their feet when the caverns twisted and shook. Roland landed flat on his back and Dawn crashed down on top of him. Roland caught her attack with the falchion with his black glass axe but discovered that his iron axe had been lost during his fall. Dawn came down with the mace and Roland caught her arm in mid strike. Dawn pushed hard with the falchion and Roland thought it foolish of this woman to try to force by brute strength anything upon him. Roland pushed back and hard. His surprise was complete when Dawn let go her falchion and dropped her hand to her waist. The momentum of Roland's push against the falchion drove his axe far wide of his body as Dawn came from her waist with a drawn dagger. The speed from the herb saved Roland's life that day.

He called his hand back down to block the intended strike to his exposed throat. Roland's arm responded with the speed of thought and caught Dawn's arm just as the dagger had sliced through Roland's chin strap. He arched his back and bucked up hard, throwing Dawn from him. He leapt to his feet and lost his helmet in doing so. Roland, now seeing by only the weak torchlight from across the room, heard Dawn's charge before he knew where she was. Roland knew what he must do.

Among the many lessons Velryk insisted on this was one of Roland's least favorite. He was taught to find that calm within himself during the bonfire of battle. Often while wearing a sack over his head, and sometimes in the darks of a nearby cave, Velryk would teach Roland to listen to that quiet voice of instinct. Roland would likely never know that the patience required for such training was as taxing on Velryk as it was on him.

Roland released his anxiety and tasted the air with his nose. He felt her on his flank and whirled to parry. Roland stopped the mace in its flight for his unprotected skull. Dawn sliced through the air with her dagger but only caught the edge of Roland's hair as he jerked back away from the attack.

Yorketh threw several more energy bolts and swirls of dark-fire at Eldryn, but his armor seemed to ignore each of them. Eldryn stalked toward the mage with his weapon ready.

Dawn reached down and took up the lock she'd cut from Roland's hair.

"I got close that time, boy," Dawn said. "Can't stand against a woman? You must be the shame of all your kin."

Roland's blood stirred, and his anger burned like the embers of a smith's fires. He disregarded everything else in existence, and rushed Dawn with the tact of a bee ravaged bear.

They all heard the words from Yorketh's mouth. Those words saved Roland's life that day for she surely had gotten the best of his emotions. 'Sectlartha' was uttered on the far side of the room from Roland. He would never forget what that word meant. Yorketh disappeared, and Dawn was gone from Roland's grasp.

Roland's faded blue eyes glared around the room but all they found was Eldryn. Roland retrieved his fallen helmet and placed it on his head. Even with his vision cleared he could not find Yorketh or Dawn.

"We had better get out of here," Ashcliff said from the doorway, surprising both of them.

"He's right Roland. This place may come down around us."

Roland looked around the room again, praying with everything that he might find the female warrior. That prayer was not answered that day.

The three hurried out of the room and down the hallways with Ash in the lead. Eldryn followed Ashcliff, and Roland trailed behind his two companions. Roland continually looked back hoping to see the female warrior.

"That fool of a mage may have awoke more than the dust and earth in these caverns," Ashcliff said. "We have to get as far from her as possible."

"Awoke what?" Eldryn asked. "A fallen champion, or maybe even a god's mount, a dragon?"

"Worse," Ashcliff said as he made the turn up into the entrance tunnel.

"This is Lucas," Roland said as they approached the starved barbarian. "He is Slandik, and another wayward traveler."

Lucas smiled, although faced no one in particular, and fell in step behind the companions.

"What is worse than a dragon?" Roland asked.

"You do not want to know and now is not the time," Ashcliff said.

The four ran toward the area of the pit that nearly claimed Roland and Eldryn. Hope for escape fell from their hearts when they saw at least twenty drow blocking their path. Eldryn turned toward the path behind them and heard footsteps in the hallway, a number of them. Twenty or more drow marched into the torchlight from the hallway that led deeper into the caverns.

"Any ideas, Ash?" Eldryn asked in a whisper. Eldryn looked both groups of dark elves over noting the well-crafted armor and fine weapons each one possessed. These were not the common soldiers he and Roland had fought in the hallways before. These were warriors.

"I'm working on it," Ashcliff replied quietly.

"Warriors of the underdark," Ashcliff said in a loud and

clear voice. "Do you realize who stands before you?"

Roland and Eldryn both gave Ash questioning looks.

"I see three sun dwellers and an old blind man who are about to die," a large drow wearing black steel alloy armor and two scabbarded Shrou-Shelds said. He was big for an elf, and thick through the chest.

"You stand before the son of Lord Velryk!" Ashcliff said with authority.

"I am Maloch of the Black Lance. I am the Knight of Shadows. I have seen the son of Lord Velryk in battle," the large drow said. "This is not him."

Roland stepped forward away from his friends toward the group that had approached from within the cavern. He removed his left gauntlet and threw it down at the feet of Maloch.

Eldryn noted Maloch's light gray eyes that almost matched the white of his long hair, and the fact that both contrasted his dark skin. His frame was much larger than the average elf, drow or fair, and Eldryn could see that there was power in the muscles of his chest and arms. What Eldryn noticed most was the absolute confidence in Maloch's steady gaze.

"Roland, what are you doing?" Eldryn asked in a whisper.

"I do not know what man you speak of, but I am Roland, son of Velryk. I challenge you to single combat, before your warriors and whatever gods you worship," Roland said. "I stand before you an honorable warrior, and I call upon that honor which your title as knight represents."

Maloch smiled.

"State the terms of your challenge then," Maloch said as his right eye brow cocked.

"The cavern is too confined for combat with the Shrou-Hayn, or the honorable weapons that you wear at your side," Roland said. "It should be dark outside. I challenge you to single combat with the weapon of your choosing in the grove above us. Should you win my companions and I will surrender to your will and be either your voluntary slaves or docile captives while we await execution."

"I see," Maloch said.

"Should I win, then I and my companions walk from here unharmed by you or your troops," Roland finished.

Eldryn gave Roland an incredulous look.

"You can't beat him," Eldryn whispered. "It is suicide."

"If you have a better plan then say so," Roland whispered to Eldryn.

"Very well," Maloch said. "I accept your challenge and terms. I do, however, have one condition. When I win, you will admit before all here that you are not the son of Lord Velryk."

Roland looked directly into Maloch's eyes.

"That I will not do," Roland said in a deadly voice. "I will not disgrace this armor, this weapon, myself, or my father, Lord Velryk, by speaking a lie on the battlefield of honor."

"Then we will prove that you do not share the blood of Lord Velryk, nor that of Verkial, on the battlefield."

At Maloch's gesture the drow nearer the entrance pulled a concealed switch that, in turn, secured the panel above the pit.

Roland turned and walked amongst the drow guarding the exit. Roland's mind raced with the implications Maloch's taunts suggested. Roland had nearly died earlier because he had failed to control his mind. If not for Yoreth's cowardice, Roland son of Velryk would no longer draw breath. He thought of that now and pushed his questions and his anger to a dark corner where his thoughts would not trip over them.

Roland continued until he reached the entrance. One of the drow slipped up and out of the tunnel with ease and lowered a rope. Maloch had reached Roland's side. Maloch took the rope and climbed up. Roland followed.

The dark elves created a ring around the grove with Ashcliff, Lucas, and Eldryn held at sword point.

Roland walked to the center of the grove, drew Swift Blood, and knelt before it. He began a quiet prayer to Bolvii. Maloch faced Roland, drew his paired Shrou-Shelds, and knelt in a similar fashion. He began a quiet prayer as well. Both warriors concluded their prayers, stood and saluted one another.

Maloch assumed a stance holding one Shrou-Sheld straight at Roland, and the other low along the side of his out-stretched leg. Roland held the Shrou-Hayn high above his left shoulder.

"Shall we limit ourselves to only honorable attacks?" Roland asked.

"You are fighting for your life," Maloch replied. "I suggest you conduct yourself accordingly."

"I invited you to this battle ground under honorable terms," Roland said. "I would not have it said that I cheated you in any fashion when I beat you."

Maloch looked Roland over again, as if he had missed something the first time. This one was too confident and there was something familiar about him.

"Well then, I release you to any methods you choose in an attempt to defeat me. My brethren and your friends shall be our witnesses."

They began to circle one another weapons at the ready. Roland started an overhead swing that followed a fat arc through the air. Maloch brought up his extended Shrou-Sheld to parry the attack, bringing his lower sword up to cut toward Roland's throat. In mid swing, Roland reversed the path of the Shrou-Hayn, which brought the hilt down and his blade in position to parry Maloch's attack.

The Great sword kissed the Shrou-Sheld that was slicing for Roland's throat just enough to knock it wide. Roland was amazed at his own luck. For that matter so was Fate who looked on with interest through her scrying basin.

Maloch's other blade had continued its arc and would be coming in for an upper cut soon. Roland quick-stepped forward, allowing the blade of Maloch's Shrou-Sheld to pass over his shoulder as Roland moved in with his weapon hilt snapping forward.

The hilt struck the nose guard of Maloch's helmet,

crushing it in and breaking his nose. Maloch staggered backward as blood flowed from his nose. Roland had to roll away to the side to avoid Maloch's blade that was coming in at an upper cut. Roland narrowly avoided Maloch's second edge as he rolled away. Maloch was removing his damaged helm when Roland came out of his roll and stood.

Roland called upon the speed the of the smoke colored blade as he and Maloch closed in on one another again. Their blades clashed, and Roland had to work feverishly to keep Maloch's Shrou-Shelds from his flesh. Roland began to feel genuine fear as Maloch's skills with his weapons became more apparent. He did not fear losing his life, he feared to fail his friends. Roland knew, without a doubt that he was outclassed by Maloch's swordsmanship.

Ashcliff began examining their surroundings, and Eldryn fought the knot building in his stomach as he watched Roland fight for all their lives. Eldryn was better with the sword than Roland, however, he knew this opponent, Maloch, was far beyond even him in skill. Lucas wore a blank expression on his face but Ashcliff noticed that the blind man's feet were positioned to attack the drow behind him to his left when the time came.

Roland slapped one of the Shrou-Shelds wide only to find the other diving again for his throat. Roland had never before worked so hard and solely in defense. Roland jerked his head back as the tip of the blade glanced off of his jaw guard. Roland quick-stepped back, but Maloch pressed his every move and his Shrou-Shelds never hovered far from their targets.

Roland had been accustomed to fighting in armor that was much more restrictive than his newly acquired suit. When he made his roll earlier to avoid Maloch's follow up attack he discovered that this new armor encumbered him no more than a leather coat but remained as hard as any steel when struck. This might be a valuable advantage. Roland thought again of Ash's tale of the first man that he had killed.

"I am done teaching," Maloch said in a calm tone. He was

not breathless, and he was not taxed in any way. Maloch would kill Roland. "I tire of toying with you."

Roland summoned the speed of the majestic weapon again and attempted an overhead chop. Maloch scissored both Shrou-Shelds up and caught the Great sword high in the air. Roland jerked the weapon back and attempted a thrust for Maloch's abdomen. Maloch scissored his swords back down and caught the Shrou-Hayn again, this time forcing it slightly down and in between his spread legs. Maloch looked over his swords at Roland's over-extended upper torso.

In his current position Roland would not be able to attempt another thrust because he had extended to the full length of his reach. Maloch smiled as he began the same scissor cut that he had used to parry toward Roland's head. Maloch half stepped forward as his blades came up. Maloch had been toying with Roland thus far, testing his strengths and weaknesses and tiring him before he humiliated him.

Roland saw the move coming and had been hoping for it. He stretched himself out in the air and dropped, turning over to hit the ground on his back when he landed. Maloch's blades had traveled over their target, but Roland was now laying down on his back at Maloch's feet. Maloch misread his 'advantage.'

Roland's sword still lay out-stretched from his defeated thrust and in between Maloch's legs. Roland, now laying on his back, cut upward into Maloch's unprotected inner thigh. The Great sword bit deeply into Maloch's flesh and sheared half way through the bone.

Maloch collapsed as one of his legs was nearly severed. Roland rolled quickly away and then stood, his sword held before him. Maloch's followers looked from one to another, unsure of what to do. Roland walked over to where Maloch had dropped. Roland looked into Maloch's eyes, which were still very much alive. Despite his injuries Maloch had maintained his senses.

"You have fought a valiant fight," Roland said as he extended his sword to Maloch's exposed neck. "I honor your skill and your conduct with an offer of mercy from one warrior to another."

"Is it truly a son of Lord Velryk that has beaten me?"

"Truly," Roland said.

"I then accept your offer of mercy, content in knowing that I was bested by that blood," Maloch said as strength dwindled from him. "Go in peace from these lands. Should you return you will be counted among our most dangerous enemies."

With that Maloch's strength waned and he fell unconscious.

Roland looked up to the drow that surround him and his friends.

"See to your leader," Roland said. "He is a skilled warrior and an honorable one."

Roland backed away from Maloch and four dark elves rushed to Maloch's side. Roland walked to where Ashcliff and Eldryn stood with looks of amazement on their faces.

"We should go now," Roland said simply.

"Yes," Ashcliff said. "We should."

The group of drow watched the four friends exit the grove with eyes full of hatred. Roland, Eldryn, Lucas, and Ashcliff made their way through the narrow passage in the lava wall as rapidly as possible. Each of them took turns looking over their shoulders, and then to the east horizon where the morning sun was only minutes away. Each of them with the exception of Lucas who only continued to gaze ahead.

"We should move from here, and quickly," Ashcliff said.

"The sun will be out soon," Eldryn said. "They will go back into their cavern and not hunt us until after dark comes again, if that is their plan."

"Yorketh and Dawn know I have the artifacts and they will try to get to us as soon as they can," Ashcliff said. "The dark elves honored their word only because their leader would not tolerate disobedience, and he was incapable of giving the order that we be killed. It was very smart of you to leave him alive, Roland. With him alive they could not elect a new leader to order us killed."

"That's not why he did it," Eldryn said. "He was being serious about the 'mercy from one warrior to another' bit."

Ashcliff looked at Roland incredulously.

"You can't trust a dark elf to do anything but try to kill you," Ashcliff said in a rare moment of lost control.

"My father raised me to judge a man, or an elf for that matter, by what he does," Roland said. "Not by who his kin are."

"Dark elves or no," Ashcliff said, still looking at Roland with unbelieving eyes. "We must get from here quickly. Dawn and Yorketh will be on our trail."

"What is the problem with that?" Roland said.

Eldryn had become accustomed to Roland's over confidence, but Ash, despite all their travels together to get here, was still marveling at it. None noticed, but, if they had looked, they would have seen an appreciative smile on Lucas' lips.

"I am tired," Ashcliff said. "You two both have injuries that need to be treated, and I think our new friend could use a decent meal or two."

"I am fine," Roland said with determination in his voice.

"Roland, I know you want to finish what you started with the female fighter, but this is not the time," Eldryn said. "Those artifacts must be taken to a safe place out of the reach of Dawn, Yorketh, and their master Daeriv. That is our priority now, remember?"

"You are right," Roland said with a sigh. "I apologize. We should get moving."

Eldryn had a moment to observe that Ashcliff and Lucas would have no idea what weight Roland's apology carried. Eldryn alone knew that Roland's apologies numbered fewer that a man's fingers.

The four companions made their way out of the narrow path through the ancient lava flow and down to the abandoned campsite that Dawn and Yorketh had left behind. Eldryn whistled in a high low pitch three times quickly and the group heard something moving from the brush toward them. Eldryn whistled again and his horse emerged from the bushes.

Roland and Eldryn checked over their equipment. Roland and Ashcliff pulled their cloaks around them to cut the winter wind that ripped at the mountainside. Eldryn found that the low temperature did not seem to bother him in his new armor. Eldryn gave Lucas his cloak and blanket. He also gave him a large piece of jerky and a water skin. They followed the path down the mountain to a clearing.

The four traveled all the next day and well into the following night with Lucas riding their horse.

"It looks to be just past midnight," Roland said. "We should probably camp here for the night and get our rest."

All were at the end of their endurance, but none wanted to admit it. Well, none but Ashcliff anyway.

"It isn't far enough from the cavern, but I could use the rest," Ashcliff said.

"I'll take the first watch," Eldryn said.

"Ash, you get some sleep," Roland said. "El, wake me when you're ready for a break."

"I suppose your father doesn't know about that move that you pulled on Maloch," Eldryn said.

"Actually, I didn't know about the move either, not until I did it," Roland replied. "That Maloch, he is a dangerous fighter. He had me, El. I don't like to admit it, but I got lucky. Well, either luck or Bolvii himself guided my blade."

"Lucky or not, blessed or not, a smart move or not, you did drop the drow," Lucas simply stated.

Roland put together a small fire and banked it with large rocks that would hide some of the fire glow and reflect the heat toward him, Lucas, and Ashcliff. Roland rolled into his cloak and pulled it tightly around him as sleep came for the tired warrior.

CHAPTER VII

Not the Whole Truth

"DID YOU HELP HIM AGAINST MALOCH?" Fate asked still looking into the basin. Her hair of quark fire waved beneath her crown of cobalt blue. It washed against unseen forces moving as seaweed on the water of a lazy beach.

Bolvii looked up from Fate's scrying basin into the turning galaxies in her eyes. No mortal could withstand that gaze and it was even difficult for Bolvii. Fate looked at him frankly. Many had been charmed by his sky-blue eyes, wild black beard, and muscular frame. Many had trembled at the first Shrou-Hayn, Oath Keeper, that hung easy on his hip. Fate was not charmed, nor did she tremble.

"I would not interfere on a field of honor where one warrior faces another," Bolvii said. "You know that."

"But Roland prayed to you, did he not?" Fate asked. She turned from the basin and glided to her throne, which sat to the right hand of that of Father Time, where she took her ease.

"He did," Bolvii responded. "He asked that I watch over his family, friends, and countrymen if he should fall. He asked that I forgive him if he should fail. He prays with his heart."

"A proper prayer for a warrior to whisper," Fate said. "So, you did not help him?"

126

"I blessed the weapons and armor that he now wears when they were forged for another," Bolvii said.

"And you approve of one so young and untested wielding them?"

"He was untested when he put them on, perhaps," Bolvii said. "He is untested no more."

"You have always favored their blood," Fate chided. "Even when they turned from you your champions still came to their call. Even when they worshiped themselves at your alters you continued to bless them."

"The whole cannot be judged by the few," Bolvii said. "They are vain, quick tempered, and some selfish. They have paid a price for that. They will continue to pay a price until they can find a path to redemption."

"You will hold them to that toll?" Fate asked. "You will not simply forgive, as before?"

"I saved a few, yes," Bolvii answered. "But I stood with you and the others when the time came for reckoning. I was there when judgement was dealt. So were my champions and some of my heroes."

"Your heroes, yes," Fate said. "Do you count this boy among them?"

"Untrained and unprepared he still held your husband's glass. He held the Sands of Time. Did he not? Does that act alone not prove his heart?"

Bolvii then saw something surprising. It was only a flicker, but he saw it wash across her face. He saw girlish deceit.

"You helped him hold the Sands of Time?" Bolvii asked, stunned.

"No," Fate said. As she continued to speak her voice took on volume and a distinct tone of command. "I did not. What I may or may not have said to Eldryn is not what I would consider interference. However, should interference be called for then it is I that will call for it! For that matter, I do not interfere! I decide! I plan! None know what it requires save me alone! Any act that would change MY plan is interference! They have choices! They make their choices! None will hold me accountable for the outcome of those choices, although many loose tongues lay blame!"

"I did not intend to accuse, my queen," Bolvii said, taking a step back and lowering his eyes. "Please understand I make no accusation. I was only surprised that you helped them. Pleasantly surprised if I may say so."

Hoping to quickly change the direction this exchange was taking, Bolvii asked, "I did not hear who Maloch prayed to. Is it still Muersorem?"

"It is," Fate replied. "Perfunctory. His prayer was chapter and verse but no heart."

"Could he still promise his soul to another?"

Roland awoke and relieved Eldryn on his watch. Roland stoked the campfire and made a walk around the site. He returned and sat close to the fire warming himself against winter's piercing cold. He repaired the chinstrap on his new, and quite useful, helmet. He studied the Shrou-Hayn and the markings on it. It was truly a magnificent weapon. He went through Eldryn's pack and found what was left of the smoking leaf. Barely enough left for El to have one more smoke. Roland returned the leaf to the pack. They would have to go to a town from here and restock, but which one. And what to do with those artifacts.

Roland woke Eldryn, Lucas, and Ashcliff when he had breakfast started and the last of their coffee boiling. Lucas savored every bite of the cooked meal. He drank the coffee as though it were nectar from the heavens.

"What do we do from here?" Roland asked to no one in particular.

"We will need to re-supply," Eldryn said. "I know you've had your reasons for wanting to avoid the public, but we must restock, and you have nothing to be ashamed of now. We must get Lucas to a town where he can rest and have time to heal."

"I can travel with you wherever you chose to go," Lucas said. "I am in better shape now than I have been in twelve years or more."

"I will not face my father until I can return victorious," Roland said.

"We have retrieved two great artifacts from ancient times," Ashcliff said. "We have saved them from falling into the hands of Daeriv. In his hands they would have only wrought evil."

Both Roland and Eldryn looked at Ashcliff strangely. That was the first time they had heard Ash mention any genuine concern whatsoever for good or evil.

"The question remains then," Roland said. "What do we do from here?"

"I have an idea," Ashcliff said. "Our first priority is to make sure that these precious items are secured from the hands of Daeriv. That means Yorketh and Dawn, and anyone else Daeriv might have sent after these ancient and holy discoveries. I mean to cast no doubt about the abilities of any man here, but we would be hard pressed to take Yorketh and Dawn if they were prepared for us. That is not to mention any of the other servants that Daeriv might send. I would hate to see our pride be the cause for these artifacts falling into his hands."

Ashcliff's eyes met Eldryn's and they both understood what, and who, he meant.

"And your 'idea'?" Eldryn asked.

"I know someone that could not only protect these items from Daeriv, but he could put them to good use against evil. I gave him my word that I would not reveal what I know of him to any man, but, if you trust me, I could take them to him in a brief time. No one would know he had the items but us and that would protect both him and the items. Dawn and Yorketh would still come after you, if that is what you wish. They will not stop until they are dead or they discover that you no longer possess the book and the hourglass."

"You are proposing to take two of the most valuable artifacts discovered in the last two great ages through those wild lands, alone?" Eldryn asked.

"Yes," Ashcliff replied with reassurance.

"Have you any better suggestions?" Roland asked Eldryn.

"Frankly I do not," Eldryn said, his eyes surveying their surroundings. "I assume we are not going to any of the churches because none of us know any paladins that we trust. You refuse to contact your father until you are satisfied that you have redeemed your mistakes. If we travel with Ash it will not only slow him down, but we will stick out as an easy target to every wondering creature and bandit between here and the coast. No, I don't have any other suggestions."

Weeks ago, Eldryn might have been ready to cross swords with Roland over this idea, but all three had grown in that time. Eldryn had grown to trust Ash, and had begun to love him as he loved Roland. Roland had always been absolute. He was rarely indifferent. He had made his decision about Ashcliff. He loved him as a brother.

"Very well," Roland said, his decision made. "Ash, do you need anything from us?"

"No," Ashcliff replied. "I have everything I need in the pack I retrieved yesterday. It will take me perhaps two, maybe three months to get there. Depending on my success, I should be able to meet you in five to six months."

"We are about four months ride from the large western town of Modins," Roland said. "We will meet you there at whatever inn is in the most northwestern corner of that town. If we are not there, we will leave word for you there."

"Don't leave it under Ashcliff. That is not a name I use freely. Leave it under Fletcher. If I cannot find you and there is no word, then I will leave word at that inn for you."

"Very well," Roland said. "Ashcliff, one day you and I will have a discussion about what you know about my father. Is he the same man that the drow referred to as Lord Velryk?"

"Yes, he is."

"And this Verkial. Who is he?"

"I have no proof, only rumors. Rumors that are often told for the great story they make, not for their basis in facts.

That discussion should be between you and your father."

Ashcliff began to gather his equipment as Lucas, Eldryn, and Roland finished their breakfast in silence. Ashcliff put a few more things in his pack and then looked up at the three.

"You may trust me," Ashcliff said seeing the worry plainly on their faces. "You have my word that I will not betray you. I will see you at the end of summer. In the fall at the latest. In the time between, watch for Yorketh and Dawn. They are both deadly in their own right. You may be better off if you can bait them into a town. If they are discovered in a city then they will surely be captured. Their evil cause cannot be concealed."

"Our long faces are not draw in mistrust," Roland said. "We are concerned for your welfare. To travel through the lands between here and the coast alone is a dangerous business."

"I have ways of traveling unseen."

"We know that," Eldryn said. "We have no doubts of your friendship or your stealth. We worry for your safety."

"I..." Ashcliff firmed the quiver that tried to take hold in his face and pulled at the edge of his mouth and his eye. He felt something caught in his throat that he had not known before.

"We will pray for you," Roland said. "We will pray for your safety and swift travel."

"We will see you at summer's end, friend," Eldryn said.

"Do you be sure that you are in Modins by the taste of next year's winter," Roland said.

Ashcliff nodded to his friends perfectly concealing the emotion that he felt swell within him. Ash, sometimes called Shanks and known to others as Fletcher, began down his road.

Ashcliff had never known anyone he could call a friend. He could not remember a time in his life when anyone was concerned for him. He had been trained, and trained well. He had been trained so that he could bring the best reputation and profit to his master. He previously had delusions that his master had cared for him but he saw things more clearly after spending two years enslaved when his master could have easily accomplished his escape. Ashcliff had been not much more than a child back then. His fifteenth birthday would come a week from now. He was much older now, and much wiser. He had found true friends in Roland and Eldryn.

Their friendship was a treasure he never thought to find, and it was a treasure he planned on keeping safe. They would not understand about Lynneare, his employer. A Shadow Blade had to keep his word to his employer. It was the first and last rule in Ashcliff's profession.

Ash traveled for months in the silence of shadows. He traveled swiftly and sustained himself on herbs that he had collected before beginning this trek.

At winter's end Ashcliff came to the port city of Stamdon, on the northwest corner of the continent of Hunthor. It was one of the points of departure for armies heading to Tarborat and other lands contested by Ingshburn to the north. He took passage on a merchant vessel to the fourth largest body of land recorded on any maps.

It was the land held by Prince Ralston, son to His Majesty Eirsett, King of Lethanor. It was a vast terrain where Prince Ralston battled to save lands already claimed by Lethanor from Daeriv. There was no confirmation that Daeriv was in league with Ingshburn, and therefore no lords considered Ralston's dilemmas worthy of aid from their armies. Ralston sent his troops out from two large cities on the small continent, Vanthor and Skult. This land of Lawrec was also the home of Lynneare, and had been for centuries before the return of the Great Men to Hunthor.

Once Ashcliff was within one hundred leagues of the coasts of Lawrec he took a charm from his pack. It was daylight now. Lynneare would prefer the dark. Ashcliff put the charm, shaped like an hourglass broken in two at its middle, back in his pack. The charm looked remarkably like the symbol adopted by the dark elves of Nolcavanor.

Nightfall finally came and Ashcliff removed the charm again. He held it in his left hand and whispered the words to activate it.

Some distance away a tall, shaved bald shadow of a man in black robes stood from his chair at a darkly stained table and looked to the southeast. His face was handsome in its own way but curious. Depending on the light he might appear twenty-five years of age at one moment and fifty in the next. He bore the frame and bearing of the race of Great Men. But no Great Men of the day were so pale and very few this lean.

"Shanks," the figure said. "After so many moons could you have finally succeeded where so many others failed?"

The seven-foot tall and athletically muscled Lynneare walked as if floating over the stone floor from his dining room to a study filled with books and magical items his knee-high black leather boots not making a sound. The pale figure took a large sack of coins from the desk in the study, put on two rings, and took up a belted Shrou-Hayn and slung it around his slim hips.

Lynneare raised his shaven head and focused his dark blue eyes as he whispered into the night. A vapor seeped between his lips as he did so. The vapor grew and swirled until it surrounded him. Once the vapor completely engulfed him, Lynneare vanished from the scarcely lit study.

On the deck of the ship that Ashcliff had taken passage the vapors collected from thin air. They began to darken and take form. Then from them walked the ancient and powerful Lynneare, The Warlock of the Marshes. He was a man that at one moment might appear to be no more than thirty years of age and in another the wrinkles at the edges of his eyes would proclaim at least fifty. Ashcliff, however, was no fool. The Warlock of the Marshes had walked this world, and perhaps others, for many centuries.

"It took me longer than expected," Ashcliff said. "However, I do have the items you hired me to collect."

"I am very pleased with your work. What are a few

months to one who has lived as I have? In this bag you will find your well-deserved payment. You may count it. I take it that my old mount is still secure in his prison."

"That fool, Yorketh, almost brought the whole complex down on our heads," Ashcliff said as he looked into the bag. "I saw no signs of the lower levels being compromised though. No one had even been near the door to that place. I think he, or it, is still secure."

"He, it is he," Lynneare confirmed.

Ashcliff felt the weight of the bag. He took one of the gold coins out and examined it closely.

"There is another thing," Ashcliff said. "The woman fighter, Dawn. You asked me to keep an eye out for her."

"Yes."

"She works for the wizard Daeriv. I suspected he would be looking for the same items and I began spying on him. I was captured, but eventually put into his service. I traveled with a female warrior who goes by the name of Dawn. She must be the same one you told me of. It was said that she had a sister who was equally beautiful, but I don't believe any could match Dawn's cruelty."

"Go on," Lynneare said.

"I believe she, along with the cantrip mage I mentioned, Yorketh, will be hunting a pair of my friends, Roland and Eldryn. If you still intend to capture her that would be a good place to start."

"Excellent."

"Are you sure you do not wish to hire me to collect her for you as well?"

"No. She is dangerous, and I must have her in custody and alive. Is she in danger from this Roland and Eldryn you mentioned?"

"She might be," Ashcliff said. "They are both inexperienced, but strong as oxen. They felled four giants between the two of them and they are the ones that killed the two headed beast that guarded those artifacts. Roland also felled the dark elf Maloch in single combat."

"They sound competent," Lynneare said, his voice rich and melodic. "You saw this Roland drop Maloch of the Black Lance in single combat?"

"Yes. It was battle to be sure, but fell him he did," Ashcliff said. "There is another thing. Roland is the taller of the two. I believe he is even taller than you, my lord. He is the second son of Lord Velryk. Eldryn is the son of Ellidik. They held the hourglass and survived it. It did cost them a few years of their lives though."

"That is another thing indeed. Does Lord Velryk know of any of this?"

"He does not. Roland is becoming a great warrior, but he is too proud to seek help from his father."

"That is good," Lynneare said.

Lynneare took two more coins of Rorkor from his pouch. Rorkor was a metal which, in its raw form, was stronger and more resilient that any alloy devised by man or god and light as ship's wood. Its proper name was Roarke's Ore. The dwarves that discovered it ages ago named it thus because it was said that it was the personal metal of the god of smithing, Roarke. Roarke's Ore was eventually shortened to Rorkor and remained so for any non-dwarf that referred to the unequalled material.

Roarke's Ore could slay unholy beasts without the benefit of holy runes or symbols and would hold an edge almost indefinitely. A point of Rorkor could pierce almost any alloy as if it were made of leather. It was treasured by all races and creatures of this world. It was, however, as rare as it was powerful.

"This is for the extra information. Information that is valuable to me. I will understand if this Dawn comes after you and you must defend yourself. However, you will not find a god that can help you if I find that you have assassinated her, is that clear?"

"Crystal, sire," Ashcliff said as he took the coins.

"Very well. You have done good work for me Shadow

Blade. If I have need of your services again how should I get in touch with you?"

"In the city of Bolthor there is a blacksmith who has a shop next to a tavern called the Rusty Nail. Go to that blacksmith and ask for two mercshyeld tipped arrows with pine shafts and Ostridge feathering. He can get in touch with me."

"I thank you again, Shadow Blade. Travel safely."

With that the Warlock breathed the familiar vapors from between his blood red lips and was gone in the mist. Ashcliff, now able to relax, shuttered a bit, breathed a quick prayer to whatever god might be listening, and then went below deck to his cabin. His first mission was complete. Package delivered and payment collected. He was indeed a Shadow Blade now.

CHAPTER VIII

The City

ROLAND, LUCAS, AND ELDRYN traveled hard for two weeks. Roland and Eldryn began slowly concerned for Lucas' health. However, they discovered quickly that Lucas could almost match even their reserve of endurance.

Roland and Eldryn also discovered their new friend, Lucas, was quite a story teller. Each night at the campfire he had a new tale of a different land. He told them of growing up in Janis, an unusual land where the tundra on the southern half was divided from the hot jungles of the north. He told them of hunting great white bears and of warriors there that rode war-cats into battle. He told them of fighting pirates between the port cities of Thorvol and Janisport, and of the fierce jungle war-riors of, the Zepute, of the city of JunTeg. He even told them a little of when he first went into the caverns of Nolcavanor, when his eyes could still see. Apparently, he had been struck by a ser-pent while wondering in the dark within the first years of being trapped there. The venom had robbed him of his sight. In the short time, the three became good friends.

When ten days of travel were behind them, they began to encounter outlying farms and ranches. They traded with a few for simple foods and wares. They were tempted to borrow a barn for shelter and perhaps share a proper cooked meal with the families they encountered. However, the thought of Yor-keth and Dawn catching them in one of those homes kept them from it. Fathers, mothers, brothers, sisters, daughters, and sons dying in a potential ambush aimed for them was not something any of them had any taste for.

They were able to make some purchases though. Lucas seemed to cherish the taste of milk as much as he had the coffee. He asked after something stronger to drink but these folks lived sparsely and only kept spirits for their use as medicines from time to time, and then used very sparingly.

"I'll give you this precious stone for whatever brandy, wine, or whiskey you have," Lucas offered one of the farmers they traded with. Lucas, apparently unwittingly, had offered the man a rock. A rock of no particular value or distinction other than the fact that it was smooth.

The farmer, who could clearly see that Lucas was blind, looked to Roland and Eldryn. Eldryn acted quickly producing a small gem that he had found in Nolcavanor. He and the farmer exchanged a knowing, yet quiet, glance.

"Sir, that is far too much to offer for such simple wine as I have," the farmer said. "It is only little more than half a bottle's worth."

"I'll take it," Lucas said.

They made their exchange, rock for bottle, and as Lucas was walking away Eldryn handed the farmer the jewel he had shown.

"Do you take me for a fool?" Lucas asked after they had walked a league or so down the road.   "I'm not sure what you mean," Eldryn said.

Lucas tipped up the bottle and drained it in a single quaff.

"I know that was a simple stone," Lucas said. "I kept them to kill snakes in the caverns. I became quite good at throwing them. The snakes were quite tasty compared to the rest of my diet. I was hoping that dirt worker would have some pity on an old, blind man and make the trade anyway."

Although Lucas seemed serious both Roland and Eldryn shared a hearty, and much needed, laugh.

"Did you really give him good coin for that wine/ water?" Lucas asked.

"I did, well a small gem stone actually," Eldryn said, still laughing.

"Roland, you travel with a good man," and that was Lucas's final word on the matter.

After leagues and days of traveling south, they finally arrived at the nearest city of Dalloth. It was the first time either boy had been to a large city. Both were amazed at the sights and sounds of the market places and taverns. They had been to Gallhallad, the home of the lord of their homeland, but that was only to spend some time at the soldiers' academy. And on those rare occasions they had no look at the city but only the martial-ing yards near it.

Now they approached a great walled city. The walls were of wood but were thick and strong. Velryk had told them both years before that the walls around a city were primarily to keep raiders out in the older days or, for cities that were near a boarder, keep out neighboring armies. He had said that in these times most city walls were to keep thieves and assassins in rather than invaders out. It was tactic he called controlled access. He explained that, much in the same way a sally port was used in vaults and keeps to prevent escape, so were the walls of the cities used to prevent looters from fleeing to the woods with their prize. When the boys were older Velryk also explained that it was a means for tax collectors to monitor exactly what goods came in and what goods were exported.

They were not disappointed when they arrived at the gate and saw that it was well manned by town guard. They also noticed that many of the guard were looking inward to the city and only a few looking outward to the roadway.

After a perfunctory examination at the gate by the guard they were allowed in. Roland and Eldryn were amazed at the sight they beheld. Merchants and mercenaries, farmers and scholars, priests and tavern girls mixed about them in what seemed a chaos of purposes.

Roland noted the stone foundations of the streets and building that must have been laid by the first Great Men and the newer construction of stores and taverns of the common men who dwelt here now. Both saw the great spires of several churches and the high stone walls of the keep toward the center of the city.

Although amazed by what they saw, smelled, and heard, all were exhausted from the road. The three found the nearest inn, bathed, and ate a huge meal. Lucas asked for a quill and paper and Roland borrowed them from the innkeeper. Lucas wrote a short note and sealed it with a ring he wore that was very dirty and worn. It was addressed in the Slandik language. Roland could speak Slandik but, had no hope of reading it.

"I want you to take this to a tavern in this town called The Blood Hair, if it still stands," Lucas said. "It is frequented by friends of mine."

"You will be well here, in your room?" Roland asked.

"Yes, I will be well."

"Eldryn should be nearby if you should have need of anything," Roland said.

"I survived in Nolcavanor for over twenty years," Lucas said. "I think I can handle an inn for a few hours."

Roland asked the inn keeper for directions and still lost his way twice before finding the Blood Hair. When he entered, he understood why Lucas had sent him to this place. He had never been to Janis but had heard many stories of the barbarians and blood thirsters from there. Some stories were from Velryk, but those were mostly for information. Velryk had schooled Roland on almost all of the races, cultures, and lands in the known world. The best stories about Janis he had heard were told by Lucas.

It seemed that within the walls of this tavern a piece of Janis had been created. The style of the place was certainly not of a western build or design. It was filled with the sons of the frozen plains who sat in chairs made of large bone and rough hides. The floors were carpeted here and there with the skins of great predators from distant lands. Each man stopped to watch Roland enter the tavern and walk to the bar. Roland delivered the letter to the bartender as asked.

Roland made his delivery and left as soon as he could. Something in him liked these men and their way of life, however, he could see that they were not given to accepting others. Roland exited and made his way back to his own inn. Then climbed the stairs to his room and slept.

Roland awoke, and he could see through his window that the sun was high in its arc over the land. He bathed using a cloth and a basin in his room. He looked at himself in the mirror and almost didn't recognize what he saw there. The months of traveling through the wild lands and the battles and struggles those travels brought to him and his friends had put age on his face along with a full beard. Not to mention the effects of the Hourglass.

Before arriving at the inn, he had begun to wonder if he would ever again be warm or rested. He had trained, and trained hard, all his life. He had been taught of the enemies he might one day face including the enemy of exhaustion. He had been prepared, but training for a deed and the deed itself were often different experiences entirely. He understood that now, or at least had a better understanding.

He had seen the change in Eldryn. El looked much the same on the outside, but some change on the inside had shone through and could be seen in his eyes.

Roland went down the steps of the inn to the dining area and found Eldryn setting alone at a table set with four full plates of food. He was setting near to the roar of the fire that burned in the large stone fireplace.

"I see that your appetite is healthy," Roland said.

"Some of this is for you too. I didn't think it would be long before you awoke. Do you know how long we slept?"

"Well past the tenth hour. I would say closer to noon."

"Accurate enough, but on what day?"

Roland looked at Eldryn curiously.

"We slept for two days," Eldryn said. "I went down to check on my horse in the stable and pay the man for his keep and discovered that I had slept while an entire day had passed."

Roland didn't miss the fact that Eldryn had checked on his horse before seeing to his own needs. He was a good man.

Roland began eating and discovered that he was hungrier than he had thought. Both young men ate three full plates of fried eggs, ham steak, cheese, and bread, and drank a gallon of milk each. Once their ravaging stomachs were satisfied, they headed out to the market place.

They purchased dried fruit, lamp oil, and several pounds of ground smoking leaf. They also purchased five pounds of coffee, four yards of leather, fifty more feet of rope, and three new heavy tarps.

Roland asked Eldryn to accompany him and advise him. They began checking stables for a suitable mount for Roland. They found a lesser war-horse, a tall and stout beast, that suited Roland and that Eldryn approved of. He was a gelding. He was black with a blazed face and well-muscled. He responded quickly to the rein and ground hitched well.

"I'll offer you thirty gold pieces for the animal, and no more," Roland said to the horse trader.

"Thirty gold? You have a deal. I'll throw in the saddle, bridle, and two sets of saddle bags."

Roland paid the man taking no note of the stare that Eldryn was giving him. Roland saddled, and bridled the fine-looking horse and the two young men went on a ride outside of town that afternoon.

"Have you lost your ability to count?" Eldryn asked.

"What do you mean?"

"Thirty gold for a horse? That animal, although a fine mount, is not worth more than fifteen gold, no more than eighteen at the most!"

"I don't like bartering. I found the horse I wanted. I have plenty of gold. I don't see the problem. Would you rather I give him one of the jewels I carry? Is that your preferred method of overpaying?"

Eldryn knew that he had no retort, which was rare, and therefore moved on with his day. They exercised their mounts and Roland got to know his horse that he came to call Road Pounder. Roland and Eldryn returned to town and stabled their horses near sunset. They went back to their inn and ate another large and fine meal.

Roland went up to Lucas' room and was surprised when a strapping and very tall Slandik warrior opened the door. His height didn't match Roland's but was still easily near six and a half feet. Weight was hard to judge given the presences of the white bear cloak that he wore, but the weapons he carried were not. A great axe of the ever-ice from Janis hung across his back and an ivory hand axe, beautifully scrimshawed, rode easily in his belt. His hair was a dark blonde as was his thick and braided beard. His eyes were the color of the deep blue waters that bordered his homeland.

"What do you want?" The young Slandik asked.

"I am here to check on my friend," Roland said with an edge in his voice. "Where is he?"

"I am here, Roland," Lucas said from a chair behind the door.

The young Slandik looked over his shoulder and made a nod to the unseen, and unseeing, Lucas, and stepped aside. Roland entered the room to find Lucas looking much better. Color was returning quickly to his face and his frame, although still frail, was regaining some of its old strength. Roland didn't miss the sight of the rich furs that layered the bed and the fine care that had been shown to the axe Lucas carried out of the caverns. An axe, at his first glance under the stone of Nolcavanor that looked over used and beyond utility, now gleamed showing itself to be a quite regal weapon. It was of the ever-ice, Roland now noticed. Properly called Kolvic, it was a mysterious material known to only come from the frozen wastes of Janis. It had the appearance of ice but never melted, the strength of alloyed steel, and weighed less than half any metal found or crafted by any race. Furthermore, if one knew the secrets, it could be shaped into nearly any useful tool.

"This is Asheim, one of my grandsons. He is named for one of our fire breathing mountains. The note reached one of my family as I had hoped it might."

"I see," Roland said. "Is there anything I can do for you?"

"You have done more than I could have hoped for. I thank you. Asheim here will see to my needs and will escort me back to my home."

"Very well," Roland said. "If you should need anything you have but to ask. If you are ever in Fordir and need help you may ask for me or my father, Velryk."

"Should you ever come to the lands of the Slandik, ask for me and my family. I would be honored if I could return some of the help you have given me."

"Will you remain in Dolloth long?" Roland asked.

Asheim looked to his elder briefly and then responded for them.

"We were here in hopes of buying steel from the dwarves, but it would seem that they only come to Dolloth to buy," Asheim said. "Those that live under the mountains are quite jealous of their wares. Still, the farther inland we travel the better price we get for our furs and seal skins. I rarely come on these trips but, hoped to speak with the dwarves myself to perhaps barter a deal. It would seem that Lady Fate put me here at the time our grandfather was returned to us. For that you have our thanks. Our thanks are not given lightly, nor is it just air passing through a man's throat. If you find yourself in Janis, then ask after us and our family. We will conclude our business here this day and head west again in the morning. I would like to have more time to visit with the man that grandfather here describes you to be, but our duties now are pressing."

Roland extended his hand and took Lucas'. They shook

hands and Roland noted a quick look of distain from Asheim that surprised him. The look passed and Asheim took his hand in friendship as well.

"Well then, may the road rise to meet your feet," Roland said. "May you be in your heaven a day before Muersorem knows your dead."

"If it comes before we meet again," Lucas said, "then may you have many sons and your death come in battle and on a warm day."

Roland met Eldryn downstairs in the main hall again and both had another ale.

"Are you as tired as I am?" Eldryn asked.

"Yes," Roland replied simply.

Both went upstairs, bathed again and had gone to bed before the ninth dark hour.

Roland and Eldryn met at the breakfast table a few hours after sunrise and ate the fill of any three men each. The innkeeper had taken to charging them three times what he charged other patrons for a meal.

"It is out of house and home you will eat me!" The innkeeper had said.

They asked the innkeeper about the welfare of their friend, Lucas.

"He spends money well and has a remarkable appetite for a man his age," the innkeeper replied.

"He was without food for some time," Roland said. "If there is any extra cost, we will cover it."

"You misunderstand me, sir. He had four women up there this morning before he and his kin left. They were the second group of four that he has requested since yesterday. He does, however, pay well."

The two companions left the inn and walked to the marketplace again that morning watching the performers and jugglers and trying foods from many different lands. Dalloth was the home of Lord Jessup. It was the only major city between the western coasts and the capital of Ostbier. Being situated between the mountain range to the north where Nolcavanor rested and the mountain range to the south which was home to a large clan of dwarves it drew a great deal of trade.

Roland and Eldryn made their way to a reputable jeweler to have the gems that Roland took from Nolcavanor appraised. They were both surprised to learn that each of the five gems were worth over two hundred gold coins. Roland agreed to sell two of the gems to the jeweler and added the sum to the one hundred twenty-five gold coins he already possessed. He divided the total with Eldryn, leaving him with two hundred sixty-five gold, and Eldryn with two hundred and sixty.

"I think I'll look into getting another good axe," Roland said. "We certainly have the money for it now."

"I could finally get a proper lance," Eldryn said. "Perhaps a new horse and a better saddle."

The two walked through the lanes and streets until they came to a large weapon shop. The building was of crafted and carved stone and of a very sturdy build. It was clearly designed to look appealing, but Roland had spent much of his early years in a jail. He knew a building designed for security when he saw one.

They entered and saw many wondrous weapons and ornate suits of armor. *This shop could have been the armory of a king, or at least a great lord*, Roland thought. Roland and Eldryn were approached by a thin man with a sallow complexion wearing robes. Both Roland and Eldryn noticed the way the man looked more at what they wore and carried than he did at them.

"What are the two young lords looking to purchase this day?"

"I'd like to find an axe to match this one," Roland said holding forth the black lava glass axe he had discovered in Nolcavanor.

"Sir, there is not an axe to match this one, not in this shop or any other," the clerk said with awe in his voice. "This is a dwarven axe of old. These markings indicate the ancient dwar-

146

ven king it was crafted for. We should very much like to purchase it. You have but to name your price."

"I am not here to sell an axe, this one or any other. However, I would be willing to pay you in gold for what you can tell me about this one," Roland's curiosity now piqued.

The clerk accepted the coin and examined the axe closely.

"This is an ancient weapon, as I said," the thin man continued. "Indeed, crafted for one of their kings. Dwarven history is not something the outside world knows much of, but the craft for making a weapon constructed of this material died long ago. I can say that with certainty. This weapon was made when men still walked among gods and all elves were fair skinned and lived in their forest homes. Most cutting weapons are forged, folded, edged, then sharpened. As you can see that would be impossible with this material. The material itself is produced by an unlikely blending of liquid metal pouring up out of the dark, hot places in the mountains. The flowing metal would then have to be very near the raw power that only gods or champions could provide. Once those are combined, a rarity I hope you understand, the environment must be just right for the resulting material to cool but, not too quickly. That forms the black glass you see here, also known as leiness. The black glass, or leiness, must be chipped by a very skilled hand until it takes on the shape the craftsman desires. A piece of it must be found without any flaw, which in and of itself is rare. Then it must be worked by a craftsman that knows his art. Once completed it will not chip again nor shatter. The edge will never dull." The clerk said.

As Roland was formulating his next question the clerk unexpectedly continued.

"An axe of this material is fit for a king, as I said, but you may have also noticed the angular engravings along the haft and the odd way the jewels are set within. This was a means of telling the story of the wielder's heritage. It's not language exactly but, craft. You see, the legend is that when light strikes the haft at just the right angle the reflection on a dark wall is an image that tells the story. Some would call it magic, and I suppose, in its way, it is. But this is all craft and skill. The right person would know what light source and angle would be needed to reveal the image. I have seen weapons from all points of the compass, but only the dwarves knew the art of painting such a picture with light."

"So, this is undoubtedly of dwarven origin and craft?" Roland asked.

"Oh, certainly," the shopkeeper said.

"Very well," Roland said. "Thank you."

"May I see the weapon you wear across your shoulder?" The slender man asked Roland.

"That weapon I will keep also," Roland said. "The leather cover remains."

"Very well, I did not wish to insult you. I was merely curious as to whether it was a true Shrou-Hayn. Some carry them, but they are rare. We even have one or two for sale to those who can pay."

"I have no interest in trading this weapon. It has served me well. I thank you for your interest."

Roland traded in his old iron hand axe and a hand full of coins for two new axes made of a strong steel alloy. He also sold one of the ten daggers in his belt so that he could carry the flame blade in the row of scabbards that held his other daggers. Eldryn purchased a magnificent lance, several bow strings, a hand full of caltrops and thirty arrows. Neither boy noticed the man browsing nearby. Neither boy noticed the way he marked where Roland placed the glass axe in his belt.

The two boys walked from the shop and Eldryn saw Roland's look of disdain.

"They are very proud of their wares," Roland said.

"You do not mind paying too much for a horse, but paying too much for a weapon upsets you?"

"Horse traders are horse traders, but weapon smiths supply the warriors of our lands," Roland said. "It is not right that they seek to make such a greedy profit from the fact that warriors must defend themselves and our lands. They take coin from men who have earned it in service or gallant combat. They sell weapons to whoever can afford them, regardless of who they fight for or what cause they represent, as long as they can pay."

"Are you saying they should be more selective as to who they sell to?" Eldryn asked.

"Not at all," Roland said. "I would not deprive any man or woman the ability to defend themselves. I'm saying they are selling to the highest bidder."

"They pay taxes, do they not?" Eldryn asked. He smiled knowing where this conversation was going. He was going to enjoy every moment of it.

"El', how long has it been since you were struck soundly in the mouth?" Roland asked.

Eldryn laughed, enjoying his complete victory.

They made their way to a stable where Eldryn looked over the stock. He found a lesser war-horse and saddle that he thought appropriate replacements. He loved his old horse, but the months of hard travel had been tough on the animal. A horse that was not a breed for warring to begin with. Eldryn called his new mount Lance Chaser.

Roland and Eldryn made their way back to the inn and found a letter waiting for them there.

The innkeeper gave it to them when they entered.

"Your friend, Lucas, left this for you."

Roland unrolled the scroll and read. Roland noted that it was written in both his own native language and that of the Slandik.

The bearers of this letter shall travel with safety through my lands. They are to enjoy the same courtesies that would be shown me by my people. Any Slandik that stands against Roland, Eldryn, or Ashcliff, stands against the house of Thorvol.

Master of the Frozen Plain
Commander of the Cat Riders
King Lucas

"How about that," Eldryn said looking around Roland's shoulder. "Lucas, a king."

"Not just a king, but The King of the Slandik," Roland said.

Thinking back on the brief, but hard, look Asheim had given him Roland now understood. It was a great insult, one that could get a man killed, to initiate a hand shake with a king.

That evening, over another large meal, they discussed their plans. They decided, or rather Roland decided and Eldryn went along with it, that Eldryn should send a letter home to let his mother know they were well. They also decided to send enough coin home to replace what was taken from the fines box, to pay for the supplies they had taken from the jail, and to pay for Roland and Eldryn's horses, because they had actually belonged to Velryk and Shaylee.

"Shouldn't we be heading home anyway?" Eldryn asked. "Why send the package if we're heading that way anyhow?"

"We are not heading home," Roland said. "Yorketh and Dawn should be on our trail. I had hoped that they would have made it to Dolloth by now and we could have had that out, but that has not been the case."

"Wait," Eldryn interjected. "You have been lounging here hoping they would catch up to us?"

"Well, yes," Roland said. "A town would be better for us and worse for them. I have also taken some precautions in my room upstairs just in case. You should consider doing the same. In any case, it would seem that they are more patient than I had hoped they would be. We can't head toward home because they might guess our destination and beat us there. When we arrived, we might be forced to deal with them while they held hostages."

Eldryn's thoughts went to his mother. He saw Roland's logic clearly.

"I propose that we head toward Modins to meet with Ash," Roland continued. "If they attack us on the trail then we will handle the situation then. If not, then we wait in Modins for Ashcliff and plan our next move after that. We will have a good lead on Ash, so we will have plenty of time on our hands. We could travel leisurely."

"By 'leisurely,' you mean bait them," Eldryn said in more of a statement of fact rather than a question.

"Yes."

In the deep hours of the night, while Roland and Eldryn slept in adjacent rooms on the third floor of the inn, a foot clad in soft black leather eased its way down from Roland's window sill. In those quiet hours while Roland and Eldryn rested deep in a sleep brought on by days of toil and capped by a hearty meal, a hand, tattooed at the wrist with a small black fly, wrapped its fingers around the blade of a short sword.

A scream startled Roland from distant fathoms in which his conscious mind had been submerged. The controlled wakefulness that he had been trained in was shattered by that scream.

As the first burglar crumpled to the floor with a borrowed caltrop buried in his foot, point protruding from the top of his boot, three more used him as a stepping stone to slip into the room like shadows. They each knew their business and knew this theft would now have to be an assassination as well.

Roland leapt from his bed, Swift Blood in hand. Too late he realized that his preparations for Yorketh and Dawn should have included keeping his fine helmet close at hand. It appeared that the other arrangements he had made proved worthwhile.

He looked around the room confused. He knew he had heard the scream. He knew a hand with a black fly tattoo grabbed at a short blade as some unknown assailant crept into his room. How did he know that there was a black fly tattooed on that hand? He had still been sleeping when the thief drew his weapon. He looked around now and the room was empty and unchanged. Unchanged? As it occurred to him, he looked to the window to see a dark form moving through it. That dark form slid into his room silently.

He should have acted then but, well, was unable to come to terms with what was happening. He was watching something unfold that he had just witnessed. Only now he was watching it happen for the first time. He watched in a stupor as the soft leather clad foot descended onto the caltrop. He watched as the would-be assassin screamed into the night. He watched as the three that followed their unlucky companion used him to pass the other caltrops on the floor and begin their work for the night.

Something prophetic? He thought. He had never been trained in magic and had never had a talent for it. What was this weird vision?

Two of these dark figures drew short blades and closed with Roland quickly. They operated under the assumption that this big dumb warrior was maybe not so dumb after all. Maybe he saw their man at the arms shop. Maybe he had been lying in wait for them. The third ignored the whole situation. He went straight to Roland's gear and began searching it with practiced fingers. He knew his part of the job.

They had accounted for Roland's size, but not for his speed or for him standing at the ready with a Shrou-Hayn in his hands. The joining of combat shook Roland from his daze. Their sure attacks were parried swiftly and the one on Roland's right found his ribs cracked by the cross piece of the Shrou-Hayn.

Roland assumed these worthies were here to distract him while Yorketh or Dawn finished him from a dark corner. While parrying and striking his eyes flitted to the empty spaces in the room searching for the ambush. His division of attention cost him.

He was reminded of another lesson when one of the

blades he faced slipped past his own and drew a thin red line of blood across the inside of his arm near the elbow. The assassin's blade missed its mark, he was sure, but it was close. Roland knew the attack. If one could slice the tendon there near the elbow the hand would lose function. If one missed, then there was always the gathering of blood vessels there. Perhaps he wouldn't bleed enough for it to slow him, certainly not enough to kill him, but it would soon make his hand slick with blood. It would make his weapon, or anything else for that matter, hard to hold.

He remembered another lesson as well. Fight the foes before you first. *Be aware of your surroundings, but not at the cost of the danger at your throat.* Even now he heard his father's voice.

Forced into tight quarters by the two assassins and their four blades that he faced, Roland fought with both ends of the Shrou-Hayn. A quick block with the cross piece of his sword where it joined the edge caught two blades while he quickly rolled the axis of the Shrou-Hayn and forced himself close to the assassin on his right. The edge of the cross piece gouged into the assassin's brow tearing the flesh in a bloody path that led deep into the jelly of his eye.

A howl burst from him as he stumbled back. He let go another howl as he happened upon another wayward caltrop on the floor.

The assassin to Roland's left worked hard to get in close so Roland couldn't use the long reach of his arm or his blade against him. Roland had a moment to think that no one had taught this fellow as he had been taught. *Watch the weapon but, fight the man.*

As the assassin jabbed and thrusted forcing Roland to parry with the cross piece and fore guard, Roland waited for the position to be right. His back would be to the thief going through his things, but hopefully for only a short time.

The time came. Roland again managed to catch both of the assassin's nimble blades, if only briefly, in one cross body block. Roland let go of the Great sword with his right hand and struck hard at the assassin's chest just over his heart with his hand open, palm forward.

The blow was hard enough to knock the assassin back yards but he traveled only a short distance when the back of his head struck the stone wall behind him. Between the heart-strike, which disrupted his heart beat, and the clash of his head against stone the quiet killer sagged as he nearly lost his grasp on the world.

Roland seized his slight frame quickly by the collar of his leather jerkin and hurled him without art into the first man to discover the caltrops. As he was attempting to regain some semblance of his wits, his compatriot crashed into him with tremendous force. The clatter of bone against bone could be easily heard.

Suddenly light shown into the room as Roland's door opened onto the landing going into the tavern. The thief, clear in his goal, was on his way out. To Roland's horror, the thief was on his way with Roland's black glass axe.

New riches in hand, the thief looked back once to make sure he was out of the reach of the Great Man. That look would cause him to miss the fact that he was headed directly toward another.

Eldryn stepped forward hard slamming his helm clad forehead into the ear of the thief. Most likely knocked unconscious by that blow, the thief's head was certainly escorted to the halls of shadow when it rebounded against the doorframe.

Roland turned his attention back to the other three. Three? There had been three. Now he only found the two that were still in a tangle together amid the caltrops. In the chancy light he saw an arm protrude from their pile, he couldn't be certain which of them it belonged to, produce a dagger seemingly out of thin air. That arm cocked to throw as Roland plunged Swift Blood through them both. The arm fell to the floor.

Eldryn started across the room toward the window which must have been the escape route the one with a gouged eye had taken. Roland shouted.

"Hold!" Roland said. "Caltrops. Bring a light."

Eldryn returned quickly with a lamp from the bannister and Roland met him at the door with a torch from his pack. They swept the caltrops aside and surveyed the window and then the alleyway beyond. There was no sign of their quarry.

"These two are dead," Roland said examining the pile of assassins he had thrust his Shrou-Hayn through. "That one?"

"He's breathing," Eldryn said pulling his hand back from the man's nose. "His head may be broken though. I thought to take him prisoner. I didn't want to use my sword unless I had to. You know I wouldn't head butt a man otherwise."

"Your Code is safe," Roland said. "It was wise. We need to know what he knows."

"Where did you get the caltrops?"

"I borrowed them from your pack," Roland said. "It seemed like a good idea. As I said, I was making preparations for our other guests."

"Well buy your own," Eldryn said. "I want those back."

"As you say," Roland said. "Shall I wake the shop keep now, or will you rouse the town guard while I wrap the wound on this arm?"

Eldryn did not reply. He turned and headed down the bannister.

"Perhaps some pants first," Roland said calling after him. "You look a bit silly in a night shirt and a helmet."

Roland tore a bit of sheet from the bed and wrapped the cut on his arm. Then he cut a short length of rope from his store and used it to tie the thief's hands and feet. He had never had a head for remembering the many knots that his father had taught him, but those to bind a man he knew well.

Then he gathered the caltrops and restored the furniture that had been shoved around to its original positions. He then turned his attention to the two dead assassins.

These two seemed well equipped for the trade. He found a small leather kit about the size of a pint wine skin. Unfolding it he found small pockets lining its interior, each held a thin metal tool of one sort or another. Lock picks. He found several daggers, two short swords, and a choking chain of fine links, all make of steel.

His most interesting find was a parchment with his name, a decent sketch of him, and an even better sketch of the dwarven axe. He also noticed that, although in different places, one on the inside wrist and the other behind the left ear, each man had a tattoo of a small black fly. He had a moment to think that the first man he had seen, the first time he had seen it, had the black fly tattoo on the web of his hand. However, this fellow had the tattoo, although of the same design, on the inside of his wrist instead.

The town guard arrived shortly. In areas further from cities, towns and seats of power the Shire's Reeve and his deputies carried a variety of duties. They were responsible for everything from patrolling the lord's lands, to fire watch, to the apprehension of cut purses and horse thieves, and adjudication in most matters not concerning the lord, or lady, themselves. However, in cities such as Dolloth, the Reeve's duties were focused more on the lord's house and politics. The Reeve of these lands had appointed a Magistrate, Lord High Inquisitor, and Captain of the Watch to Dolloth. Those three stations would have their own officers to carry out what was required. In this case the Captain of the Watch was responsible for the enforcement of the lord's laws, apprehension of any and all criminals found within the walls of Dolloth, and the jailing of same.

Roland knew he would be speaking with someone from the Inquisitor's office some time soon. Perhaps tomorrow. However, for now, it would be the town guard under the Captain of the Watch that would take custody of the remaining assailant and assess the situation. No need to call an Inquisitor every time someone was killed over a wager, or a woman.

The two fellows were young but, who was he to think such a thing? So much had happened he had a hard time remembering he had probably been in this world less time that either of them. They were of the more common man races that populated much of the central regions of Lethanor. They sported matching leather jerkins and maces that bore the seal of Lord Jessup.

"You're the Roland this man told us of?" one asked as he jerked a thumb toward Eldryn.

"Yes," Roland said. "It looks like they were trying to steal the axe."

Roland showed them the parchment.

"And you killed those two there?" the other asked.

"Yes," Roland said. "There was a fourth that escaped. Any idea where I might search for him?"

"Anywhere outside Dolloth," the first replied. "Any searching done here is done by the Capt'n or them 'quisitors. You'll be around tomorrow."

"Certainly," Roland said. "We can be found here."

"I wasn't askin'," the first said. "I was tellin'. One of the 'quisitors 'ill be by tomorrow."

Eldryn moved quickly to intervene when he saw the color of Roland's face darken.

"We'll be here," Eldryn said. "You'll be taking the bodies?"

"Yep."

The two guards drug all three out to the bannister where the corpses and the prisoner were piled onto a tarp to be hauled down the stairs and away.

"I think we'll be taking that axe for, um...evidence," the second said.

"The only way you'll get this axe will be to take it," Roland said. "You can tell that to your 'quisitor' too!"

It seemed that for the first time these two actually took in the size of Roland, and what he had accomplished on his own, in the dark, and against several assailants. They left without another word.

"Such slovenly, goat-headed, dung-healed..." Roland began.

"Can you imagine Tolbert walking in on this scene?"

Eldryn asked.

"What!?"

"I was just thinking of your father's deputy, Tolbert. Can you imagine his response to walking in on this scene? Two men dead, an assassin escaped, and a prisoner to jail that's as dangerous as that one likely is."

"I take your point," Roland said.

The next morning as they were finishing breakfast, on the house and in private dining as a form of apology from the inn keeper for the attempted theft from the night before, a short man of stout build dressed in black silk trousers and a white cotton shirt approached them. He was being shown the way by their waitress.

"I am Scurlough," the short man said. "I am an inquisitor here. I hope I have not caught you at a bad time."

To be fair Scurlough was taller than Ashcliff, much closer to six feet in height. He was of the common blood of men, with combed back brown hair and eyes that matched. At first look he would appear fat to the casual eye, but Roland noted the calloused hands and strong shoulders of a man accustomed to work. *A man gets fat in his gut and his ass*, Roland thought, *not in his shoulders*. Roland put his age at perhaps forty.

"Not at all," Eldryn said. "Please, join us."

"Don't mind if I do," Scurlough said nodding to a waitress. "You have a familiar bearing," Scurlough said looking at Roland.

"I suppose many of the Great Man race do," Roland said looking down and away.

Scurlough saw right away one thing and thought a second. One, *this Roland was no good at lying*, and two, *men on the run were unusually much better liars*. Either this Roland was stupid, or he was honest. Although there was a third possibility. He might be both.

Roland knew that Velryk often received dispatches from Ostbier about matters concerning the front, or criminals that had eluded capture. If Scurlough put together who his father was then he would likely include what he learned in his next letter east. Velryk would know a good deal more about his son, and much faster, than Roland had intended.

"I take it you were raised to be a warrior?" Scurlough said. "A lord's son?"

"No," Roland said, not sure if he was lying. "Our fathers served together. Eldryn's father died in battle. My father thought we should be prepared for the trouble with Tarborat."

"And your father is?" Scurlough asked.

"Possibly dead," Eldryn cut in. "He still serves and we have not had word from him for some time." *It's really not quite a lie*, Eldryn thought.

"I see," Scurlough said. "Perhaps to the matter at hand. Do you know why the thieves targeted you?"

"No," Roland said. "I assume one of their number spotted the axe. I take it this isn't a common occurrence in Dolloth, or in this inn anyway. Otherwise, I doubt the hospitality would have been so generous by the innkeeper."

"You are correct in that it is not common," Scurlough said. "This axe then, is it of particular value?"

Roland produced it from his belt and removed the lamb skin cover from it. He had taken to covering it the way he 'concealed' Swift Blood. He handed it across to Scurlough.

"This is a fine weapon indeed," Scurlough said. "Not just of rare material but rendered by a skilled hand as well. These symbols along the haft are interesting. Have you spoken to any of the churches about its origin, or perhaps a shop about selling it?"

"We did speak to a tradesman at the armorer's just down the street," Roland said.

"I see. He didn't offer a fair price?"

"It's not for sale," Roland said. "I was just curious as to what he could tell me about it."

"Ah, well, in that case I can be of some help. I know a monk here of the Church of Bolvii. He is well read on the subject of rare weapons and has studied many languages. I can make arrangements for you to meet with him in a day or two I'm sure, if you like."

Scurlough handed the axe back to Roland. Roland noted that Scurlough carried what appeared to be no more than a decorative dagger but, this man knew how to handle a real weapon as well.

"I don't think that will be necessary," Roland said.

"Who did you get it from?" Scurlough asked.

"From no one," Roland said. "We discovered it."

"Ah," Scurlough said. "That makes more sense. Where did you discover it?"

"The mountains to the north," Eldryn said. "We were traveling and happened upon a scene of battle from long ago. There were many broken weapons and other articles vanquished by the weather and time. The axe Roland found, however, was in very good condition."

Scurlough did not miss that when it came time for a lie, this one chimed in. Furthermore, the fact that this one didn't exactly lie was not lost on him. He had interrogated many who knew how to leave holes in the right places in their tale and he had the truth out of all of them. However, this was not supposed to be an interrogation.

"The Black Fly," Scurlough went in another direction, "have you had dealings with them before?"

"Never heard of them before," Roland said. "I assume that was the reason for the tattoos?"

"Many that we have discovered have had them," Scurlough said.

"Discovered?" Eldryn asked.

"We have never taken one into custody before," Scurlough said. "We have found their bodies from time to time and reports of them or their criminal acts. You have never crossed them or any other thief or assassin before?"

"By crossed, you mean had a conflict with?" Roland asked.

Scurlough thought that he would need to know a lot more about these two Great Men. They had the trappings of lords, or their close kin, yet had known or transacted with thieves or assassins before. They appeared to be between their twentieth and thirtieth years but, he had never heard their names before. He was confident, if the bigger one had been involved in anything significant or sinister, that at the very least a description of his size would have given him away. However, Scurlough had never heard of them and that troubled him.

"Yes," Scurlough answered. "Have you wronged, or been wronged by, anyone of that ilk?"

"No," Roland said.

Eldryn wasn't as certain as Roland. He hated himself for it but, he could not avoid the thought that Ash might have double crossed them.

"Well then, I would say that it was a robbery, plain and simple," Scurlough said.

"What else would it be?" Roland asked.

"The Black Fly aren't known for plain and simple," Scurlough said. "They are dangerous. You would do well to be wary of them. Inquisitors are not sent to investigate thefts. However, do to the fact that the Black Fly was involved I am investigating."

"Has the prisoner told you anything?" Roland asked.

"He has told me much," Scurlough said. "Thanks to him I have discovered two of our guards that were working in league with them. I have also discovered that they possess at least one copy of a key to our inner chambers and cells. You see, the prisoner was murdered last night before anyone could question him."

Scurlough waited for a reaction from them. After seeing none he continued.

"If you haven't crossed this sort before," Scurlough said, "then you have now. Watch for them for I assure you they will be watching for you."

That evening Roland and Eldryn drank in the tavern with a colorful group of mismatched and misled travelers. They sat in on a game of cards with a tracker, a fur trader, two mercenaries, and a dwarven warrior. The tracker and fur trader, both women, worked with one of the sell-swords along the rivers and lake south of Dolloth and were happy to tell of that area and their finds. The other mercenary worked as a guard for a caravan from Modins and had a few tales, clearly borrowed from others, about the seas, pirates, and distant lands. The dwarf mainly grumbled to himself about the luck of men as his pile of coins dwindled.

Roland, wishing to know more about the dwarves for a specific reason, asked a few questions about culture, family life, and what types of books the dwarf read. None of this gained any ground.

"That's a fine hammer you're toting there," Eldryn said. "Mercshyeld?"

"Aye!" the dwarf exclaimed. "T'was me father's crafted for him by me gray father, Derin the Squint Eye. Named so for the squint he was known for when examinin' good steel."

I'm Eldryn, son of Ellidik, and this is my good friend Roland," Eldryn said. "I gather that you are great son of Derin the Squint Eye but I don't know your name."

"Aye!" the dwarf exclaimed. "That's cause I ain't told ya! I be Ungar Hammer Strap!"

Roland marveled at Eldryn. One remark, one simple remark, and the dwarf was chatting along with the rest of them.

As it turned out the dwarf was of the Stonebeard Clan that resided in the mountain range that ran south of Dalloth, separating it from the southern areas of Hunthor. Dwarves rarely claimed any land above ground, but instead kept themselves to their mines in the mountains. There was at least one clan of dwarves or another in each mountain range in the known world. As far as Ungar's father, he had been Ultik the Bent Finger. There was a funny story about that moniker that

Ungar promised to tell but never got around to telling.

"If I had an item that I thought should be in the hands of the dwarven people, how would I go about getting it to one of their leaders?" Roland asked of the dwarf.

Eldryn looked at Roland with disbelief.

"That would depend on what item you speak of," the dwarf said dropping his jovial tone. "If you have 'an item' that belongs to us, I would know how it came to be in your hands. I would have the name of which of us it was taken from. I would take it in order to return it to my kin."

"This item you will not take," Roland said.

"I am Ungar Hammer Strap," the dwarf said as his dark eyes glinted. "No man will tell me what I will or will not take. The only person I will accept commands from is Vigorr, King of the Stonebeards!"

"Well met, Ungar," Roland said matching the dwarf's volume. "However, this item I will give to King Vigorr myself, or it will not be given at all."

"If you have something of our King's, you will surrender it immediately and hope that I am in a merciful mood."

Roland removed the oiled leather cover from the black glass hand axe and drew the weapon. Everyone at the table began to back away. Roland hoisted the weapon and drove it into the table top, easily sinking the edge two inches into the thick oak.

Ungar looked the axe over with eyes as black as the coal that stained his cheeks and hands. Age dropped from his face. His eyes took on the look of a child viewing a cart full of rock candy. They looked out of place surrounded by the long rough beard and hard skin.

"How will Ungar return to his people when it is said that an axe of their kings was lost to their people because of his bluster and stupidity?"

Ungar continued to stare at the sparkle on the dark surface of the leiness.

"You would make this a gift to King Vigorr?" Ungar

asked, his tone had lost all malice.

"I would," Roland replied.

"I shall show you the way," Ungar said. "If you would permit me."

Roland retrieved the axe and placed it back in his belt.

"Then we will leave in the morning for the home of the Stonebeards," Roland said.

"Sir, I would know the name of the warrior that would return such a legend to my people."

"I am Roland."

"Aye, I heard that the first time. But a fella' totin' that axe, a fella' that'd give a gift like that, that fella's got a name that folks would'a heard."

"Not yet they haven't," Roland said. "I do plan to make a name for myself such as you describe."

Ungar bought a round of drinks and then another. His mirth seemed to know no bounds, and dwarves were not known for their generosity. He and Roland became fast friends that evening, with Eldryn looking on in amazement at Roland's luck. The card game continued and Roland and Eldryn both lost several of their newly acquired gold coins. Finally, the time came to turn in.

Roland could not see through the dense mist. He knew the woman warrior, Dawn, was out there. She came out of the mist towering several feet over him. She grabbed him by the throat and threw him like he was no more than a child.

Roland leapt to his feet, but could not charge. His legs seemed pulled to the ground by a thick mud. He drew his Great sword. Once Swift Blood was in his hands Roland held it before him in a feeble defense. The sword began to shift and change in the mist. Roland squinted to peer at his weapon, and brought the blade close to his face to examine it. To his horror the end of the blade became the head of a viper and struck out at his face. Roland threw the wicked beast from his hands.

Dawn laughed as she strolled toward Roland. She was

laughing when she struck his face knocking him down into the thick mud.

Roland struggled to free his hands and finally got his axes from their scabbards. Roland held the axes in front of him.

"Your friends will die because of your failure," Dawn said. "Your father will be eternally ashamed of the son he tried so hard to raise properly. He weeps even now because of your weakness and cowardice."

Roland attempted an attack with the axes but both became serpents. Roland cast one aside but the other bit deeply into his hand. Roland looked on in terror as the reptile bit the end of his thumb off and swallowed. The snake forced its head beneath his skin and continued to swallow Roland's arm, slithering under his skin.

A scream rose in Roland's throat.

"Roland," Eldryn shouted. "Awake!"

Roland jerked from his bed soaked in sweat. He glared around the room and cringed away from the sword that he had leaned next to his bed.

"Roland, are you well?" Eldryn asked. "You were screaming in your sleep."

"I am sorry to wake you," Roland said, still unnerved to his core. There was a tremor in his voice Eldryn had never heard before. He was still trying to separate dream from reality. "It was a bad dream, nothing more."

"I've never known you to have bad dreams," Eldryn said, concerned.

"Nor have I. It has, however, been a busy time for us."

"It has at that, friend," Eldryn said with a smile. "You are well, so I will return to bed. Should you need anything…"

"I am no child that needs tending in the night," Roland said more sharply than he had intended. "I will be fine."

165

CHAPTER IX

Demons Inside

THE LATE NIGHT, AND HEAVING DRINKING, caused all to stay in bed much longer than they had intended. As Roland descended the stairs to the dining area, he saw that all the other morning traffic had come and gone. He also saw that Eldryn and Ungar were just beginning their meals. He ordered and joined his friends.

"Sir Roland, a man came round this morning looking for you," the waitress said. "A monk I think they call them. Said he was with the Church of Bolvii and that he had some questions he wanted to ask you."

Roland looked across the table at Eldryn and both began to package their breakfasts in their napkins preparing them for the road. Ungar Hammer Strap, whose years of morning dew were long behind him, took the cue well and began wolfing his breakfast down instead.

The group saddled their horses quickly, paid their stabling fees, and rode out of Dalloth heading south. Ungar led the trio astride a white-haired mule leading another mule burdened with crates and bundles.

"We are but a little more than two week's ride from the entrance to our lands," Ungar said. "I do not intend insult; however, I must blindfold you before I take you in. No man can know where the entrance is."

"We understand, and would not ask you to violate your customs," Roland said.

"What is it that you haul back to your people?" Eldryn asked.

"We are excellent weapon smiths and we craft fine armors," Ungar began. "However, we always have a great need for vegetables, grain, wheat, and other herbs. Farmers we are not. We have water aplenty, but we also have to pay dearly for milk, when we can get it."

"I would imagine that the amount of coin you earn from your weapon sales is more than enough to pay for the vegetables you need," Roland said.

"No," Ungar said. "It is dwarven custom that we will not sell to any that are not friends to the clan. It was not always so, but is now. Not many stilts are friendly toward the dwarven race these days. There's some in the churches that say we weren't intended by Fate or Time. That's how it started. That we're some kind of extra thing. Not part of their plan. Well, over time that came to be preached as though if it's outside of their plan then it's the work of Muersorem. Not many in the church hold to that way of thinkin' but, some do. Some do that's high up in their cathedrals. We have to trade our extra ale and spirits for the few supplies we can get."

"It seems you fellas had some trouble with the churches of your own," Ungar said.

"We would rather not answer any questions they would bring with them," Eldryn said. "Not exactly trouble but, a disagreement on who should know what."

"If we're not there to be questioned then there is no trouble with the churches," Roland said. "If we refuse to answer questions for them, then there may be."

"Aye, been little to no kindness between the church folk of men and me own kin," Ungar said. "Been that way since me Da' was young. Always figured it be a trouble between man and dwarf. You two seem good enough folk to me. What's the stone

167

in their boot over you about?"

"We had a disagreement with a paladin of Silvor..." Eldryn began, hoping to cut off the response he knew would erupt from Roland.

"Disagreement, hell," Roland said. "And it's more than that and you know it, El.'"

Then, to Ungar, Roland said, "The churches, all of them, have been more interested in building spires and couching fat priests and clerics than feed the people, caring for refugees, or soldiering against Ingsburn. Some say it is the gods themselves that are vain and greedy, but I don't believe that. I've read the book of Bolvii and studied the books of Silvor and of Roarke some. What I have read is about honor, charity, and justice. I didn't read a passage one that said anything about stained glass in the temple with gold and silver alters. I read about humility before the gods but nothing about groveling before a priest. I read about how a man's neighbor is one that is in need and one that comes in times of need. There was nothing about the color of their skin or the heritage of their race! I read..."

"Ok, Roland," Eldryn said. "I think he gets it."

"It makes me angry to think about, El'," Roland said. "I tell you..."

"Clearly it gets yer blood up," Ungar said. "I think I may come to like you, Tall Walker. A speech like that, well, maybe you ought to be preachin' in one of them fancy cathedrals your own self."

Roland's face grew dark but before he could speak, he was cut short by the burst of laughter from Ungar and Eldryn. Eldryn's laughter helped him reflect. It always gave him perspective. The laughter continued for almost a minute before Roland joined them. The idea of him in a robe with a cup or book in his hand instead of a sword or axe was pretty funny.

Each night the demon dreams cursed Roland's sleep. Rest had become a scarce thing for him. He usually slept only a short time before a nightmare would startle him from his slumber. He could rarely go back to sleep because the uncommon terror the dreams brought with them was always hard to shake. It stayed with him longer each time. His heart felt sick and afraid even under the light of the noon day sun.

Roland could not eat and could not think of anything other than the seeds of fear the nightmares planted in his soul. He was not a man accustomed to being afraid but these terrors seemed unaffected by his courage. His mind began to deny reality and accept imagination.

The trio rode for two weeks with Roland becoming more pale each day. They were finally within a day's ride from the entrance that Ungar had told them of. They rode late into the night that night, hoping to get close enough that the following days ride would be a short one.

Eldryn had noticed that Roland seemed to be getting ill. He seemed to become hollow and had stopped talking three days prior. He had always been quiet, but the last few days he had been completely silent. Roland had also begun drinking far too much from their stores of brandy and whiskey.

This night Ungar was to take the first watch, Eldryn the second, and Roland, as always, the third. Eldryn awoke to begin his watch and found Roland sitting near the low burning fire, staring blankly ahead.

"What are you doing up?" Eldryn asked. "It is second watch, right?"

"It is," Roland replied in a dead tone. "You did not miss your watch. I just didn't feel like sleeping."

Eldryn noticed the jug in Roland's hand.

"Ale is one thing, but brandies and whiskeys are another. That stuff will use you hard."

Roland looked absently at the jug.

"I am fine," Roland replied, turning his gaze back into the fire.

Eldryn felt concern for his friend, but knew of no way to help him. He did not even know what was wrong with him.

Ungar came back to the fire from checking on the horses. He looked at the two and knew something was wrong.

"Young Eldryn," Ungar said. "We should move the horse pickets before I take my rest. They will need to be moved to better grass."

Ungar and Eldryn stepped off into the dark leaving Roland staring blankly at the fire as he took another large swallow of the burning spirits in his clay jug.

"Your friend has been cursed," Ungar said flatly. "Someone walks in his dreams. I hear him during my watches. I am surprised you slept through it. Some enemy has a token of him and has cursed him."

"A token?"

"Yes, something that belonged to him or a piece of him. An old shirt, or a piece of jewelry, or a lock of hair. It takes something personal to curse someone in this fashion."

"What can be done?" Eldryn asked.

"You find the witch what done it and you kill 'em. But your friend will continue to lose sleep, and he will begin to doubt himself and all around him. I have seen what those inner demons can do to a warrior."

"Can anything be done to help him sleep?" Eldryn asked.

"Strong drink can work, but it is trading one devil for another. A dwarf loves his drink, but to drink of the strong spirits at each meal will steal a warrior's wits and battle skill."

Eldryn and Ungar returned to the fire, both giving Roland concerned looks. Roland did not notice. He continued to stare into the fire.

Ungar shrugged and pulled his cloak around his shoulders against the wind. He made his way to his bed roll and slept. Eldryn continued his watch in silence and Roland sat, unmoving, with that unsettling blank stare on his face. The hours passed and it was Eldryn's time for more sleep before they moved on.

"Will you be alright for your watch?" Eldryn asked.

"I am fine," Roland replied. "I am not so weak as to bring

shame on my father."

Eldryn looked at Roland with genuine concern in his eyes. He did not know what to say and decided it best not be discussed in that evil hour of night. Eldryn, comfortable from winter's chill in his gifted armor, propped his saddle up and laid back into the bow of it. Eldryn looked to Roland one last time but Roland did not look from the fire. Eldryn was worried for his friend, but the days of riding and short sleep were wearing on him as well. Sleep came for Eldryn, and he slipped deep into that dark water of rest.

Roland dropped an empty jug onto the ground next to the fire. It was his watch and watch he would. He took the majestic helm that was his reward from Nolcavanor and strapped it onto his head. Roland could see clearly into the dark and all around the camp. The effect was a little dizzying, until one got used to it.

Roland found himself sitting in front of the dying fire with his Shrou-Hayn across his knees. He tried to find comfort in the holy symbols of Bolvii carved into the hilt and the strength and grace of the weapon. However, each time he looked on it he waited for it to become the serpent that would eventually burrow under his skin and eat its way to his heart. Roland had suffered the dream every night since the first night in the tavern. Each nightmare was a little different, but always the snakes were there. And always his father was ashamed of him. His failures were ever-present.

If it had not been for the mystical qualities of his helm, Roland would have died that night. As Roland sat, apparently fixed upon the blade across his knees, a shadowy figure came from the dark that surrounded the camp. The figure approached Roland's exposed back and raised a black bladed sword high, confident in his strike.

Roland saw the creature just short of too late. If Roland would have had to rely on his wits at that moment, he would have been dead. However, Roland's training and honed muscles took over for his mind much like the eyelids will blink in reflex to protect the eye. Roland took Swift Blood by the hilt and spun, remaining in his low crouch.

Roland's speed, fed to him by the mighty weapon, caught the unnatural thing off its guard. Roland's strike cut deeply into the shadowy form's middle. Roland pulled as his blade sliced free of his opponent's torso and followed the first attack up with a chop that severed the creature's head. As it fell to the ground, Ungar and Eldryn rose with weapons ready.

Roland stumbled near the creature. He tried to focus his eyes on the thing but it seemed to elude them. The only thing Roland could see clearly was the bastard sword the thing held, and 'Roland' inscribed on the blade in the high language of the gods.

"What are you doing?" Eldryn said with great concern. "Who are you attacking?"

"It is there, on the ground before me," Roland said, fear creeping into his voice. "Do you not see it's blade?"

"Roland, are you feeling ill?"

"I see it too," Ungar said. "It is not plain to normal sight, but the heat from its body is still there. Even with dwarven or elvish eyes they're hard to see when they move. It is a demon more of shadow than of our world. One that crosses from plane to plane at will. That is your name burning on its weapon, is it not?"

"It is," Roland replied.

"It is a Soul Stalker," Ungar said. "They are demons forged to be assassins. They are sent after one target. It is very rare that one does not complete his mission."

Ungar looked at Roland.

"How did you defeat it?" Ungar asked.

"I saw him just before he struck down with his weapon," Roland said. "My reflexes took over from there."

"You saw him?" Ungar asked.

"Yes," Roland replied, tapping his helmet.

"That is a powerful item indeed if it allowed you to see that creature. There are helms that see into the dark, and helms that see both before and behind a warrior. But a helmet that sees into that plane is a helm to be treasured. Would you favor me with the story of how it came into your possession?"

"I would prefer to tell that story before your king," Roland said. "Please understand. I know your people will need the tale, but I am tired."

"Very well."

Ungar and Eldryn went back to their make shift beds as Roland stood and stared at the dissipating figure laying on the ground in front of him. He was dangerously beginning to doubt his own sanity. If Ungar had not also seen the Soul Stalker...

Roland was scared. He took up the blade the Soul Stalker had been wielding. He walked to the nearest tree and stabbed the blade several inches into the solid wood. Roland then grabbed the hilt in both hands and bent it sideways until the weapon snapped. Roland hurled the hilt and partial blade far out into the night.

The sun began to push against the dark in the east and Roland began putting breakfast together for the group. He woke Ungar and Eldryn and the three ate in silence, Ungar and Eldryn taking turns to look at the scorch marks on the earth where the Soul Stalker had burned into the ground. They all examined the violated holy symbols that were left traced into the dirt and ash.

"From here I must blindfold you," Ungar said. "It is not a sign of mistrust, it is simply a precaution of our people."

Roland and Eldryn gathered their equipment and saddled their horses. Once they were in the saddles Ungar took the reins to their horses and passed them the blindfolds. They removed their helmets and tied the dark cloths in place.

Roland and Eldryn both attempted to keep a mental track of their route but Ungar had done this before. Within the first ten minutes of the trip neither of them had any idea of where they were. They traveled like this for more than four hours when Ungar finally brought them to a halt.

"From here we must walk," Ungar said. "I will help you dismount and then I will stable our mounts."

Ungar helped each man down, and then took up the reins to the horses and led them directly toward a rock face. Once there, Ungar whispered something to the rock and it developed stony legs and arms and stood. The stone elemental took two ground trembling steps away from the cavern and Ungar led the two horses and his mule into underground stalls. Each animal was fed grain and then led to the stone water trough.

Ungar returned to an uneasy Roland and Eldryn. They could hear the grinding of stone, but took some small comfort in the fact that their horses didn't bolt from the area.

"Rest assured, friends," Ungar said. "All is well."

Ungar joined Roland and Eldryn's hands and then took Roland's hand. The two warriors staggered behind him in darkness as he led them up a narrow path. Ungar arrived at sparse brush growing out of the rock and tugged on it hard and to the left. A panel of rock slid away and Ungar began down the tunnel it revealed.

The group twisted down a short corridor before being confronted by the outer guard.

"What dwarf steps in these halls?" The challenge came from the dark within the mountain.

"It is I, Ungar, son to Frumgar, grandson to Studor."

"Enter the halls of the Stonebeards, your home."

"I have brought two outsiders," Ungar said. "They wish to see Vigorr, our king."

"That you must take up with the King's guard. You may enter."

Ungar led Roland and Eldryn past the two outer guards and then removed their blindfolds.

"From here you may see," Ungar said. "You will witness the glory of the dwarves."

Roland and Eldryn placed their helmets on their heads. Roland had to remain in a crouch most of the time, and Eldryn had to duck occasionally.

They made their way past rich veins of silver and gold, and through hallways skillfully carved with the history of dwarven warriors. Finally, they entered a large hall lit with torches and lamps where Roland could stand to his full height at last.

Over one hundred dwarves ate and drank at long oaken tables arranged along the large hall. Roland's attention was drawn to the table at the head of the hall where a dwarf in fine mercshyeld armor sat with a gold, gem encrusted goblet before him.

Ungar led the way to the table. The dwarf setting next to what Roland presumed was the King spoke.

"Ungar, we recognize the renowned warrior, son of Frumgar, grandson of Studor. We also understand that you have brought the precious wheats and grains we need. What business do you have before the king?"

"My companions wish to speak with the King," Ungar said.

"We have no business with a man so tall who is clad in such arrogant armor," the dwarven general said. "He is a boy of those that angered the gods and separated us from Roarke. I'll wager that his father does little more than defile the gods and keep whores. Or do the tall walkers keep boys such as him for whores now?"

"I have been insulted far too much," Roland said as, it seemed, his limited patience reached its end. "I am Roland, son of Velryk of the lands of Gallhallad. I come here as a friend and have made no judgments of the Stonebeards nor any other dwarf. I come here bearing gifts for the dwarves, but have been treated worse than a slovenly servant."

At this all the dwarves in the hall rose to their feet. The King himself stood and eyed Roland dangerously. The visual threat had all but the desired effect on the tall man. Even if Roland's sanity had not been at its brink, his temper would still have been a volatile thing.

Roland drew the ancient dwarven axe from his weapons belt.

"Vigorr, King of the Dwarves," Roland said. "I come to give this axe as a gift back to the people whose skill crafted it. I come as a friend and fellow warrior. However, if I am to continue to be treated like a rogue and dishonorable man then I shall begin to act as one. I would have this axe find its home in your revered armory, however, it may find its home in your skull!"

Roland held the axe high and every dwarf in the room drew in a quick breath. Eldryn felt every muscle twitch with the feeling of certain death. Roland extended the hilt of the weapon toward Vigorr who took it gingerly, as if afraid it would turn into smoke upon his mere touch.

"Roland, you come as a friend and truly you are one to all dwarves," Vigorr said taking the weapon and examining it. "You have my apology. As one warrior to another, will you accept that apology and forgive our manners."

"I will," Roland said.

"This weapon belonged to one of the first three kings of the dwarves, King Vech," Vigorr said to Roland as much as too his people. "He traveled to Nolcavanor with his friend of the Great Man race, Lord Ivant, in the days before the Battles of Rending to set right the wrongs of the Great Men. He did not return. This axe is an artifact of my people, a holy item! This axe is a legend!"

Roland recounted the story of Nolcavanor, leaving out the part about the holy book and the hourglass, for the dwarven king. He was certain to include the contributions of King Lucas and their friend, Ashcliff. All in the hall sat silent, absorbing his every word. Although many mugs sported fine ale, they sat stilled.

Roland came to the end of his story at the point where Ungar had blindfolded them. Roland was not a conversationalist. In fact, he was quite terrible at it and usually left that to Eldryn. But, when it came to telling a tale, he was very skilled.

One would think the two talents connected. One would be wrong.

"Let this be heard by all," King Vigorr said. "Roland and his friends, Eldryn and Ashcliff, shall be known as friends to the dwarves in all lands. King Lucas and his house of Thorvol shall be our trusted allies. They shall receive all of the hospitalities our people can offer until the end of their days."

A great roar went up from the crowd of dwarves. Vigorr showed the axe to several of his advisors and generals. Roland and Eldryn were bombarded with offers of ale and cooked meats. The supper gathering of the dwarven clan was transformed into a spontaneous celebration almost immediately as dwarves who had been absent were receiving the word and pouring into the hall. Roland and Eldryn only understood about half of what was said, neither of them spoke the dwarven language with much aptitude. They did gather, however, that they were being welcomed and cheered.

The celebration continued well into the night. As dwarves stumbled off to bed or lay on tables snoring, Roland and Eldryn were led to an emptied storage room.

"The King apologizes for the room, but it is only our Great Hall and a few storage rooms that men like you can stand up in."

Roland and Eldryn were given plush mattresses and heavy blankets. They stripped their armor and laid their weapons close at hand. Roland gave his sword and remaining axes a second look as he pulled the blankets up to his chest.

"Roland, what is it?" Eldryn asked.

"It's in my dreams El," Roland replied with a quiver and an unusual weakness in his voice. "It has been more than two weeks now since I have slept more than ten minutes at a time. The nightmares that come are not like the dreams of a child. These seem so real that when I awake, they continue to tear at my heart and gnaw at my sanity. I didn't tell you, but I was greatly relieved when Ungar saw the Soul Stalker too. I was scared that it was all in my head. I thought I might really be losing my mind."

"Ungar said that he thought you might be cursed," Eldryn said. "He said that if an enemy has a token of yours, a piece of jewelry, an old shirt, or some sort of personal item they can curse your dreams. He said that he has seen it drive brave warriors mad."

"Did he say if there was a way to stop it?"

"He did," Eldryn said. "You must find the enemy and kill them. Does anyone have a token of yours? Can you think of anyone that could do this?"

Roland thought back and then his gaze steeled.

"A lock of hair, that could be used as one of these 'tokens,' could it not?"

"It could."

"Dawn cut a hand full of hair from me when we battled in Nolcavanor, when she cut the chinstrap on my helmet. I must find a way to stop this. If she torments me from a distance, she will drive me mad without ever having to face me."

An idea burst in Eldryn's mind and showed through to his face.

"What is it?" Roland asked.

"Lord Ivant. You remember the stories as well as I do. The Great Man that was a warrior who worshiped in Bolvii's church before and during the Battles of Rending. The legend said that he carried a Shrou-Hayn that he called Swift Blood, and that his armor was the color of smoke."

"So?"

"The stories said that he wore a green gem on his brow. The fallen champions could not harm him with certain magics. Many of his men lost their senses under the mental attacks of the fallen and other demons, but Lord Ivant was somehow immune to those attacks. What if it was because of the lexxmar he wore in his helmet, in the helmet you wear now."

"Now that you say it, I realize that none of the dreams or visions have come to me while I have worn it," Roland said. "You really believe this was Lord Ivant's armor?"

"It must be. He traveled with King Vech. It was King Vech's axe you found there, and the armor and sword match the descriptions of those that belonged to Ivant. Try sleeping in your helmet this night and see if the dreams are warded off."

"It is certainly worth trying. I would do many unspeakable things for one good night of sleep."

Roland pulled on the helmet and buckled the chinstrap. It would be uncomfortable, but not too much so. Roland fell to sleep with his hands still on the chinstrap. He slept a long and dreamless sleep that night.

Eldryn noticed more color in Roland's face the next day, and his eyes seemed much sharper.

"Shall we see what the dwarves are having for lunch?" Eldryn asked.

"Lunch?"

"Yes, lunch. I have already shared breakfast with them hours ago. I thought that perhaps you could use the sleep."

"Yes indeed," Roland said through a yawn. "El, I feel like a new man."

"Well, let's get something to eat then. They are anxious to view the image of the axe but would not do so without you."

Roland and Eldryn made their way hunched over in the short tunnels until they reached the Great Hall where they received a hero's welcome. Roland ate like no man ever had before. Even the sturdiest of the dwarves were amazed at his appetite.

Roland was indeed a new man after the restful night, however, he would carry the new lines around his eyes and the gray streaks at his temples for the rest of his days.

As Roland finished his fourth plate and third flagon of water, it would be water only for a while, King Vigorr stood and called for a silence in the Hall.

"We gather together as clan and friends to share food and fellowship," King Vigorr said. "We also gather for an event many thought would never come to the Stonebeards again. We gather to view the Line of the King!"

At this a cheer rose from the crowd that shamed the great storms. Clerics, smiths, and generals gathered near the throne where a large mirror, about the size of two hearty dwarves, had been placed. Not a mirror of silver, Roland saw, but a mirror of pure Roarke's Ore. It was finely polished and without flaw. Close by, four lamps had been placed and each burned with a different color of fire.

King Vigorr held the axe while the others maneuvered the mirror and the lamps. The first lamp was brought up and a light of deep red reflected from the axe, to the mirror, to a wall of slate behind the throne. The light was the dwarven color of forging. Upon the wall was a marvelous image of a regal smith at work on a great anvil. Roland saw that the object of the smith's work was a dwarven warrior.   Those more educated in the matter saw the signs and symbols that indicated this was an image of Roarke crafting the first of their race. With an almost imperceptible movement, Vigorr adjusted the axe and the image moved. Roarke's hammer struck again in the Hall of the Stonebeards. The Hall was silent.

The lamp was lowered, another brought up, and the axe was tilted, slightly. The light of this lamp was of lush green, the dwarven color of growth or learning. The next image was of the same smith, Roarke, teaching the craft of smithing to the first of their kind. It showed seven dwarves at anvils, hammers in hand, surrounding a much larger anvil where Roarke worked. Eldryn noticed that each of the seven anvils had a different marking on it and among them was the symbol of the Stonebeard clan. Again, with a gentle tilt of the axe, the hammers of the first seven fell in unison with Roarke's. Eldryn decided that the man in the shop in Dolloth was wrong. This was magic indeed.

That lamp was lowered, and the third lamp was brought up. This lamp shone in a blue hue, the dwarven color of life and propagation. The axe again was repositioned. The next image revealed a scene of a dwarf, Eldryn was confident it was the one from the Stonebeard anvil in the previous scene, at his work station with a much younger dwarf working at his side. The motion in this scene was the old dwarf talking while the younger nodded his head. A father teaching a son.

The final lamp was raised, this time held up in conjunction with the rest. The combination of the lights shined as a white light, a holy color of Roarke. As this scene was revealed many of the dwarves around them began to weep. Concerned at first, Eldryn relaxed when he saw their tears streaming into their beards and around their smiles. This image was of the same dwarf walking past an anvil. The motion showed him young at one side of it, older as he worked at it, older still as he taught from it, and even older than that as he walked past it. The final motion of the image showed the same dwarf as he walked from his anvil into the workshop of Roarke where other dwarves, Eldryn presumed his ancestors, waited for him.

This was no magic of the sort that moved objects across a room by thought alone, or that changed lead to gold. This magic was much more potent. This magic warmed the hearts of hundreds of the toughest race of the gods. This magic moved people to rejoice and sing. This magic caused brother to forgive brother and eased the grief of the widowed.

This was no simple magic as the sort that could teleport a man great leagues or cast a bolt of lightning. This was the kind of magic that could heal a people and remind warriors what they fight for. This was the kind of magic that sparked love in its purest form. Not the love that a husband felt for his wife, but the love that a cavalier holds for his country. The kind of love one neighbor has for another that he has cared for. The kind of love that causes evil men to lay down their swords or good men to take them up.

Eldryn, until the end of his days, would not forget this time with the dwarves.

At the supper gathering King Vigorr called a silence to the hall.

"Listen my clan, and new friends alike," Vigorr began. "No dwarf has ever received such a gift as we have received from these Great Men. And no dwarf has ever been honored with a gift that he did not return a gift in kind. We cannot match the majesty of the axe Roland and Eldryn have returned to us, however, we offer them these humble presents as a symbol of our appreciation. First a ring for each signifying their friendship with all dwarves so that they might be known to all as a trusted friend among the great smiths and miners of the world."

Roland and Eldryn were each presented with a Roarke's Ore ring with the dwarven symbol of hammer and anvil engraved on its rich surface. Roland was given an extra ring to be given to Ashcliff and Eldryn an extra for Lucas.

"Then to you, Eldryn son of Ellidik of the One Eye. I am told that you are a cavalier in the ways of the Shyeld, and would practice the honorable ways of that ancient battalion and the old Code. To you we give four horse shoes crafted by our finest smiths. These shoes will make your steed faster and more sure footed than any other."

A dwarf, clad in a dingy leather apron, approached Eldryn and presented him with four black mercshyeld horse shoes with runes carved into each. Mercshyeld used for horse shoes!

"Then to you, Roland son of Velryk the Just from the Line of Ivant the Eld," Vigorr continued. "It is a warrior's heart that you possess and a warrior's armament that you wear. Our humble gift does not deserve to go adorn with such fine craftsmanship of old. However, it is our hope that you will find use in these boots of boiled leather sole and hard steel toe and heel. These boots will allow you to stand in combat without concern of your feet being cut from beneath you. These boots will allow no blade to pass through them. No injury will come to you where these boots cover you."

The same dwarf in the leather apron walked toward Roland bearing a pair of beautifully made knee-high, dark-gray leather boots.

"To the dwarven people you will be known as Roland Tall Walker the Oath Keeper, and Eldryn Stone Rider. These gifts we offer in humble appreciation for what you have done for our people. The axe of the legendary King Vech has been returned to us, and with it the story of our line, our fore bearers. It has told, and will continue to tell, a bit more of our story to our following generations. If there is anything else that you would request from me or my people you have but to ask it."

Roland burned with questions about what the king had said. Those words, 'son of Velryk the Just from the Line of Ivant the Eld,' rang in his ears. He knew this was not the place or time. He was shamed to know so little of his own family history when surrounded by such a display of dwarven ancestry. Very well, if he was indeed as the king had called him, he would act worthy of the name and title. It was not lost on him that Oath Keeper was also the name of Bolvii's sword. He reined in his own curiosity, which he knew, deep down, was vanity.

"King Vigorr, and all Stonebeards, hear me," Roland said. "You have honored us with your hospitality and kingly gifts. I am equally honored to call the Stonebeards allies and friends."

Eldryn, knowing Roland perhaps better than anyone, was always amazed at how he seemed to know the right thing to say at the right time. It wasn't conversation. Roland was terrible at that. It was…diplomacy. Any other man speaking as he did might have been killed when they first met Ungar in that tavern weeks before. Any other man might now struggle for what to say in the face of such kingly gifts. But not his friend, Roland. The words he needed seemed to always be there waiting for him.

A great cheer went up through the dwarven mass and another celebration seemed to be beginning. Roland talked briefly with Eldryn and then approached the King's table.

"King Vigorr, I and my friend, Eldryn, have been honored by your reception and hospitality. However, I regret that we must move on. We have an appointment in Modins that we must keep and therefore we must continue our journey."

"I understand that a young warrior has much to do. In your travels, should you ever need the clan of the Stonebeards you have but to call upon us. You have my leave, Tall Walker the Oath Keeper."

King Vigorr assigned one of his personal guards to escort Roland and Eldryn through the maze of caverns.

"I thank you, Your Majesty," Roland said with a bow.

Roland turned to Eldryn and they sought out Ungar who was being cheered and toasted at a table nearby.

"We must be on our way, friend," Roland said.

"I and my clan are forever in your debt," Ungar said to Roland and Eldryn.

"Perhaps we will meet on the road again someday," Eldryn said. "Until then keep yourself well."

With that Roland and Eldryn, led by their escort, began the winding walk that would eventually deliver them to the face of the mountainside.

A dwarven smith that had been minding the animals in the stone stables offered to shoe Eldryn's horse for him.

"I would be very grateful," Eldryn replied.

The smith shod Lance Chaser and the two friends were on their road to Modins once again. It was late afternoon when they rode out of the stable and past dark by the time, they made their way off of the mountain and down to the forests surrounding the range.

"I have to say this, Roland," Eldryn began. "How did you get so lucky with the dwarves? I was sure that Ungar would kill you that night in Dolloth. Then the way you spoke to the King in front of all of his people. I thought for certain that we would be killed."

"You remember what father taught us about dwarves," Roland replied. "He said that they shared a lot of characteristics with mules. They are stubborn, blunt, and tough. They would set themselves on fire just to spite you, and they will bite you whenever they get the chance, unless you let them know that you will not tolerate being bitten. It is just a matter of responding to them in a manner that they are accustom to. They feel that if a man puts up with being insulted then he deserves the insult."

"You could have let me in on some of your insight."

"I don't think that would have worked as well. They wouldn't have noticed your shocked expressions, and would have thought that my words were hollow."

Eldryn gave Roland a curious look.

"Very well," Roland conceded. "Most of it was due to my temper. However, I did remember the lessons father taught us about dwarves. And everything worked out in the end."

They set up camp and Eldryn picketed the horses while Roland began the fire and maneuvered stones to bank the heat. Roland slept in his helmet again. The rest was never so wonderful.

CHAPTER X

Friends?

T HEY TRAVELED WEST ALONG THE mountain range for days without incident. Traveling in the forest with the mountains to block the southern winds was much more comfortable. The two friends enjoyed the break from the brutal weather and the new, pleasant scenery. Eldryn hunted and both young men ate well.

On a morning ten days after leaving the dwarven stronghold they saw smoke on the horizon more to their north than west. A lot of smoke. They turned their horses in that direction. A short ride brought them upon a boy running through the forest. Roland guessed him to be no more than nine or ten years old.

"What is the matter, boy?" Roland asked. He noticed that the boy's face was tear streaked, and new tears welled in his blue eyes. His clothes were torn and stained with soot. His short cut blonde hair was a nest of ash.

"Our village," the young boy said through barely controlled sobs. "A horrible wizard is burning it."

Roland took the boy up and put him behind him in the saddle.

"What is your name, boy?" Roland asked.

"Petie."

"Take this," Roland said as he handed Petie one of his

daggers. "Petie, every man was once a boy and was scared at one time or another. What makes them men is that they stood when they were scared, and they fought against what they feared."

Petie took the dagger from Roland and looked directly at him. Petie choked his tears back and stiffened his quivering lip. Roland nodded and he and Eldryn started their mounts on a gallop toward the burning village.

They rode into a clearing at the outskirts of a small community on the edge of the forest backed up against the mountains. Roland and Eldryn saw an elf with long blond hair wielding a broadsword and screaming as he took deliberate steps north up one of the three trails that passed through the small town. This elf, clad in finely crafted chainmail of some exotic alloy, continued to scream hauntingly as he marched north. They felt fairly confident until they watched the elf summon a green ball of energy to his left hand and then release it toward a small hut. The hut burst apart in green and blue flames.

Roland watched as the remaining inhabitants of the small village fled north out of town. Roland began walking his horse forward.

"What are you doing?" Eldryn asked.

"We cannot allow this," Roland replied.

"How do you plan to stop him? There is no way we can take him."

"We have to try."

Roland rode his horse to the center of the small trail directly in the elf's path. When the elf looked up Roland thought he saw something that he recognized in the mage warrior's eyes that was painfully familiar. A doubt of sanity. It was clear that this elf was plagued with some kind of mind disease. Roland calculated his odds of taking this dangerous fellow by force. Those odds did not seem to favor him, especially when he had a child to protect. Then an idea came to him.

"Friend I cannot let you continue with this," Roland said.

"Why do you think you can call me friend?" The elf spat. "All of my friends are dead, save one. ALL OF THEM! DEAD! Pay me tribute or die."

"I call you friend because we share a common enemy and that makes us allies, as is in 'Thoughts on War,'" Roland said. "I can offer you rest from that enemy."

"You, a simple-minded mortal, would attempt to trick me, the Almighty Gallis Argenti?"

"Surely a wise elf could tell that there is no lie in what I say."

"So, you hope to ply me with flattery?" Gallis Argenti asked. "A tribute or I'll leave your death to be the last so that you can watch what I do to your friend and the child there. Let's start with that magnificent helmet you wear. Pass it over."

Roland removed his helm and handed it out to Gallis. There was a moment of hesitation. What would he become if this mage warrior destroyed the helmet? This helmet was his only bastion against inevitable insanity. The moment of greed, and no small amount of fear, passed.

He thought to himself how lucky, or blessed by Bolvii himself, he was that Gallis Argenti had asked for the helmet first. He had decided to give him whatever he asked, hoping that he would put the helmet on. However, Roland didn't know if he would have the strength to give up his sword to meet that end.

Gallis took the helmet and eyed Roland dangerously. He said a few arcane words and moved his hand over the helm.

"You may begin unclasping that great sword now as well," Gallis Argenti said. "I think I'll take that and any Rorkor you have. Perhaps I'll kill you anyway. I hate spies!"

Gallis Argenti placed the helmet on his head and the tight lines around his mouth and eyes relaxed immediately. He slumped to the ground in a sigh of relief. The people from the village continued to flee the small town.

Roland dismounted and handed his reins to Petie who still sat in the saddle. Roland approached Gallis Argenti and then knelt beside him.

"Rest easy," Roland said. "You have no enemies here and I will see that you are not harmed."

"How can you say that?" Eldryn asked. "You have heard of Gallis Argenti. We saw his posters in Dolloth. He is dangerous, and a wanted criminal. There would not be such a high price on his head for no reason. We should shackle him now while we have the chance."

"This warrior fights the same enemy I fought for only a few weeks. If my battle had continued there might have been a high price on my head. Would you still have offered me help no matter what I might have done in that state?"

"You are a good man, Roland. I don't think…"

"You can not know!" Roland shouted. "Until the inner demons chase you in your sleep, you can not know."

"I am alright KyrNyn," Gallis Argenti called out in a sleepy voice. "They mean us no harm and I have found a reprieve."

Roland and Eldryn were both surprised when a tightly muscled common man appeared from almost non-existent cover behind them. He walked over and stood over Gallis Argenti.

"He is my friend," KyrNyn said. "I have stuck by him even though the inner demons haunt him. You will both die if you attempt to capture or harm him."

Roland looked at KyrNyn, fixing him with his faded blue eyes. He wondered how this man planned to kill them while wearing no armor and toting no weapon. Hopefully, it would not come to that.

"I understand your friend's pain," Roland said. "He will not come to any harm or capture at my hand this day."

"The towns people may have other ideas," Eldryn said. "Perhaps we should move him to a safer location."

"You have a good point," Roland said. "Petie, perhaps you should try to find your father."

"My folks are dead. They were killed by an ogre raid several months ago. I have been a worker for the town ever since.

I have nothing here but work. I work for everyone and some of them feed me. I don't want to stay here. Could I leave with you? I'm strong. I don't eat much. I'm good at catching rabbits."

Roland looked the boy over. Petie was standing there, tears gone, holding the dagger Roland had given him as if prepared to use it on Gallis Argenti. Roland saw intelligence in the boy's eyes, and something else. Roland saw a strong will.

"Very well," Roland said. "You may travel with us for the time being, but you will do as I say just as though I were your father. Agreed?"

"Yes sire," Petie said.

Roland picked Gallis Argenti up and laid him over his saddle. KyrNyn collected his horse from the edge of town and followed Roland and Eldryn south out of the small village.

"Where is Gallis Argenti's mount?" Eldryn asked.

"His mount can take care of himself," KyrNyn replied. "He would be better handled by Gallis himself. His mount can be very dangerous."

They traveled until dark and then began to set up camp. Roland and Eldryn went through their usual routine. Petie began to gather firewood and then helped Eldryn with the horses. KyrNyn checked Gallis again and found that he was sound asleep.

"We went into the town to have a drink of whatever they might brew there and have a hot meal," KyrNyn said. "One of the village men recognized Gallis and got greedy. Several of them organized and attempted to kill us while we ate. Gallis, as he is prone to do, got a little out of hand, and after the group that ambushed us was dead, he began tearing apart the town."

"What happened to him?" Roland asked.

"His story is his own to tell," KyrNyn said. "He does, however, suffer from the haunts that you seem to understand."

"The helmet will not cure the problem," Roland said. "The rest it gives, however, is like breath to a drowning man."

"Good gods!" Eldryn exclaimed drawing his magnificent Shrou-Sheld. "What is that?"

Eldryn pointed to a large shadow in the woods near the camp. He kept his sword handy and began stringing his sectot bow that he retrieved from the caverns of Nolcavanor.

"Rest easy," KyrNyn said. "That is Gallis's mount."

"It looks like some kind of cat. A huge cat!"

"It is," KyrNyn replied simply. "Some of the greatest of the warriors from Janis ride them into combat. We can all sleep without concern tonight. Quick Claw will watch for us."

Roland gave Petie his extra shirt to wear, which covered the boy completely. He also gave him a blanket and a rope belt with a scabbard for the steel dagger. The companions all stretched out for a peaceful rest.

KyrNyn cracked his eyes open and found the rest of the group resting. He made his way around the camp on silent feet and began to go through Eldryn and Roland's packs. He found the letter written by Lucas and examined it closely for several minutes. He heard Roland stir and replaced the letter quickly.

Roland awoke to find everything around him bathed in oppressive darkness. He felt his bedroll slithering all around him and the air was thick with the smell of decaying flesh. He leapt from his bed.   As he jumped, he slammed into a large fang. Roland struck the ceiling of something and then realized as terror seized his heart that he was in the mouth of some huge creature. Roland pushed up on the roof of the creature's mouth only to find that it gave way in his hands as the rotting flesh pulled from the bone. Roland grabbed one of the fangs and heaved up with all his strength, forcing the mouth open.

He saw that he was over thirty feet up in the air, but Roland jumped from its mouth just the same. He landed on the run. When he looked over his shoulder his knees felt weak with fear. He looked on one of the old mounts of the gods. A dragon. Not just any dragon, but one that had defied death and now walked in unlife.

Roland had never imagined something so purely evil.

Nor could he imagine anything deadlier. Roland looked upon an undead mount of the champions. A great dragon that was bone and rotting flesh. There was nothing but death in its puss colored eyes.

Roland charged into the curtain of night, fleeing blindly in panic. He rounded a tree and could hear the beast behind him. Roland struck something in the dark that was solid as stone. Roland looked up to find his father, Velryk, towering several feet above him.

"My son, the mighty warrior! Ha," Velryk scoffed. "You are a coward and you run from battle like the scared child you are!"

Velryk took up his axe.

"I'll not allow my son to be a coward and make our name no more than another insult for cowardice, another mark for a yellow fighter."

Velryk swung the axe and Roland could only stare in a mixture of shame and terror.

"Roland!" Eldryn exclaimed.

Roland jerked awake, covered in sweat.

"You were screaming," KyrNyn said. "Are you well?"

"I can take it for now," Roland said, shaken.

Roland took a coffee pot from his pack and began brewing the dark drink.

"I'll watch the rest of the night," Roland said.

KyrNyn gave Roland an understanding look and everyone else went back to their bedrolls. Roland spent the rest of the night looking toward the whiskey bottle in his pack. He had set his mind that he would not touch it, but it was more of a fight than he anticipated. Roland won the battle, but it was not a battle easily fought. Roland welcomed the sun when it began its journey in the east.

KyrNyn awoke and walked over to Roland.

"I'll remove your helm from Gallis Argenti," KyrNyn

said. "I think you and your friends should be gone when he awakes. I know that he would do no harm to me, but I cannot guarantee the same for you."

"You know there are priests in the larger temples that can help him," Roland said.

"Yes, but he refuses. He is my friend and I will be here for him, whether he chooses to be healed or not. He is not as blood-thirsty as they say. He just tolerates very little. The price on his head invites fools and with each fool that he kills the bounty rises."

"Very well. We will be on our way."

Roland and Eldryn gathered their belongings and ex-changed looks as they watched Petie helping them break camp. Roland put Petie up in the saddle and then climbed up behind him.

"Are you reading for a long day, boy?" Eldryn asked Petie.

"You'll not find me complaining, Sir Eldryn."

"Just Eldryn, Petie, just Eldryn," Eldryn said as he rus-tled Petie's hair.

The three rode with the rising sun warming their backs.

Gallis Argenti stirred from his first restful sleep in sev-eral years. Years and decades meant little to an elf, unless it was time without meditation or sleep. Gallis's mind had driven him hard for over twelve years. The only sanity that remained was his friendship with KyrNyn and his love for his cat.

"What happened, KyrNyn?" Gallis Argenti asked.

"I think we encountered friends," KyrNyn said.

"How can you say that?" Gallis Argenti asked as the lines of strain began to draw themselves around his eyes again. "Surely my rest was a trap. They must be spies."

"They did not harm us," KyrNyn said. "And there was something else."

"What?"

"I found a letter on them," KyrNyn said. "It was signed

by your friend, Lucas. Apparently, he has been returned to the surface of this world from which he vanished so many years ago. The letter called them friends of the house of Thorvol."

"Could we have found friends that can be trusted?" Gallis Argenti asked.

CHAPTER XI

The Orphan

THE THREE RODE TOGETHER FOR THREE WEEKS through the forests and plains of Lethanor and crossed a great river. During their journey Roland and Eldryn both began to respect their adopted traveling companion. They discovered that Petie was quite strong for his size and was actually a very skilled hunter. Roland had taken to instructing the boy in the use of the axe, and Eldryn, being the better swordsman, taught Petie the use of the bastard sword. Petie, no matter how strong, was still small for the actual blade so Roland had carved him a wooden sword to practice with.

Eldryn began teaching Petie how to ride and the tricks and tactics associated with mounted combat. Roland continued to sleep wearing his helmet.

Petie also began joining Roland and Eldryn for their morning exercises. They taught him how to stretch and the routines that would develop both his muscles and his balance and speed. They also began to teach him to strengthen other aspects of true warriors.

Roland had read many books however, his favorite was Arto's 'Thoughts on War.' Roland began telling Petie of the General Arto and of how he took a handful of Great Men, and a small tribe of common men, and conquered league upon league of the lands around the capital now called Ostbier. He told him of how Arto used his mind to fight his enemies as much as his sword, and of how he had time and time again defeated superior numbers in battle through tact and planning. Roland had brought two books with him on his journey, 'Thoughts on War' and 'Philosophy of the Blade.'

Roland had been very lax in his reading since leaving his home so many months before. However, now he took those books up again, this time not as the student but as the teacher.

It was a bright morning, and Eldryn had taken Petie on a hunting trip while Roland packed what could be packed of their traveling gear and led the horses to water at a nearby stream.

As Roland returned to the camp both horses became increasingly nervous. Being trained war horses neither of them made a sound nor fought against Roland's hand. However, Roland had learned enough about the wild to know that horses usually smelled trouble long before their riders became aware of it. Roland noted their tension now and loosened Swift Blood in its scabbard.

Roland approached the camp cautiously and saw two demons sniffing through their packs. The first fallen champion was black skinned and stood nearly twelve feet tall. It carried a whip in one clawed hand and had heart red eyes. The second fallen champion was shorter than the first, standing only eight feet tall, with scaly red skin and eyes that were the absences of light. It wielded a barbed mace in one hand and a heavily built crossbow in the other.

Roland thought of trying to seek out Eldryn and Petie but dismissed the idea. He had heard that demons could run much faster than any man and judging by their height he assumed that they would have an incredible stride. If he started looking for El and Petie the demons might find them first. If he yelled to Eldryn and Petie then he would give up his surprise.

Therefore, Roland did what he thought to be his only avenue. He called out to Bolvii as he charged the two demons.

The red demon loosed a crossbow bolt that struck Roland high on the shoulder and glanced off his armor. The black skinned demon held out his hand and chanted in a foul language. Roland felt the wave of hate wash through his head and then it was gone like a swift spring breeze. The gem on his helm illuminated in a bright green glow.

Roland feigned toward the red demon, which had dropped his crossbow and taken his mace in both hands, and made his attack toward the black demon bearing the whip. The whip-wielding demon lashed out with the leather instrument of torture and the magically burning weapon slapped against the high top of Roland's leather boots. The whip wrapped his leg, but the hissing burn did not affect him.

Roland saw his predicament and changed his attack. He knew that if the creature maintained a hold on the whip that he would be hurled into the air any moment. He called upon the speed of Swift Blood and spun a thrust to the side, turning it to cut toward the black skinned demon's arm. The blade cleaved the arm in one smooth stroke and the creature cried out and drew away.

The red skinned demon had an opportunity and seized it. He struck Roland hard on the back with the barbed mace, knocking him to his knees, stunning him.

The red demon revealed a mouth full of fangs as it smiled in its triumph. The barbed mace came back and then swung forward with vicious force. The mace crashed into the back of Roland's helm and slapped him hard into the ground. Roland's eyes rolled as he struggled to hang on to consciousness.

The black skinned demon had retrieved his whip from the grip of his severed limb. The two demons exchanged knowing smiles as the red demon kicked Roland's sword from his hand.

The black demon knelt and wrapped the end of the whip around Roland's throat. He stood and hauled Roland up to a standing position. Roland struggled to clear his vision while his hands clawed at the choking demon leather.

R.J. Hanson

The red demon drew back his mace again and laughed. He was beginning his swing when he screamed out in pain. The red demon whirled around to see Eldryn preparing another Roarke's Ore tipped arrow. The red demon bellowed a stream of curses as it turned and started for Eldryn and young Petie standing next to him. Petie's iron tipped arrow took the demon in the thigh, but the creature seemed not to care.

Eldryn prepared the next arrow and its flight was true. The arrow struck the demon in the belly. Flames erupted from the wound as acid spewed from the gash.

The black skinned demon decided it was time to conclude his business. He lowered his remaining arm and prepared to jerk up, which would tear Roland's head from his body.

Roland drew the flaming dagger and slashed at the whip. The leather severed just as the whip had begun to tighten around his throat. The black skinned demon staggered back with the unexpected momentum. Roland struggled to get the writhing end of the whip off his neck.

Petie stepped forward and loosed another arrow that took the reeling demon in the shoulder. The demon turned toward Petie and scowled.

Eldryn drew his Shrou-Sheld and charged the creature. There are not many men who are skilled enough with a blade to parry a whip, but Eldryn managed it. As the slithering whip came in to grapple his blade, Eldryn slapped a portion of it, and turned the edge of his blade against the encircling leather. Eldryn cut through the whip and followed up the parry with a devastating attack that cleanly severed the fallen champion's head. Both creatures began to sizzle and smolder into the ground. Roland finally tore the whip from his throat, leaving a bloody gash where it had attempted to strangle him.

"Demons? Here?" Eldryn asked.

"No doubt sent by our well-wishers who come to visit me at night," Roland replied.

"That is a demon? That is what they look like?" Petie asked.

198

"Yes, Petie, those are demons," Roland said. "Let this be a lesson well learned. A man that can stand alone is a strong man. However, a man with hidden allies, like you and Eldryn where to me just now, is a dangerous foe indeed."

"Spoke Arto," Eldryn quipped.

Roland shot Eldryn a disapproving look.

"Remember this young Petie," Roland said as he disregarded Eldryn's sarcastic comment. "Remember that even fallen champions can be defeated if a man is not afraid, and he is skilled with his weapon. An evil man cannot remain against a man that defends the weak, and fights for a just cause and who will not admit defeat. A man that fights for a just cause can never admit defeat for his surrender is his defeat. A just warrior that will not quit will never know defeat, although he may be bested in combat."

"I don't understand," Petie said.

"There is no defeat if a man faces evil and dies fighting it," Roland said. "If a man dies then it is because Fate, in her wisdom, has decided to take him. The only defeat a just warrior could ever know is cowardice. 'He who lives more lives than one, more deaths than one must die.' Do you understand now?"

"I think so," Petie said. "A coward dies each time he turns to run. A weak warrior dies each time he quits."

"You are a smart lad," Roland said as he placed his hand on Petie's shoulder. "What is a warrior's most valuable weapon?"

"His mind."

"And what is a warrior's most trusted ally?"

"His courage."

"Excellent."

Roland smiled at Petie and Petie stood tall and proud. The three companions gathered their belongings among the smoke rising from the smoldering demons. They rode in silence most of the day.

That evening, after Petie had gone to sleep, Eldryn walked out to Roland who was gathering more firewood.

199

Eldryn lit a roll of smoking leaf and handed Roland one. Roland bit the end off of it and chewed it. He then maneuvered it into his jaw and looked back toward the camp at a sleeping Petie.

"He is a fine boy," Roland said.

"He is at that. You know we must leave him in Modins. Our road is much too dangerous for a boy, no matter how smart or strong."

"He learns fast, El'," Roland said, trying to hide the emotion in his voice. "We are young but… we know things that we could teach him."

"You know I'm right," Eldryn said.

"Before the Hourglass I hadn't thought of a family, of sons," Roland said. "I feel for him as I did when we traveled the Sands of Time and I saw…well I'm not sure what I saw but I know what I felt. I love him, El'."

"So do I," Eldryn said. "But you know I'm right."

"We will see," Roland said.

"You know who you sounded like?" Eldryn asked, skillfully changing the subject.

"What are you talking about now, El?"

"You sounded just like your father when you were talking to him this morning about the demons."

"You're just saying that to get my blood up," Roland said, knowing there was truth in it.

"You know I'm right," Eldryn said through a slight laugh.

"Aye, and just so. You are right. But this one it might not be wasted on. This boy is a smart one, and strong."

"Always doubting your own wit," Eldryn said.

"There is no wit, you yourself have said so. I have been called an ox all of my life. There is truth to that label."

"Roland, I know no man who is as hard on himself as you are," Eldryn said. Then, maneuvering the subject skillfully, "I wonder if this is a bit of what it's like for you father, or my Ma'."

"What do you mean?" Roland asked.

"You know what I mean. We've only known this boy for a short time, but I worry for him. I hope for him. I'm proud when he has the right answer or shows bravery as he did earlier. But mostly it's the worry. I feel it too, Roland."

Roland nodded, not wanting to muddy how he felt about Petie with clumsy words.

The two friends enjoyed the silence of the night, and the calmness that came with the smoking leaf. Eldryn looked to the horizon where the mountains butted against the stars. Roland spat into the grass and then walked back toward the camp. Eldryn followed and they rolled their bedrolls out.

"Take your four hours of sleep," Eldryn said. "I'll wake you two hours after midnight."

"Sleep," Roland said looking off into the night. "A man doesn't know what true riches are until he has been deprived of his sleep."

Roland put two more sticks into the fire and pulled his bedroll up around him. He slept soundly until Eldryn woke him at two past the midnight hour. The morning came, and the three friends gathered their belongings as they had so many times before. Breakfast was prepared, and packs were loaded onto horseback.

Roland led them out of their camp, traveling west and slightly north. Roland now wore a black cloth around his neck to cover the wound from the demon's whip. The wound accurately marked him as a man someone had attempted to hang. However, most men that carried that sort of mark needed hanging. He did not want to be confused with that sort.

Ten days after their encounter with the fallen champions they cleared the forests and made it out onto the plains surrounding Modins. They were still leagues and weeks away from the great port city, but that time would be spent traversing these flat lands.

They found that these plains were not so flat after all. Roland noted that while looking out across the lands everything appeared flat there were actually several great gullies and some canyons cut into the earth.

Without the forest or mountains to protect them from the onslaught of winters last weeks they took to sometimes traveling with those canyons for the wind break it provided. Being naïve to the trail, they also took to camping in them. That mistake would mean death for some and life for others.

One night, in the early hours before sunrise, Roland began building up the fire. It had been very cold with a norther blowing hard and pelting them with freezing rain.

They had camped near a small stream at the bottom of a canyon around a bend and out of the north wind's direct path. Roland was stoking the fire with collected driftwood that he found all around. If he had been paying attention things might have gone differently.

Roland gathered driftwood from near the stream but also from much higher up the bank. Several feet higher than where they had encamped.

As the coffee and the stew of jerky and potatoes began to come to a boil Roland heard a voice on the wind. *Waves and waste-landers come. Be ready Roland son of Velryk the Just, Tall Walker and Oath Keeper. Be ready.*

Roland bolted upright from his position over the stew pot. He kicked Eldryn's foot and shook Petie's shoulder gently.

"Something comes," Roland said.

"You see, boys," a voice from the dark around them spoke. "I told you I smelled someone cooking us breakfast."

"We are but poor travelers," Roland said. "We are always happy to share what little we have, though."

Roland edged himself away from the fire and put himself between Petie and where he judged the voice to be coming from. He started his hand toward his helmet which sat so far away near his pack.

Eldryn, who had made a practice of sleeping in his armor to ward off the cold, did have a blanket over him to shuck the freezing rain. Under that blanket he also protected his fine sword and bow.

"Now now, what sort of host reaches for his armor when

guests arrive," the voice in the dark spoke again. In short order an arrow lodged into the ground between Roland's hand and his helm. "We'll make this easy, fellas. Just put down your weapons and walk on down your road. You'll be leaving behind your packs and fine horses, of course. But we'll be lettin' ya walk away. I'm friendly like that."

Roland was smart enough to note that the arrow that struck the ground near him had come from below him near the stream. He also now realized he could hear the rushing of water. He had been hearing for several moments now.

"We don't have much," Roland said addressing the voice from the dark. Under his breath he said, "El', see to the horses. I'll get Petie."

"We are but poor travelers from Fordir," Roland continued. "We will lay our weapons down but, I must know, how did you come upon us so quietly? You came along the edge of the water, didn't you? That must be it."

"You've done enough talking, big man," the voice said. "It's time for moving."

"Agreed," Roland said. "El', now!"

As Roland scooped up Petie in one hand and his helmet in another Eldryn rolled from his pallet and sprang for the horses that had been hobbled. The first volley of arrows struck the ground around them but, if Roland was right, it would be the only volley.

Eldryn reached out with his sword and cut the hobbles loose. He took up the halters of Lance Chaser and Road Pounder and the first waves rounded the bend in the canyon.

Roland and Petie were swept up in the blast of freezing waters. The heavy rains from the north had created a flash flood in the lower canyons that ran north to south. Roland struggled against the numbing waves that threatened to take him. As he swam, as much as splashed, he saw that Petie was limp in his grasp.

Rage, a deeper rage than Roland had ever known, devoured him. His muscles strove like titans against the killing waters. He was struck again and again by debris the flood had collected. He was slammed against stones and trees as the rushing waters carried him south. He twisted and turned to protect Petie from those assaults.

In all his life he had never struggled so. It seemed that the world itself was against his every move. It may have been minutes or hours since he began this war with the killing tide, he could not tell. He only knew one thing. If it meant his death so be it, but he would see Petie to dry land.

Eldryn awoke with the sun high above him. He was wet, but not cold. Thank whatever gods that had bless his armor, he was not cold. He saw Lance Chaser and Road Pounder grazing not too far away. He could see their muscles shivering against the cold and their coats were still slick with the freezing water.

As he made his way to his feet, he discovered that his leg had taken a bad turn. Sharp pain stabbed up his side and he barely managed to stand. Wavering there he called to the horses who responded dutifully. He rubbed them down and checked their legs for cuts or breaks. Somehow, they had made it through with only minor scratches.

Then his thoughts went to Roland and Petie.

"Roland!" Eldryn called. "Petie!"

Eldryn scanned the plains around him to no avail. He hopped onto Lance Chaser bareback and took up Road Pounder's lead rope. He again surveyed his surroundings.

"Bolvii, if ever you would hear me then please hear me now," Eldryn said. "Please let them be well. Please. Roland loves you and Petie is coming to love you. They will be your heroes! Any gods that hear me, I will trade my life for theirs! I offer you my soul!"

Bolvii was listening. So was another.

Eldryn thought that the morning had become cloudy. He didn't realize he was weeping.

Eldryn had ridden for the rest of the day and well into the night. He had determined to ride south for that was the direction the damned waters would have carried them. It would have been better for the horses to be warmed by a fire, or at least placed in some form of shelter. However, Roland and Petie were out there, or their bodies were.

While there was daylight left, Eldryn scanned the sky as much as the plains. He looked for vultures in the air or bodies on the ground.

Deep into the night he heard the howls of wolves. He was tired. Bone tired. More weary than he had ever been. Hunger and thirst clawed at him. Lance Chaser stumbled on exhausted. Eldryn knew that he might well be riding his horse to death. His heart ached.

Cavalier that he was, Eldryn had learned from an early age to respect his mount. Treat them well and they will serve you well. Watch them and watch out for them. Now that served him well when he noticed Road Pounder toss his head to the west.

Eldryn road up a group of wolves stalking toward something laying in the dark. The wolves maneuvered themselves in a semi-circle around him. At some point he had strung his bow and he knocked an arrow in it now. As his attention was on the wolves before him, he detected motion and then heard a yelp from behind.

One of the wolves had attempted to ambush him and his horses. Road Pounder had sent that wolf flying with a sound kick. At that the rest of the wolves back away a bit. They backed even farther when Eldryn dropped one with an arrow strike through the shoulder.

Eldryn dismounted, slung his bow, and stumbled forward, sword in hand. The wolves backed away until he discovered the bodies of Roland and Petie. Roland was on his back and still clutched Petie in one strong arm, holding him across his chest. There was blood. So much blood.

Eldryn began to weep again even though he believed he had been wrung out of tears. He fell to his knees and crawled forward to hold them. He wiped blood away from Petie's cold cheek. Petie had a gash below is left eye. As his weeping became sobs, he kissed and mopped blood away from Roland's forehead. A blow that would create that sort of wound would kill a man for sure.

"If you tell anyone that I let you kiss me there will be a reckoning," Roland said.

Eldryn's weeping halted, hiccupped, and continued as he saw that blood still flowed from both Petie's wounds and Roland's.

"How many days?" Roland said.

The words shocked Eldryn.

"Three," Eldryn said at last. "You both were used pretty hard by the flood. I made a broth of the herbs we had from Ash. I couldn't exactly remember which ones did what so I mashed them all together into a soup. I poured what I could down your throat and Petie's. Damn, Roland. You had me scared."

"Petie is alright?" Roland asked, still not opening his eyes.

"I think so," Eldryn said. "It looks like an arrow cut his cheek pretty bad. May have even knocked him out. I did what I could to stitch it and the wound on your forehead."

Roland's hand reached up and felt his face. His fingers found the wound, that would become a scar known far and wide, that ran up from the outside of his left eye brown to his hair line.

Roland drifted off to sleep again. Eldryn camped on the plains for the next three days before he had someone around that he could talk to. Roland roused first and healed miraculously as he drank deeply of the broth Eldryn had made. Petie awoke a day later. That day Roland and Eldryn took turns giving the boy worried looks.

"El', you were right. You are right."

"What do you mean," Eldryn asked.

"Our road is too dangerous for a boy," Roland said. "I see it now. I suppose I knew it before but didn't want to admit it. I have an idea."

Eldryn didn't care about Roland's idea. He didn't care about much more than having them with him and alive. Eldryn had prayed and Eldryn had been heard.

Although few remembered, champions, fallen and otherwise were aware of the pleas made to the gods.

Petie rose the following day and they spent the next four days camping there and casting about for lost equipment. Roland's helm had washed ashore a little more than one hundred yards south of the camp. He was very glad to have it back. The bulk of their equipment had been lost to the water, but their weapons, armor, horses, and, most importantly, Petie, had survived. There was no sign of the highwaymen.

The three friends rode into Modins a little more than two months later. The smell of spring and the ocean salt was in the air. The world awoke all around them as new life came out of winter's death grip.

All of Roland's wounds had healed, but Roland still carried a nasty scar on his forehead and around his neck. The scar around his neck he concealed with the black cloth. Petie had been arguing with both Roland and Eldryn since he had discovered that he could not travel with them farther than Modins.

The argument continued as they approached the gate in the city walls.

"I will be fine. I did well against the demons," Petie said. "You said so your own self, Roland."

"Yes, you did, young warrior. But there are things you must learn that Eldryn and I are not qualified to teach you. And we were lucky with the fallen champions. Skill is good, but 'if a man may pick any ally, make that ally good fortune.'"

"Spoke Arto," Eldryn said. That particular quip had become something of a usual joke among the three and each of them chuckled.

"I have not told you about this until now," Roland said. "However, I think you would have a good chance at getting into the academy of Silver Helms here in Modins."

"How can I? I have the skill, but I haven't the money for that."

"I do," Roland said. "We go straight for the academy, and, if you pass their tests, then I will pay your tuition."

"I will not accept the charity!" Petie said defiantly.

"I am a warrior, I give no charity to another fighting man!" Roland barked. He heard his own father's voice in his sharp reply and regretted it.

"Once you graduate seek me out and you will earn the coin I spend today," Roland continued in a softer tone. "However, I will expect you to make the most of their training, for I will need you and you will need those skills."

"I am to serve in your army when I am trained?" Petie asked.

"I have no army yet, but nor are you yet trained. You learn, you study, and you work, hard. I will have a place for you when you are ready."

They rode through the gates and, after asking a few town criers for directions, located the Academy of the Silver Helm. Roland rode into the marshaling yard and approached an official there. They talked briefly and then Roland returned to where Eldryn and Petie sat on the horses.

"I will be back in a moment," Roland said.

Roland walked toward a well-built stone office near the wall of the academy grounds. He entered and found a very stern man within, appearing in his forties, conducting an inventory of practice weapons. He appeared to be of the Great Man race as well, approaching seven feet in height. He had short cut salt and pepper hair. The skin on his face was a road map of a life lived hard. Roland observed that the rank on his arm indicated that he was a Master Sergeant.

"I am here to see about enrolling a student," Roland said.

"Have you the coin for his room, board, and tuition?"

The Master Sergeant asked, not turning from his inventory.

"I have this," Roland said as he produced one of the gems he had taken from Nolcavanor.

The Master Sergeant turned and looked the gem over carefully.

"I am Master Sergeant Walkenn," the hard-built man said.

"I assume that will cover the costs, if he is accepted," Roland said. The boy in him wished for Walkenn to regard his fine armor and weapons in high esteem. The growing man in him saw the vanity in that wish and was a bit ashamed.

"Yes, this will do," Walkenn said in his ever flat tone. "Is the boy ready for the tests now?"

"Yes, he is," Roland said. He did wonder what it would take to impress such a man. Those thoughts took him again to his own father. Walkenn, it seemed, shared that trait with Velryk.

"Bring him to the marshaling yard. I will meet you there shortly."

Roland nodded and exited the office. He walked toward where Petie and Eldryn waited.

"You will tell no lie," Roland said. "They will ask you who your father is, and you will tell them. Your first father... what can I say about a man that I did not know? I am sure he was a mighty man, to have such a son. However, he is dead now. I, Roland, am now your father, and that is what you will tell them. They will not accept orphans, however, you are no longer an orphan. You are my son, from this day forward."

Tears brimmed Petie's eyes. Head Sergeant Walkenn walked from the stone building carrying a small backpack burdened with rocks, and an hourglass.

"Boy come here," Sgt. Walkenn said.

"I am Peterion, son of Roland," Petie replied with indignant pride in his voice.

Sgt. Walkenn looked at Peterion with steel in his eyes.

"I give no damn if you are the king's favorite whore," Sgt.

Walkenn yelled. "You will do as ordered, and you will jump to it!"

Peterion leapt from the horse's back in a smooth dismount, just as Eldryn had taught him, and ran to where the Sergeant stood. Roland could easily mark the pride on Eldryn's face at the swift execution of a move El' himself had spent hours teaching Petie.

Roland felt a bit of shame then. The warrior's road was no place for a boy and this was the proper decision. However, Roland had been so concerned with how he would miss Petie he had not taken into account how the boy had taken a place in Eldryn's heart as well.

"Yes, sir," Peterion said still wiping at his eyes.

The Sergeant gave Peterion the pack and Peterion hoisted it upon his shoulders.

"You will run this course, boy," the Sergeant said as he indicated a series of ropes, short walls, and a muddy pit arranged in a large circle around the yard. The course was, by Roland's guess, at least two leagues long and perhaps more. "You will finish before the sand falls from this glass."

"Yes sir!"

Sgt. Walkenn turned the glass over and Petie sped off. Roland and Eldryn both watched with the anxiety that only a nervous parent can know. Twenty minutes went by as Roland and Eldryn looked on. Petie struggled through the obstacles with determination.

While Petie ran, Sgt. Walkenn placed the hourglass in a pouch at his waist and withdrew another. He waited and, when Petie was in sight with the course almost finished, he held the second hourglass high.

"You failed, boy. Your time is up."

Petie growled and pushed himself even faster along the course.

"Perhaps you didn't hear me, boy. You failed! You lost! You can leave now! You did not make it!"

Petie shouted an obscenity, perhaps his first, and ran

even faster. He crashed into the final wall with exhaustion that spread into every muscle. Petie growled again and forced himself over the wall. He continued to run the last forty yards back to the point where the Sergeant, Roland, and Eldryn waited.

"You are defeated, boy. Quit."

Petie pressed on even harder, calling strength from deep within him. He made his new hate for this Sergeant burn fuel to his legs and lungs. Petie finally reached the three onlookers. He collapsed at their feet, sucking in wind as his lungs starved for air.

"Why didn't you quit, boy?"

"A warrior never quits," Peterion said as his chest heaved in gasps. "A warrior only knows defeat when he quits. You can shove that glass, and the sand that's in it!"

"You have a fine son here, Roland," Sgt. Walkenn said as he turned to Roland. "We will accept him into the officers' training here."

Roland looked at Peterion with pride bursting from his seams.

"You will do what these men tell you, and you will learn. I will return for you when the time is right. If something should happen to me, then seek out your grandfather, Velryk, in Fordir."

The Sergeant's head jerked toward Roland at those words.

"Lord Velryk in Fordir? You are the son of Lord Velryk?"

"I am."

"Then your son is welcome, Sir Roland."

"There is no sir, just Roland. I thank you Master Sergeant."

Roland nodded toward Petie, who worked hard to hold back his tears. Petie stood, stern and ridged and watched Roland and Eldryn ride away. Roland stopped at the gate and looked back to Petie. Petie held the dagger Roland had given him tight in his hand. Since the first time he held it, it had given him strength against his fears.

"I will come for you when it is time, son."

CHAPTER XII

Reunion

SPRING HAD COME TO THE CITY OF MODINS and, like the land surrounding it, the city was in full bloom. However, the luster of Eheno, named for the god of joy and blooming, the fifth month of 1649, seemed empty to two tired travelers. Roland and Eldryn made their way toward the northwest corner of Modins and found an inn there called Hell's Breeze. They rented two rooms and ordered large meals. Roland asked the bartender if there had been any messages left for him, but there were none.

Roland left a note at the desk under the name Fletcher. The note listed their room numbers and where they planned to stable the horses. The note was signed with a simple 'R.'

They put up their horses in a stable that was behind the inn. Once back at the inn, Roland and Eldryn sat down to their meals but they only pushed their food around with their forks. Neither of them wished to eat.

"I already miss him, Roland."

"As do I," Roland said. "We both know it has to be this way. Our road is not the road for a boy so young."

Roland's thoughts turned to Velryk then. Could that be how he felt? Instead of holding Roland back, could he have been trying to protect him? No, that was a foolish thought. Roland was tough. He had proven that time and again these past few months since leaving home. Still, his thoughts troubled him.

They nibbled at their meals in silence and, for the first time either could remember, left ale in the bottom of their tankards and food on their plates when they walked from the table. Each man went to his own room where they bathed and then went to bed.

Roland pulled his helmet on and strapped it in place. He was actually starting to get used to sleeping in it. He looked out his window toward the setting sun. Roland then climbed into bed and he pulled the covers up high over his head to blot out the light and fell to a deep sleep. The helm allowed him to see through the shade of night, which meant that in order to sleep with the helmet on he had to cover his head with something for it to be dark. Therefore, Roland drew the covers up and realized this was his first time in a real bed in what seemed like an eternity.

Dawn smiled to herself. Roland had been managing to block most of the Dream Twister spells that she and Yorketh had placed on him. He was probably using some leaf that burglar gave him. Leaves, however, would not stop a well-placed dagger.

She and Yorketh had decided that regardless of how young they were, Roland and Eldryn should be handled separately for safety's sake. They waited for an hour to make sure that Roland would be in a deep sleep. After an hour had passed Dawn and Yorketh walked up to the staircase, which led to the boys' rooms. Yorketh had gone to the tavern across the street and put gold up to buy the drinks for the next three rounds. That act had literally cleared this inn of its customers.

They crept to Roland's door. Yorketh whispered and touched the door lock with his king's finger and ring finger. The bolt slid open silently and the two entered. This was going to be too easy.

Dawn, her dagger ready in hand, aimed carefully. This

would be the end of the mouthy brat. Dawn hurled her dagger with deadly accuracy.

Roland was startled awake by a loud clang and a blow to the back of his head. His ears began to ring. The dagger had struck the back of his helmet. He heard the chanting and rolled out of bed just before '*dactlartha*' and the cold fire of dark energy ripped through the mattress and pillow where Roland had been.

"El," Roland yelled. "To arms!"

Anger flushed through Dawn. She hated this boy for his impudence and his luck! She began around the edge of the bed as she drew her falchion.

Roland had been lucky. He had dropped onto his pile of armor and equipment. He took all of it up in one armload and grabbed Swift Blood with the other. Roland rolled again and stood. Dawn smiled an evil grin and started for him. Roland hated this, but he didn't have much choice. These odds would mean his death. Roland lowered his helmeted head and charged for the large window in the room, which was a full story above the alleyway. Dawn and Yorketh stood in disbelief.

Eldryn had just grabbed up his Shrou-Sheld when he heard the window break. He opened his window and looked out to see Roland laying in the alleyway with his equipment strewn all about him. Despite the situation Eldryn stifled a small laugh. He would never get used to seeing Roland in his nightshirt and wearing a helmet.

Unsure of what to do, Eldryn decided that he should be at Roland's side. They had faced many battles together in just that fashion. He grabbed his pack and shield in one hand and his sword in the other. He stepped to the window ledge and jumped. He landed hard.

Eldryn looked back up to Roland's window and saw Yorketh preparing another spell. The bolt of energy loosed from Yorketh's hand and Eldryn had just enough time to raise his shield. He was knocked to the ground by the force of the bolt.

Roland winced in pain when Dawn's second dagger hit a few inches low of its mark and struck him in the thigh. Roland and Eldryn scrambled down the alley as two more daggers struck the ground behind them. Yorketh and Dawn looked at the long jump and decided that the stairs would be better.

"Look," Dawn said, answering Yorketh's expression, "they are not even armored. They are weak without their shells."

Dawn and Yorketh hurried down the steps and out the front door of the inn.

Roland and Eldryn made it to their horses and saddled them hurriedly. Roland's whole leg was going stiff but, with El's help, he managed a pretty good shuffle. They ran a rope through the straps of their armor and packs and secured them to their newly purchased saddles. Roland tore a piece of cloth from his nightshirt and removed the dagger sticking in his leg. He tied off the wound in an attempt to stem the bleeding. Roland looked at his new dagger. *This is an expensive way to collect new knives*, he thought. Roland placed the new dagger, a frosting blade, in the empty slot on his belt left by the dagger given to Petie.

Roland and Eldryn turned their mounts and started for the door of the barn. When they reached the door, they were surrounded by swirling acids somehow magically contained in twenty-foot-high walls. They wheeled their horses to find Yorketh and Dawn standing behind them.

Yorketh shouted *'istuderth'* and Road Pounder and Lance Chaser froze, paralyzed. Dawn stepped forward with her mercshyeld falchion in one hand and her enchanted iron mace in the other. She had a smile smeared across her face.

Roland raised his Shrou-Hayn high over his left shoulder, holding it in both hands. Eldryn raised his shield with his left arm and held his Shrou-Sheld in his right hand loosely. Both dismounted and stepped forward.

Yorketh whispered another arcane word of command and Eldryn felt the quiet speech rinse through his mind and seize his nerves. Eldryn's entire body shuddered and he collapsed to the ground.

Roland also felt the word of command travel into his ears and echo through his thoughts. However, the ancient syllables drifted past with no more effect than a gentle summer's breeze. His leg was still stiff and hurt like there were biting worms in the muscles. He shuttered at that thought and forced himself to focus.

Dawn came in fast as Roland hurled an overhead chop at her. She brought up her mace and falchion crossed to block. The momentum of Roland's attack dropped her to one knee. Roland pivoted Swift Blood on Dawn's weapons and swung his sword hilt in. The jeweled hilt struck her sculpted nose with wicked force. Dawn's head snapped back and a broken nose sprayed blood across her mouth and cheeks.

Dawn's falchion pulled away from the cross block and slashed toward Roland. Roland attempted a quick-step back but the edge of Dawn's blade found his unarmored thigh. Steel sliced through flesh and muscle, biting deeply into Roland's leg.

Roland staggered back and fell to one knee. If he had heard the word spoken through the roar of pain in his head, he might have been able to prepare. Might have. A blast of black and green flame struck Roland's right shoulder. His right hand fell from its place next to his left on his sword's hilt. Roland called his arm to action, but the bolt of cold black fire had struck it numb.

Dawn rose and forced her eyes to focus through the blood and pain that fired in her nose. She walked toward Roland with the knowledge that she would kill him. Dawn thrust with her falchion and Roland hauled the great sword up with a single hand to swat away the attack.

Dawn's mace followed on an arc behind Roland's parry and struck viciously against his bare left shoulder. Both combatants heard bone snap. Swift Blood fell to Roland's lap gripped by a hand that would not heed its masters call.

Roland felt the warmth of his own blood draining out of

his leg and seeping out of his shoulder. He felt his strength fading. Roland glared ahead at Dawn. He knew that he would die at her hand, but he might have a chance to take her with him. If he could head butt her, striking her armor hard enough to shatter the crystal in his helmet, the resulting burst of energy would be enough to destroy them both. However, the gem was placed and mounted so that it was protected from just that outcome.

Yorketh began another word.

"Quiet," Dawn said through teeth stained red in her own blood. "This one I will execute with my blade."

Dawn smiled and brought her falchion out to her side. She began the arcing swing that would severe Roland's head. Roland sat, focusing his hate for this woman into fuel for his final act. Roland was no more surprised than Dawn when a dark figure kicked the blade of the falchion up.

As Dawn's arm rose a right hand grabbed her wrist and twisted it violently. The falchion fell to the ground. Dawn swung the mace toward the new assailant. The dark figure drove his forearm into the elbow of Dawn's captured arm, twisting it viscously and breaking it.

However, Dawn's swinging mace reached its destination, knocking the wind from Ashcliff's lungs and throwing him back and away from her. Dawn screamed in pain. Her arm dangled, displaying a grotesque bend at its center that was quite unnatural.

Ashcliff hit the ground but came up in a roll. He scrambled to his feet to stand next to where Roland knelt. The two old friends exchanged nods. Ashcliff, whose face was always a mask of one emotion or another, succeeded in hiding his horror at seeing Roland's incapacitating injuries.

Ashcliff reached into his sleeves and drew out two slim daggers.

"The second plan," Dawn shouted through gritted teeth. "The second plan, now you jackass!"

Yorketh shouted 'sectlartha' and all the world became a jumble of images and gravities to the occupants of the barn.

Roland and Ash looked around them to find that they were in a field not far from the coast judging by the sounds of the nearby ocean. They noticed that Eldryn's body and the horses Road Pounder and Lance Chaser were behind them. They saw Yorketh and Dawn standing a few yards away ahead of them. They also saw twenty men clad in various armors wielding an array of weapons.

Ashcliff wasted no time. He hurled the two daggers and two men fell dead. Roland steeled himself against what he knew would come. He sat on his knees as his strength drained in a red flood from his body. He would take enemies with him this day.

A Great Man, by the looks of him, walked toward Roland in confidence. Roland waited, focusing his mind through the pain in his body and the blur in his brain. The Great Man smiled and hoisted his blade high in the air. Roland flexed the fingers of his right hand. He gripped Swift Blood in the numbed right hand and swung it in an irregular arc that severed the Great Man's left leg. The Great Man screamed out and fell back, unable to keep his footing because now he only had one.

The swing over balanced Roland and pulled him to the side. The Shrou-Hayn crashed to the mud and Roland hauled it back toward him with only his right hand.

Three came at Ashcliff. He was ready for them. The first thrust a saber at his chest that Ashcliff slapped aside with the back of his bare right hand. Ashcliff continued the move and struck out with the same hand, striking the attacker in the throat. The first man fell to the ground, dead. The second attempted an overhead cut with a broadsword towards Ashcliff's unarmored neck. Ashcliff quick-stepped inside the arc of the attack and struck the assailant in the nose with a callused palm. The second attacker was dead before his corpse began to fall. The third man swung his morning star from behind Ashcliff and it struck Ashcliff hard on the knee. Ashcliff dropped to the ground as the knee bent inward. Ashcliff twisted his torso and punched out with a quick fist that struck the inside of the third man's knee. Now both were crippled. Other assailants drug the third man away from Ashcliff's reach.

Ashcliff drew two more daggers and two more men fell dead. Yorketh whispered another arcane word and the suggestion coursed through Ashcliff's ears and seized his spine. Ashcliff trembled, locked in place by his rebellious nerves.

"Move back," Dawn shouted. "Everyone, move back!"

The crowd of men stepped back away from Roland and his friends. Eight archers stepped into the opening, standing thirty feet away. Roland saw no path that could lead to victory. He called to Bolvii for the strength to take one more with him. Somehow Roland lurched from the ground, hauling Swift Blood in one arm, and charged the archers. The last thing Roland remembered was the piercing pain of arrows, and the comfort of knowing that one more enemy fell beneath his blade.

Roland awoke in the dark. He tried to sit up, but pain shot throughout his body. His vision blurred, and dizziness swam through his head. He could hear distant voices. *Is this the home of Bolvii?* Roland thought to himself. Sleep came for him like the charge of cavalry.

Roland slept.

Untold hours later Roland again awoke to the feel of a moist cloth on his forehead. He opened his eyes and the blur had cleared. He was now certain he was dead for he looked into the eyes of an angel. She was an angel that was somehow familiar. When she smiled Roland felt peace wash throughout his soul. She was a slim, light skinned beauty with long, raven black hair and sky-blue eyes. Roland's angel stood and drifted from the dark room he was in. He tried to speak but discovered that he was still very weak. Sleep came for him again as he collapsed back into the silk that surrounded him.

EPILOUGE

Penitence?

A DARK FIGURE WALKED ACROSS THE remains of a bleached stone foundation, his long starlight shadow very dim in the night. This foundation was all that was left of what was once a grand cathedral. A cathedral once dedicated to Father Time. Moonlight shined off the tall figure's pale and shaved head. The shade of the skin on his veined but powerful hands matched the night-covered white stone.

An armored dark elf approached the lone figure, his white hair streaming out from underneath his helmet, his soft boots making no sound. The Warlock of the Marshes could smell the exhale of the approaching drow. That smell teased his disciplined appetite.

"It has been ages," Maloch finally said. "Why do you request this meeting now, priest?" the label of priest spat as an insult.

"It is my understanding that you had a sort of 'contact' with a young warrior some months ago," Lynneare said. "He was in your caverns and took something from there. Is it not so, Knight of Shadows?"

"I know the one you mean," Maloch said. "He isn't very skilled but he is strong, and lucky. I would rather have the favor of a god than skill any day."

"I understand that since that time you have left your followers behind."

"What concern is it of yours?" Maloch interrupted with venom in his voice.

"I know that you still blame me for your curse, and the curse put on your people. I have accepted responsibility for my actions and have lived eons with the mistake. If you cannot forgive me, then forget my wrongs for a time. Let us talk as the friends we once were."

"Very well," Maloch said, staring off into starlight and back hundreds of years. "There was something about him that was familiar... Something... Did you know that he challenged me to a duel? Ridiculous, is it not? He fought not within the bounds of the old Code but, still he was merciful and honorable. Those were traits I thought had been lost, that we drove, from this world forever. He showed mercy and honor. It reminded me of better days. It reminded me of days when I was an honorable elf, of days when I stood for what was just. I could not stand to think of those times and stomach my brethren in their depraved sins and hatreds. I set out on my own. I searched for answers once, thousands of years ago. My searching has begun again."

"Do you know why the boy seemed so familiar?"

"No, it was just something about him."

"Did you not recognize the armor he wore. The weapon he carried?" Lynneare asked.

"Lord Ivant's?" Maloch asked. His mind went back thousands of years. His heart wanted to believe but, his practical nature was afraid of the implications. "Surely not."

"They were indeed," Lynneare said. "He died in that room the day the battles came to their ends. He has laid there with the original holy sacraments since that time."

"I wish I had known," Maloch said. "I might have..."

"You could not have," Lynneare said cutting him short. "We are still cursed. In that other time and place the Hourglass bestowed the ability to see the past and the future. The final vision I received was the blood sacrifice my line would have to make for the king. My blood for the king's blood. I will crave blood until that sacrifice is made. I am sustained only by blood until that act of repentance is made. The rub is that the sacrifice be made of love. I have toiled since that day."

"I had an agent remove the holy sacraments," Lynneare continued. "I did not know it was you that lived in those caverns, otherwise things might have been easier. I tried to look on The Book of Fate and Sands of Time but could not. You would have surely perished if you had entered the alter room. That curse is still very potent."

"So, it was Ivant's armor that triggered those old memories," Maloch said. "That makes sense I suppose. I haven't thought about him in centuries. I curse the day we betrayed him."

"I think it was more than the armor," Lynneare said. "I had years of training and prayer before I could touch the Hourglass or the Tome. I had seen them destroy those foolish enough to handle either with anything less than educated reverence. Even with my gifts and practiced prayers they were a considerable challenge. My agent tells me the boy and his friend both were able to touch the Hourglass. Roland...he was able to glimpse what it had to show...he was able..."

"What do you mean?"

"I believe that boy, Roland, has mighty blood in his veins."

"He said that he was the son of Lord Velryk," Maloch said. "Velryk was always a dangerous and shrewd enemy. It is said that even Ingshburn has a justified fear of Verkial, his general in the east. I can say that Verkial is formidable. I have faced him personally. If Roland is truly Velryk's son, and Verkial's brother, then his blood line is mighty indeed."

"I think it goes beyond Lord Velryk and General Verkial," Lynneare said as his eyes stared into the night air. "What do you do now, in your wandering of the land?"

"It will sound absurd..." Maloch began and broke off.

After a few moments he continued, "I am attempting to make atonement. I realize I have no hope of forgiveness, but one does not repent in search of forgiveness. He repents because he knows he has done wrong and is shamed. I have sinned...I have..."

"Penitence, then?"

"Yes," Maloch, no longer of the Black Lance, replied. "Penitence."

"My curse has passed to many," Lynneare said. "Each of my children carry some aspect of that curse. I have prayed for many years, Maloch. I believe the Infinite Father has given me an answer."

"Yes?"

"I needed to know your heart before I told you of this," Lynneare said. "I may have a way for us to return to his service. My youngest daughter suffered the thirst more than any of my children, however, my continued penance to the Father of Time along with prayers, and centuries researching, have granted me a miracle. She craves the blood of men no longer. You might again wear the symbol of the hourglass on your breastplate in battle."

"How?" Maloch asked, attempting to hide the eagerness, the need, in his voice.

THE COST OF VANITY

In the days before the Shore Drift, the Father of Time and his bride, Fate, created the world from the void and populated it with three races. They created the elves, which would endure the passing of time, as the great sectot trees, and be of the forest. They fashioned the dwarves, who would age as the mountains they delved in. Then they gave life and soul to the men, who would live briefly, but love and build as passionately as the gods themselves.

The elves, fair and vain, saw themselves as equals with the champions and only worshiped the gods that remained in the heavens.

The dwarves were content in their mining. Their love and worship were reserved for precious metals, rare gems, and the fine art of smithing taught to them by the god of stone, Roarke.

In the days before the Battles of Rending, when the land was one, gods and their champions roamed the earth with men. The gods and champions showed men many things. They saw the eagerness in man's heart and taught him various skills. They taught them the secrets of iron, and steel. They taught them the mysteries of the three great oceans. Some took the fairer and stronger of the men as companions and lovers. Those couplings spawned a race not intended by the Father of Time or Fate. The Great Men rose from the old land, when it was still one, out of the passion of men, champions, and gods.

The Great Men mastered steel, and conquered the storms of the unending oceans. They built vast cities to honor

The Father of Time, Fate, and the gods and champions that walked among them. Their accomplishments amazed even the gods remaining in the heavens. Their best soldiers rivaled the champions in their prowess with sword and axe, mace and arrow. Their artisans broadened the imagination of the champions, and sculpted the grace of the gods in metal and stone.

As all men do, Great or otherwise, they succumbed to pride and vanity. In their vast cities, they held on high regard their generals and kings. They worshiped their heroes of war in the same halls they worshiped the Infinite Father. They bartered their congregations to the gods that would teach them more and grant more blessings. They traded their worship for power that was offered by vain and evil champions. They gave the champions their first tastes of jealousy, tainting the hearts and twisting the souls of the angelic creatures. They enslaved the lesser common men and scorned the elves and dwarves.

The earthly gods saw the vanity of the Great Men and were shamed. The heavenly gods would not tolerate the insults. The champions of the land were sent against the Great Men to destroy their cities, burn their ships, and purge the land of their people. Most common men, elves, and dwarves were spared, but they watched as a golden age fell.

The magnificent cities of the Great Men were pushed into the oceans. Knowledge was lost, art was destroyed.

The history of the world and the calendar of the gods decayed. The measure of Time was forgotten. Some champions faced their own kin in the Battles of Rending.

Some of the Great Men remained faithful to the Infinite Father of Time, and continued to worship Fate. They had split from those who would enslave and persecute. Those Great Men surrendered their arms to the champions, pleading for mercy. Bolvii, a god of war, watched the champions, who were once valiant, murder the faithful. Bolvii was shamed. He found no glory in execution. He felt no malice in his heart toward the faithful of the Great Men, but found forgiveness there instead.

Bolvii disguised one of his own ships of war and sent the

Great Men that had remained faithful to an island in the west that he had fashioned separate from the works of Fate. Bolvii hid this island in the mist from the eyes of the other gods. There the Great Men built a city to honor Fate, the Infinite Father, and Bolvii.

The island of Lethor was home to the faithful Great Men for several generations during the times of the Battles of Rending and the Shore Drifts. Their history and time were kept in the spoken word only. Bolvii forbade the tangible trappings of religion and would only allow sincere worship. History and time were lost to them as was their vanity and pride. They emerged from this period of vague measure as a race with a clear conscience, a genuine love for the gods, and a desire to see peace and justice restored to the home of their grandfathers.

Some of the Great Men who remained behind fought viciously in the Battles of Rending. Some champions aligned with their descendants and opposed the strength of the earthly gods and their champions. They fought, but saw their doom. At the end of the Battles of Rending, and during the times of the Shore Drifts, those Great Men and their champion allies fled north to a far land. They hid there with the enchanted aid of the traitorous champions from the sword of the earthly gods, and the eye of those heavenly. They waited for the day when they once again might emerge from the shadow and challenge the gods for the rule of the land.

Bolvii counseled the faithful to spread among common men, elves and dwarves. He told them that some champions and evil Great Men would still hunt them. When the Great Men took to the sea again, they found that the land was no longer one. They found that the Shore Drifts had split the land apart and changed the face of the world. They discovered nine lands and many tribes.

Seeing the folly in trusting those earth bound with their knowledge, the earthly gods returned to their home in the heavens leaving their mounts, the mighty serpents, to roam the lands untended. They still looked over those who remained faithful, and from time to time sent their champions to the aid of their followers. However, the gods would not walk again with men until the time of the Awakening.

Bolvii returned home to the heavens as well. He sent his champions frequently to reassure the faithful among the Great Men. Bolvii knew that evil was still in the world. Bolvii was sure that the bloodlines to lead and rule would be from the Great Men, and they would be evil's chief nemesis.

Of the nine new lands, only three were of great size. Those were known as Tarborat, Janis, and Hunthor. The other six were a series of large islands that surrounded those three which came to be known as the land of Ozur.

Tarborat was a vast grassy plain, with great mountains near its center, and bordered by sheer cliffs. It was here that the evil Great Men fled with their champion allies.

Those champions were far from their gods, and their grace wilted. Their visages became dark, and the evil in their hearts was reflected in their appearance. They stalked the land as demons. Some still served the Great Men. Some stalked the land alone and sought revenge for the purity that had been stripped from them. They raped innocents, and spawned perverse and gruesome things to walk the earth. Some haunts that resulted from that revenge were burned by daylight, and thirsted for the lifeblood of men. Some creatures birthed by that hate became man and beast, changed by the phasing of the moon.

In Tarborat, some of the Great Men mixed with the common people. The Great Men, who were leaders of the Tribes of Tarborat, kept their blood pure. Among them rose a mighty and wicked king.   Ingshburn was a powerful warrior who commanded a score of demons. He stood almost eight feet tall and wielded a heavy battle-axe in only one hand while known to conjure with the other. He organized his forces and systematically conquered the plains and mountains of Tarborat. Elves of the plains and dwarves of the mountains of Tarborat fled the land. Some were captured and enslaved.   Ingshburn's demons used the elves and dwarves in horrible ways. Ingshburn's sorcerers mastered some of the roving demons and sent them against island tribe after island tribe. He conquered three of the six islands before he met opposition.

Janis was the smallest of the three great continents. It was caught on the border of seasons in the fits of magic, the lower half of the land frozen year-round and the upper half a tropical sprawl. It was home to many different creatures and two tribes of common men.

One scattered tribe had taken to the jungles of Janis. They were called the Zepute. They wore thin skins, and stalked through their deadly lands in small groups.

The other tribe had taken to the borderlands of the frozen south. They were called the Slandik. They were a tough and hearty people who existed in tight communities where they depended on each other for survival in the harsh environment.

The two tribes warred when they encountered one another, but those encounters were rare at best.

Hunthor was the largest of the three continents. The High Ranges shared the northern half of Hunthor with a lush and enchanted forest, Suethiel.

The High Ranges were the largest range of mountains encountered by man or beast both before, and after, the Shore Drifts. The ancient homes of the dwarves were carved into the bones of the majestic peaks.

Suethiel was home to the slim and graceful sectot trees, and the majority of the elven population of Hunthor.

The southern half of Hunthor was a flowing combination of forest, hills, and plains, divided here and there by swift rivers. It had been inhabited by roving clans of common men for ages after the Battles of Rending.

Great Men from Lethor began appearing on the shores of Hunthor long after the Shore Drifts had been forgotten in the common man's history.

The Great Men lived among the scattered tribes and only a very few kept their blood pure and separate from the common men. Of those few that did keep themselves pure in blood, there arose peaceful leaders in the tribes. In time, those leaders combined their people and built cities. Some of the glory of the former world was returned. Those leaders tried to make amends to the elves and dwarves of the land, but the long-life span of those peoples brought with it a long memory.

More than a thousand years after the Great Men returned to the lands of Hunthor they were of two kingdoms, led by brothers. The calendar of the gods was restored, and the Age of Brother Kingdoms began.

The kingdom of Lethanor, called so to honor the refuge that Bolvii provided the Great Men, prospered for another thousand years. The kingdom of Ozur, called so to honor the warship of Bolvii that carried the Great Men to sanctuary, also prospered. Among both lands, many common men and Great Men alike held lordship over smaller fiefdoms.

Then they learned of Tarborat, and of its king, Ingshburn. An all-consuming war began between the Brother Kingdoms and Tarborat. It was a war that had been destined since before the days of the Battles of Rending, a war that Fate foresaw. That war saw the fall of Ozur. That war has been waged for centuries.